TROUTFLY

R.G. Dierks

ISBN: 1-4196-9477-4
ISBN-13: 9781419694776

Visit www.booksurge.com to order additional copies.

Prologue

The year is 2020. A global terrorist network, the Transnational Organization of Victorious Asian/Arab Islamic Republics, is intent on shaping the destiny of a great nation and threatens the outcome of a presidential election. History provides the backdrop for the epic struggle between the West and radical Islamic extremists. The nation's capital is under siege. Deception and greed orchestrated by enemies across the globe reach deep into the American halls of power. The character, leadership, and loyalty of quiet professionals willing to risk it all in the defense of freedom reaches across generations to display the sacrifice of fathers and sons.

Chapter 1
Royal Wulff

Clayton Harcourt learned about the impermanency of life at an early age. He no longer had anything to prove to his family or the rest of the world. He just wanted to spend his days doing what mattered most. He relished the freedom to perfect his angling skills away from urban crowds. Time melted away when he ventured deep into the forest. A narrow trail behind his cabin led to a pristine mountain stream, where trout lived in the wild. He liked to ply his art in the quiet hours at dawn. He was a purist who imitated nature with dry flies. He loved to watch the upright wings of a Royal Wulff twinkle against the early morning light. He knew trout snatch other fly patterns at the edge of a riffle, but the regal elegance of his favorite fly visible just above the water line epitomized perfection.

Clayton spotted a rise about fifteen feet upstream, and decided to mend the line with a quick flip of his wrist to prevent drag. As intended, he slowed down the fly's journey alongside the current. Without warning, a rainbow bit. He steadied his feet on the slick gravel. Reeling deliberately, he moved toward the water's edge, focusing on the quick movements of his prey. He persisted until, resigned to its fate, the trout quit fighting. Clayton felt the throb of the line pressed against his fingers. He scooped his catch. The rainbow sparkled with blinding force. After pulling the barbless hook from her upper lip, he cradled his trophy against the current and released her back into the stream.

Clayton was as meticulous about his pastime as he had been about his work. He moved behind two large boulders to check his gear. The line to leader connection was perfect – ideal for the transfer of energy necessary to reach the fly and propel it forward in a straight line toward its target. He clipped off the battered Royal Wulff. The hackle looked like a tiny tuft of calf's tail caught in a barbwire fence. He tied on fresh tippet with a double surgeon knot. With a steady hand, he secured a new fly to the end of the tippet. The improved clinch knot seemed strong, and he rubbed a dot of floating gel on the wispy wings. He tucked his fly box into his vest pocket and waded back toward the head of the riffle, the best place to look for holding lies. He listened as the stream rushed past him.

Clayton had learned his first fly-fishing lessons at his grandfather's side. He had followed grandpa Harcourt up rugged trails and across meadows. Before he was ten years old, he had learned to read water. Wading into slow and fast currents, the youngster discovered the mysteries of mayflies and caddis hatches. Not much later, he figured out the meaning of patience.

While daydreaming his way through boring lectures at Yale, pictures of his favorite Colorado streams would come alive. Sometimes, he felt so homesick that he nearly dropped out of school to return to his beloved West. The river, however, had taught Clayton the value of persistence. He would close his eyes and envision the Arkansas flowing free and unrelenting. The great big boulders resisted the fast current and provided shelter to big browns, but the river always won the battle of endurance.

After catching a second rainbow, Clayton hiked back to the cabin. He had been up since 4:30 am and had skipped his favorite ritual of checking the oil futures market. Instead, he had rigged a light rod and headed up the trail, before the sun came up. This day marked two years since he had lost his wife. The initial grief had eased, but her absence carved a void in his existence that only nature could fill.

An eagle soared high above the pines. On this late summer morning, Clayton smiled as he watched a herd of elk move swiftly toward the edge of the forest. It was time for these majestic animals to take cover. The walk down the steep trail invigorated him. He approached his place, paused, and looked beyond the mountain peaks as if to snap a picture of the storm clouds rolling in from the distance.

When he walked into his cabin, the first thing he noticed was the flashing light on his cell phone.

"Check oil futures. I'll call you back."

Market volatility was at an all-time high with the rise of political uncertainty and social turmoil in oil-producing regions across the world. The U.S. was building a coalition of oil importers to put pressure on oil producers. The goal was to reduce demand and keep oil prices down. It was a costly strategy, but it seemed to be paying dividends. For weeks now, oil prices were stuck in a narrow trading range. Clayton logged on to his laptop. Oil futures were sharply down. He was long the October 30 put, and knew his move last week would cushion the blow. He checked his e-mail and found another message:

"We need to talk."

Clayton sat back across the stone fireplace and just as he tried to figure who was trying to get a hold of him, the phone rang. The voice was familiar and the e-mail message now made sense.

"I need to talk to you. I'm in town. Can we meet today?"

The choppy sentences, the commanding tone – this was definitely Tom Munroe, his former boss. Clayton clearly remembered Tom's words on his last day at Langley.

"Nobody ever quits a job like yours, Clayton. You'll be back."

"Not in your lifetime."

Clayton never regretted his decision to quit. And now, Tom was in Driggs, just a few miles from the cabin, asking to see him.

"Tom, if you are here on vacation, you are welcome to come up to my place to enjoy the view or hook a rainbow. If you are here to talk business, I'm retired and no longer available."

Clayton had no desire to talk to Tom or for that matter little desire to see him again. He was certain Tom felt the same way about him. They had nothing in common outside of work. When Tom persisted on getting together, Clayton knew that this was not a casual visit.

"Give me a chance to explain, I'm begging you. I need your advice. The president asked me to see you. Please Clayton."

Tom never begged, never asked for anyone's advice. The voice was firm but calm. Clayton needed time to collect his thoughts.

"OK, meet me at the Grand Old Grill on Main Street, in one hour."

☼ ☼ ☼

After graduating with honors, Clayton had joined the CIA as an East European analyst. Most analysts did their work in Washington, isolated from the creative intelligence-gathering jobs of agents in the field. Early in his career, Clayton showed a unique talent for analysis and creative problem solving. He had a gift for operational challenges and moved with great ease from the analytical to the operational side of the business. His superiors recognized Clayton's intellectual dexterity and gave him challenging lab and field assignments.

When the Cold War ended, a temporary duty assignment in Egypt led to jobs in India and Pakistan. After twenty years with the agency, Clayton realized that government work limited his quest for new challenges. His work was intriguing – a constant puzzle demanding problem-solving prowess and analytical skills. He viewed his job as multiple chess games played simultaneously against multiple opponents, some of whom cooperated to defeat one another's enemies. Clayton felt that the very nature of his work required taking risks to come up with the most comprehensive set of decision-making scenarios. Yet the intelligence business was increasingly constrained by endless bureaucratic red tape. The agency rewarded risk-averse behavior in the field and behind each desk.

The Washington bureaucracy frustrated Clayton, and he began to think about leaving his government job. He was an avid student of market trends, and in his spare time he managed his family's trust account. He invested aggressively and enjoyed testing his knowledge of probability theory to profit from the increasing volatility in the equity markets. For him, trading was a sport like fly-fishing – it required patience, skill, confidence, and stamina. It was an art form. Before executing each trade, Clayton played out in his mind multiple potential scenarios and calculated his risk/reward for each move, always pinpointing an exit strategy before he executed a trade. He never let emotions get in the way. Ice ran through his veins when he made investment decisions. Uncertainty was a big part of the game.

✲ ✲ ✲

Tom's unexpected visit under the guise of seeking advice did not make much sense. Clayton showered, shaved, and put on his old jeans and worn out t-shirt. He made his way into town, alert about his surroundings like a veteran traveler in a new city. He drove up to the parking lot behind the downtown café, and noticed three black SUVs with tinted windows parked along a side alley. They seemed out of place.

Clayton walked into the small establishment and noticed the secret service agent sitting at a table facing the entrance. Tom, heavier but expansive as usual, sprang to his feet and walked toward Clayton. At the table near the fireplace, a down-to-earth man dressed in khaki pants and white short-sleeve shirt read the newspaper. His silver hair was the only sign of his age; his lanky frame portrayed a disciplined life. The President of the United States looked like one of the regulars who met for coffee each morning in downtown Driggs to catch up with the latest news.

"Clayton, it's good to see you." Tom beamed as Clayton approached him, and added, "Mr. President, Clayton Harcourt."

"Great to meet you, Clayton, I've heard about your work of some years ago. Please join me, take a seat."

Clayton had designed an innovative analytic model early in his CIA career, and the agency was still using his basic framework to estimate political risk. He had long forgotten that professional feat. Lately, he was more inclined to think about places where trout lived. The president spoke softly, his dark blue eyes fixed on Clayton's pale green eyes.

"You must be wondering what brings us here. Let me get to the point."

The president's business background came across—he was direct and got to the bottom line right away.

"I need you to come back to Washington. I know how strongly you feel about the West. Just like your dad. You were born while we served together in Vietnam. Sometime, I'll tell you more about those days."

Clayton was shocked. His dad, Jack, never returned from Vietnam. Jack's best friend, Ken Baines, made it back but said little about the war. He never talked about Jack. The close-knit Navy SEAL unit got together for reunions every year, but Ken Baines never attended. After five decades, the memories were still raw, and the old sailor was now too weak to travel. Clayton had visited Ken a few years back hoping to hear what happened to his dad, but he never had the courage to ask. Now, Mack Cumberland, President of the United States, was opening a door to Jack's past and giving Clayton hope for answers to questions buried deep in his heart.

"Heck, I wish I could spare a few days up here just fly-fishing with you, getting to know you better. Jack would like that, I think." The president paused and added, "Our country is in peril. I need your help." Mack Cumberland wasted no time to deliver his closing pitch.

"Clayton, I knew that if Tom called you to ask you to serve your country once again, you would have declined. I know how much this place means to you. I am asking you to serve again and protect what your dad loved so much, our freedom."

The president's tone was grave. The blue eyes were piercing. He reminded Clayton of his dad's sacrifice. While living in Washington DC, Clayton had walked along the Wall to touch his father's name carved in stone. The Wall gave him a sense of purpose; it reminded him that Jack and other heroes like him were the reason a great nation fulfills its destiny. Clayton's sense of duty to country was as solid as the etchings on the Wall.

"How can I help, sir?"

The president turned to Tom and said: "Go ahead. Tell him."

The world had become increasingly complex since the fall of the Soviet Union. Russia and China were once again engaged in a struggle for supremacy not unlike the Sino-Soviet rivalries that plagued their tense interactions during the Cold War. Eastern European countries now embraced democracy and free markets, showing the first signs of economic success after joining the European Union and becoming strong allies of the US. The games Clayton had played against his East European opponents were simple compared to the multidimensional games played across the Middle East and South East Asia.

The war on terrorism was still raging in various hot spots around the world. Many radical Islamic leaders were in custody, while some fundamentalists remained at large and had stepped into leadership positions. Large clusters of reluctant terrorists continued to provide a fertile recruiting ground for an increasingly militant leadership. The next generation of radicals was in training for a long struggle. The *madrassas,* Islamic fundamentalist schools, continued to operate across Africa, Asia, and the Middle East, stirring hatred against the United States and the West. Multiple efforts to rebuild failed states yielded mixed results. The violence in the Middle East continued, while Central Asia sank deeper into chaos. Tom adjusted his reading glasses and sipped some water before resuming his briefing.

"The rebuilding of war-torn countries in the Middle East and Central Asia is slowly reducing the threat of terrorist attacks against U.S. interests around the world but we have uncovered new domestic threats. Three nations seem to be part of a complex terrorist network determined to strike the economic nerve centers of Western civilization first and then to direct simultaneous paramilitary attacks against selected political targets across the United States and other allied nations. Behind this plot is a Machiavellian alliance of China, Saudi Arabia, and India. These American allies appear to be playing a double game of deception."

Clayton listened attentively but could not stop thinking about Jack. He wanted to know more about the man he sought to emulate since childhood. He had heard how his father had lived; he was curious as to how he had fought and died. He caught himself no longer hearing what Tom was saying. Knowing that he had missed part of the briefing, Clayton struggled to focus back on Tom's words. Tom was still talking about China, Saudi Arabia, and India.

"On the one hand, they pledge to stand by the U.S. in the fight against global terrorism, but under the cover of mutual friendship they seem to be leading a global alliance of Muslim, Hindu, communist, and nationalist anti-Western fanatics intent on destroying liberal democracy and capitalism." Tom's briefings were never brief.

"These governments share anti-Western sentiments, have nuclear capabilities, and control vast oil reserves."

Tom went on to explain that China resented America's rising power after the defeat of terrorism and the liberation from autocratic regimes in Afghanistan, Iran, Iraq, and North Korea. China had found a willing partner in Saudi Arabia, now increasingly under the control of radical fundamentalists and an anti-Western Wahhabi elite. After testing their first nuclear long-range missiles, the Saudis were betting on a partnership with China and India.

"India transferred nuclear technology to Saudi Arabia in return for exclusive access to Saudi oil. India's demand for oil imports continues its double-digit growth, but its economy lags due to a weak financial system. Meanwhile, a revitalized Silicon Valley continues to attract India's best and brightest. This brain drain fuels resentment against us. India is fearful of the U.S.-Pakistani alliance. Kashmir is still a sore point. The alliance with the Saudis and China gives India a convenient leverage against the U.S."

President Cumberland scribbled on a notepad as Tom spoke. Clayton struggled to concentrate and pushed aside questions about his father. He expected that the president would find the right moment to talk about Jack Harcourt, some day, somehow.

"When we imposed the oil trade embargo on Saudi Arabia, we hoped to isolate them, to give them a chance to stop their covert financial support for terrorism and to stop them from pushing forward with their nuclear weapons program. Our move backfired," reported Tom, peering over the top of his reading glasses.

The president's jaw tightened. Clayton recalled that the liberal majority in Congress had gained public support for the Oil Protection Act, right before the midterm election. Protectionist sentiments were on the rise across the land, and Congress wanted to appease constituents in the home districts. Liberals who wanted to maintain their tenuous grip on the Senate and the House saw the Oil Protection Act as a tool to limit the power of a popular president. The bill reached the president's desk a week before voters cast their mid-term election ballots killing any chance for a veto. Tom checked his notes and continued his briefing.

Supporters of the Oil Protection Act argued that reduced Saudi oil imports would not affect U.S. gas prices. Increasing oil imports from Russia and Azerbaijan would keep prices down at the gas pump. That was the theory before ethnic conflict embroiled Central Asia in civil war and demand continued to outrun supplies. Oil prices continued to climb. The U.S. built a coalition of reluctant allies to put pressure on oil producers. Tom explained that this solution was not sustainable in the long run. World stability could only come once the enemies of the West were defeated.

The U.S. had begun to pull its armed forces away from Central Asia and the Middle East, but U.S. deployments to these troubled spots resumed when Saudi Arabia fell into China's arms.

Clayton looked across the table and noticed that the president had closed his eyes and was leaning back in his chair. Yet he seemed to be listening. Tom's voice was almost a whisper. The president opened his eyes and jotted down some notes.

"China seems to be the leading partner in this new terror alliance with a long-range plan to regain Middle Kingdom status. China is intent on neutralizing Russia to take over the vast, oil-rich region along their extensive mutual border. The forces of nationalism are pulling Saudi Arabia, India, and China together, canceling out any cultural differences among them. In turn, these nationalist motives give TOVAIR, a growing multinational terrorist organization, a unique chance to piggyback on this agenda." Tom took a sip of water and cleared his throat.

"TOVAIR, the Transnational Organization of Victorious Asian/Arab Islamic Republics, represents a highly decentralized joint venture of multiple terrorist organizations aligned with Saudi Arabia, India, and China. Network members share a fanatical hatred of the West. They have shifted their operational targets from failed states like Afghanistan and Somalia to a broader universe of developing nations. We suspect that this network of terror draws direct support from the Saudis and their Sino-Indian allies."

Clayton could not help but think about TOVAIR as a cancer. Like Linda's cancer, this deadly scourge hit without warning. It spread. Surgical removal did not intimidate it; remissions never lasted long. For a split second, TOVAIR became a reminder of another loss in Clayton's life. His mother's long battle against breast cancer ended while he was a sophomore at Yale. She had been his mentor, his best friend, his main link to Jack. She spoke of Jack often. She made sure Clayton grew up spending much time around his grandfather. Jack's father was a reserved man. He seemed aloof to strangers, but his few friends knew he was steadfast. His family was the center of his life. He taught his grandson the very same lessons he had instilled in Jack, his only son.

Tom paused long enough to take another sip of water. Clayton wondered what role the president expected him to play in the fight against TOVAIR. Just as he was about to ask, Tom continued:

"Now, you must be wondering where your expertise comes in, right?" Clayton did not respond. Tom Munroe glanced at his notes and announced:

"Here is what we know so far. Remember Ahmed Assoud, your local liaison during your TDY in Karachi?"

Clayton remembered his temporary duty assignments in the Middle East. Assoud worked at the U.S. embassy and was responsible for identifying local contacts within the Pakistani counter-intelligence service. His father was an army general who was now retired after leading a coup in which he took control of a democratically elected government. During a decade of military rule, General Assoud worked closely with the US on defeating terrorism in the region. He managed to defeat Islamic fundamentalism within his own borders through swift action. Once he accomplished his mission of bringing back order, he paved the way for democratic elections. His son Ahmed was now CEO of Al-Aldinah, a telecommunications, oil, media, and financial conglomerate based in Riyahd, Saudi Arabia. The pieces of the puzzle were now falling into place. Tom continued:

"Evidence shows that Al-Aldinah serves as a front organization to finance the activities of TOVAIR. When we drilled down the data, many points led to multiple global financial avenues used to deploy and hide TOVAIR assets just below the radar of our counter-intelligence, and we found a New York link."

Tom paused, adjusted his reading glasses, and cleared his throat before letting a name hang in the air like fog on a river's edge. "Will Rogerson's Eagle Investments."

Clayton heard the words spoken calmly, deliberately, and he felt a knot tightening in the pit of his stomach. Clayton's first thought was: "There must be a mistake, Will must be in the dark about this. I cannot believe he would accept such clients..." Clayton's thoughts raced back through time.

During a Christmas holiday, one of his childhood friends from Colorado, Will Rogerson, offered Clayton a partnership in a hedge fund he had been running for a number of years. Clayton did not have to think much about this chance to move on. He submitted his CIA resignation and moved to New York.

Until the moment he heard Tom mention Will Rogerson's name, the war on terror had been a distant subject of intellectual interest for Clayton. Now it became personal. As if thinking aloud, he said:

"Right after I joined Eagle Investments, Will traveled to London for a meeting with some European clients. When he came back, he was very upbeat and mentioned that our assets under management were going to triple. Will had met a French industrialist who was looking for an aggressive manager. The name was Francois Duveau or something like that..." Tom interrupted Clayton in mid sentence.

"Duvenoix. We know. Born in Algeria, he is a French citizen. We believe that he was affiliated with Al-Qaida, went underground after the Afghan war a decade ago, and resurfaced in southern France. He operates out of London and Paris. His Eagle accounts continue to grow. We think he uses Eagle Investments to hide TOVAIR profits from other sources. What we don't know is how much your friend Will knows about this French connection."

Clayton listened carefully, and somehow, the words "your friend" felt like a nasty wasp sting. Will had been a close friend, but since Linda's death most of Clayton's contact with him or anyone else he had known in New York was minimal. He exchanged e-mails with Will about investment ideas. When he moved to Driggs, he had closed out his account with the Eagle hedge fund. Surely, Tom knew all of that.

"Clayton, we want you to contact Will and see if you can get back into business with him." Tom's command confirmed Clayton's thoughts. "But you'll need to figure out a way to work with our InterIntel team and maybe do some overseas consulting for us at the same time."

InterIntel was the interagency analytics team bringing together the best analysts from the intelligence community – elite commandos using state-of-the art technology. They worked closely with small teams of interagency field agents to solve the most intricate puzzles about terrorist operations worldwide. InterIntel worked in close cooperation with similar analyst units around the world representing friendly intelligence services. This global web of highly trained problem solvers fed actionable intelligence and other real-time, critical information to a central data insight center somewhere in the Rocky Mountains. There, data mining programs drilled for valuable nuggets of raw intelligence, which in turn analysts dissected and reassembled around the clock.

Clayton began to think about the logistics of getting back to the business he had left behind long ago. Tom's briefing had ended, but it was clear that the time to act would come soon.

"What's your timeline?"

"We would like you to contact Will today before we return to D.C.," Tom said as he handed Clayton a cell phone. As he dialed Will's direct number at Eagle Investments, Clayton began to sketch the story line. It had to be convincing; if Will was in any way, shape, or form connected to a terrorist organization, the ruse had to be credible.

"Yes?"

Will always answered his direct line with a short question, making the caller feel that he had just interrupted some important work.

"Hey, Will. Clayton here, how's the market?"

"Old buddy, we are in the money today. The Dow just closed down 135 points and our short positions saved the day. What's happening in the Western front?"

Clayton paused before calmly announcing:

"Good, OK," he paused. "Fishing is great, but it's not enough anymore. I've had a long time to think about the future, and it's time for me to get back into the game. I miss the market action. I miss the challenge of bringing in new business. I miss our early morning calls scoping out the moves for the day. I miss the adrenalin."

He paused deliberately as if delicately presenting a fly to a skeptical rainbow. Silence followed. This was not the time to talk. Clayton let the pause grow like the special moment just before a tug at the end of the fly line, when time sits still and one can hear an ant move. Then, he proceeded with the close. He was ready to set the hook.

"I need your help. Any chance I can rejoin Eagle Investments? I would like for us to work together again." Clayton paused and thought, *"Let friendship sink slowly like the Hewitt method of letting a nymph drift underwater to a feeding trout. The speed at which the fly sinks depends on its weight...*"

After a short pause, Will spoke, his voice quivering: "Well, would love to... but before I commit to anything ..." Another pause. He cleared his throat and now sounded as if he was standing on firmer ground:

"I have new partners now and it would only be fair to bring your offer up, see what they think. Business has changed since you left; we work mostly with international clients." Will sounded distant and Clayton began to have doubts about his old friend.

"Let me call you back after I check with London and maybe we can work this out." Clayton concluded that Will was no longer a free agent, able to call his own shots at Eagle Investments.

"Great, let me know." Clayton sounded upbeat.

"Sure thing– I'll be out of the office until the end of next week but I'll call you when I get back."

Clayton had not pushed Will for information about the new partners. He knew that Tom's team would be tracing calls to London immediately after he hung up.

✲ ✲ ✲

The phone call had cut the bonds of friendship held together regardless of time and place. Clayton and Will were always able to connect, to pick up a conversation wherever they had left it off. Like the time they met in Denver after Clayton's first year away from home. Will stayed in Colorado and enrolled at Colorado State. Their reunion that summer was joyous and filled with adventure. They climbed the Rockies and camped in the wilderness. Another reunion came ten years later, when Will traveled to D.C. from San Francisco. He was a successful investment manager for some mutual fund company and had just accepted a position in the options trading department of a major Wall Street firm. After Will and his wife Judy settled in New York, they took the train down to D.C. to spend a weekend with Clayton. Their lives could not be more different but the two friends felt closer than at any other time. Will spoke about being a father, and shared the angst and joy of the enterprise. Will and Judy brought pictures of their children and shared stories about their family outings and accomplishments. Clayton remembered that visit and recalled thinking that his bachelor life was just right. His fear of commitment was like a tall wall; he avoided the climb. But that was before he had met Linda. Now he knew the cost of that climb, the joy, the pain, and the loss.

Barely a week into his new position at Eagle Investments, Clayton had met Linda Knolton, the love of his life. She was a rugged individualist, had a dry sense of humor, and like him was passionate about the West. She made her living in the Big Apple but her cobalt eyes would sparkle as she recounted childhood memories of camping in the Salmon River Mountains under a blanket of stars. Like Clayton, she never considered the East Coast her home. Soon after their wedding, they traveled to Idaho to visit her family. Near Driggs, they found the perfect log cabin - a cozy retreat nestled in the mountains with grand views and open skies - a place to call home and retire some day. Their marriage became a refuge from the fast and demanding professional lives they pursued in New York. When they came home to their 5th Avenue penthouse after a fast-paced, seventeen-hour day they rejoiced in each other's company, and made plans to return to their world up in the mountains. In a few years, early retirement seemed assured. They began to talk about raising a family, in a place where they could still leave doors unlocked.

On an early summer afternoon, Linda had called Clayton at work. He could hear fear in her voice. A routine medical exam had uncovered leukemia. The prognosis did not look good. Linda held on to her good spirits. Chemotherapy followed. She was not able to do much as her cancer spread. It was just a matter of time. Too weak to travel, Linda resigned herself to spending her last days in New York, and Clayton seldom left her side. When the end came, Linda slipped away in her sleep. Clayton held her in his arms, unable to cry, and decided that it was time for him to take her home to Sandpoint, Idaho, where Linda grew up.

After the funeral, Clayton drove away alone and cried for the first time in his adult life. The cabin near the Grand Teton helped him heal and reconnect with his faith. The longing for meaning had always come at times of great loss. Now, in God's country, he felt close to his creator.

He settled into a daily routine of fly-fishing and reading. The quiet sport gave him solace and renewed his will to conquer pain. He loved the sound of riffles and the trickle of thin ribbons of water barely flowing into the steep mountain creek at the edge of his property. Here he felt close to his roots. He just loved the sound of an early morning breeze whistling past the pines. He loved to watch the golden wheat hills across the distant valley and the ghostly Grand Teton peaks nearby. Each day, New York loomed more distant. He gave up his hedge fund partnership. As time passed, he found greater and greater pleasure in his solitude. The quiet sport became a way of life. Clayton did not dwell in the past and one of his favorite sayings was, "You cannot live back there, you live here now."

✲ ✲ ✲

After talking to Will, Clayton was not sure he still knew his old pal. Clayton shifted his attention to how he would navigate the road ahead. He believed that Will was innocent until proven guilty, and knew that finding that proof would now be his job.

Tom interrupted his Clayton's thoughts. "There is no time to waste. We'll track the London call. Pack up and be ready so we can pick you up in one hour. We are flying out this afternoon. We'll pick you up at…"

The president interjected. He stood up and walked past Tom and a stocky Secret Service man.

"Clayton, mind if I ride with you to see your place?"

"Sir, you cannot..." The Secret Service man, visibly upset, was about to tell the president that his idea to ride up to the cabin with Clayton was a bad one.

The president appeased him. "Relax, Jimmy, I'll be alright, besides you guys will follow close behind. I would like some time alone with Clayton."

"Yes sir, as you wish." Jimmy's response was short and crisp.

President Mack Cumberland seemed relaxed as Clayton drove out of town. The sharp edges of the Teton Mountains pierced the soft clouds against the sky. Clayton wanted to ask so much about his dad, there were so many questions. The president broke the silence.

"What a place! No wonder you decided to come home. I grew up in Montana, so this place feels just like home. How's fishing?"

Clayton gave the president a succinct account of the water, trout, and bug conditions in the area and promised to show him some of his favorite spots on the Henry's Fork.

"Good, I'll take you up on that. It's been a long time since I've been able to get away. Perhaps we can come back soon after we get this business under control."

The president paused for a moment and lit up his pipe, looking around and hoping Jimmy and his detail were lost somewhere in the forest. The Jeep pulled up to the front of the cabin and a black SUV appeared not far behind.

Mack Cumberland walked into a bright room with a high cathedral ceiling, wood beams, and a glass wall facing a huge deck. A stone fireplace on one side of the room seemed to separate the forest from the inside of the rustic cabin. On the other side, books lined the wall from floor to ceiling. The president took a deep breath of mountain air as he stepped out on the deck. The views of a horizon bursting in bright red, orange, and pink were delicious. He felt comfortable around Clayton. He liked the quiet man who was his own son's age. He wanted to tell Clayton how much Jack had looked forward to holding him in his arms. He could not find the right words.

Leaning against the redwood railing and taking in the majestic views, President Cumberland remembered the ambush, the shots, the rush of adrenalin, and the blood everywhere. Then, he remembered another ambush, the one he missed, and the one that killed Jack. He could still see Jack's limp body and feel the pain of his own guilt. He remembered Ken Baines bleeding, staggering across the jungle, and carrying his best friend, Jack Harcourt, over his right shoulder, tears streaming down his face.

"Mr. President, how about a cup of mud, I mean coffee, sir. I just made a fresh pot."

"Mud's good. I'll have a cup."

Clayton handed the president a mug filled to the brim. Their eyes met again. The two men stood silently looking across the vast land, like hunters alert to any movement along the edge of the forest, just a few yards below the deck.

"Clayton, it's so good to finally meet you. Your dad would be proud of you. Someday I'll tell you more about our time in Vietnam.

Clayton understood. The time was not now. Like Ken Baines, the President seemed unable to unlock the haunting memories. Clayton would not push; the right time would come. He would wait and wonder as he had for a lifetime.

After a long pause, the president continued: "Son, I need to tell you something very important before we head back. You heard Tom's briefing. You now have a rough idea of what we are confronting. You'll get a full report on TOVAIR while we fly back to DC."

It was beginning to sound to Clayton as if he was actually going to fly back on Air Force One.

"Tom's been with the Agency for over thirty years. As you know, the bureaucracy has a way of becoming stuck in a particular way of thinking. The old-boy network is protective. The analysis I get is often stale."

The president's eyes narrowed as he strained to look into the distant mountain range surrounding the valley below. He turned to Clayton and said:

"I need a fresh point of view. Keep your eyes and ears wide open, I want your assessment of InterIntel. This is Tom's baby. It was his idea to set up a vast global network of analysts working with the most sophisticated tools. Many of these tools are a product of bio-engineering innovations. Some are quite accurate; we can plot 'what if scenarios' with greater precision, calculating multiple outcomes. We can mine data in ways unimaginable even a couple of years ago. We can literally travel across the data, plotting data visually to identify non-intuitive relationships. Move around it, and discover bits and pieces hidden behind words or numbers. The marriage of biology and engineering has given us windows to knowledge that we never dared open until now. But even the best of our technology has limits."

The president paused to watch a young fawn appearing at the edge of the tree line. A doe followed close behind and they slipped deep into the woods. Mack Cumberland lowered his voice like a hunter waiting for his prey in a blind.

"I'm from the old school. We cannot fight terror with technology alone. I'm afraid we are winning battles and losing the war with our reliance on the high-tech wizards. I trust your judgment, Clayton. I've read your work. I think you have the right instincts, a nose for spotting trouble before it happens. I cannot rely on anyone in the bureaucracy to give me a straight answer as to why InterIntel is not working."

Clayton was a good listener. He registered every word, every change in tone, and he sensed the president's deep sense of frustration with bureaucratic inertia. The president felt isolated from the competing bureaucratic interests outside the White House. He understood that those conflicting forces limited his ability to make decisions.

"You might think my political appointees could tackle this. I trust them but I don't have anyone with the depth of your technical knowledge to understand what is going on in the bowels of the system." Mack Cumberland leaned forward as if to get a closer look of the forest below and after a brief pause continued:

"I have a hunch. InterIntel is not meant to work. Can't quite put my finger on it. I want you to keep an eye on Tom. Just a hunch. This whole business with your former investment partner is just a side-show, as far as I am concerned. We need to find out what this French connection is all about, their motives, and their financial links to terrorism. But I am equally concerned with what is going on inside our own intelligence community."

Clayton understood the president's words. The Commander in Chief's motives were less clear. Cumberland's eyes narrowed again as he searched for movement at the edge of the forest:

"I'm interested in finding out why we cannot come up with reliable data. Is it our sources? Is it our analytical tools? Is the problem systemic? Is someone sabotaging our process from within? We need answers. Our efforts to reduce and ultimately eliminate terrorist threats seem stalled. I want an action plan by next week. Hope I'm wrong but as that famous Shakespeare line goes – something is rotten in Denmark."

Clayton quickly realized that his job description had just changed. The problem was bigger than figuring out Will's motives, his possible deception and ties to a terrorist organization. The president seemed to hint that Tom had a hidden agenda. Maybe there was an even larger national security problem rooted in InterIntel. Was President Cumberland cooking up a Nixonian conspiracy to build up his own legacy? Were his instincts right? The CIA and its new web of partnerships with the intelligence community at home and friendly services abroad were not producing the promised results. Tom would resent any second-guessing about intelligence estimates and more importantly, any questioning of the entire system he had masterminded. Any hint that Clayton reported directly to the Commander in Chief would close doors, instantly shut mouths, quickly bring the old-boy network to a defensive position at best or an offensive one at worst.

"Mr. President, if you are right it will not be easy to untie this Gordian knot. Do you have anyone I can work with at InterIntel?"

"Give Mort Rourke a call when we get to Washington. He's FBI, a former Marine, and a straight shooter. Mort has been around a long time, and I've been able to talk him out of retirement. Please report directly to him."

"Yes, sir."

"Thanks, Clayton. We need to figure out how to win this war."

"We will, Mr. President."

Cumberland liked the can-do attitude. Jack's son was a chip off the old block. Clayton walked across the room to the wall lined with books. There were books all the way across the top of the stairs leading to the bedroom loft overlooking the main room. Without much of a search, he reached for a hardcover and handed the president a worn copy of Haig-Brown's *To Know a River.*

"Here, sir, perhaps you'll enjoy some of my favorite river stories. I'll start packing. The fellows outside are starting to look antsy. Make yourself at home."

The president looked relaxed as he sat down on the old leather chair in front of the fireplace.

"This feels like home. What a great place you have here. We'll come back soon to put a Royal Wulff on the water." From the loft upstairs, Clayton responded while packing his canvas duffle bag.

"Yes, sir, we will."

Chapter 2

Capital Puzzles

Air Force One smelled of rich, soft leather. The understated elegance reminded Clayton of his visit to an officer's club in Charleston, South Carolina years back – the thick carpet, the cherry wood newspaper racks, the clocks showing time across four time zones, the sparkling crystal and gold-trimmed china. Clayton sat back as the aircraft climbed away from the familiar Western landscape below. Somewhere, down there, tucked away among the thick forest was his favorite mountain water flowing unencumbered. This was going to be a long journey away from home.

Tom interrupted Clayton's thoughts.

"Here is the report. We'll discuss it after you have a chance to take a look. When you're done come get me. I'll be in the next cabin, some press folks need babysitting."

The report was about five inches thick, filled with color-coded tabs. Clayton thumbed through it and decided to finish his cup of coffee before tackling the material in earnest. For now, he looked out the window and noticed the fighter jets flying in formation, escorting Air Force One, protecting the Commander in Chief and his entourage.

Twelve hours earlier, Clayton had released a nice rainbow back into the water. He now wondered what his dad would think of that. He recalled that Grandpa Harcourt always preached about "catch and release." More than likely, Jack had heard the same lessons from the old man. A passion for conservation ran in the Harcourt family. As a young boy, Clayton had struggled with his father's loss but he felt a deep sense of pride in the man who had fought for the values he held dear. Pride and faith did not seem compatible but together they helped Clayton overcome the lasting pain of his father's absence. He looked forward to the time when Mack Cumberland would find the right words to tell him about Jack Harcourt. He looked out the window one more time as if to catch the last spot of faint light over the mountains, reached for the briefing book, and settled in for the long flight back to D.C.

✲ ✲ ✲

Mort Rourke hung up the phone and finished typing the e-mail to Jeff. He kept it short, after all he was at the office, and he liked to keep his personal business separate from work. He had glanced at the attachment and noticed a letter Jeff had sent to Citicorp about a mistake in his direct deposit six months ago. Mort had promised to follow up at the bank's Bethesda branch, just a few blocks from Jeff's townhouse and wrote: *Got your e-mail, son. I'll take care of it on my way home. Proud of you, Dad.* Mort was proud of his oldest boy, a highly decorated Navy SEAL now serving somewhere in the Gulf.

Jeff Rourke had secured an oil field during the Iraqi war a few years back and was now on his fifth tour in the region. Before each deployment, Mort would remind his son of a lesson passed on by his own father, a WWII prisoner of war:

"The most dangerous times in war are the beginning and the end."

This war was different; it was dangerous at all times. Jeff was fluent in Arabic, Mandarin Chinese, and French, and he communicated often with his dad about the volatile political situation in the region. He commanded an elite team of interagency field operatives in the Middle East. His son's first-hand account of events and insights about individuals often led Mort to ask probing questions during the daily morning brainstorming sessions.

Mort's team of interagency analysts incorporated these questions into their models but often their analytic outputs would either ignore Jeff's questions or give answers with low probability of correlation to events in the field. Mort often wondered about this recurring pattern but figured the "Whiz Kids" knew what they were doing. After all, he had made a quantum leap from law enforcement to intelligence analysis. His learning curve was still a bit steep when it came to using the latest technology to connect the dots. Yet, Mort had an uncanny sense for asking the right questions.

Mort Rourke had joined the FBI shortly after returning from Vietnam and earning a Purple Heart. His priorities were his faith, his country, and his family, in that order. He married Susan, his high school sweetheart, and a year later Jeff was born. Two years later, the twins arrived. Molly and Christy were now married and had their own families. Mort loved to spend time with the little ones, Jenny, Vicky, and Mark. The kids lived in California and Oregon. Visits were limited to Christmas and summer vacations. He and Susan stayed connected with the "Grands" via the Internet. Susan beamed whenever she downloaded the digital images of the three happy little faces. She liked to read their goofy messages aloud. Mort would laugh and praise the kids for inheriting his sense of humor.

Susan wanted Mort to retire so they could get a place closer to the kids. She kept telling him how much they could enjoy retirement: playing golf, traveling, spending time with the twins and their families. That was before the war against terrorism heated up again. Jeff shipped out to the Gulf, and Mort postponed his retirement at the request of the President of the United States of America.

Mack Cumberland and Mort Rourke became friends during their first tour in Vietnam, and Mort agreed to stay on out of loyalty to country and friendship. He began working almost around the clock, obsessed by his duty to find the culprits of the simultaneous attacks on innocent civilians from coast to coast. American casualties mounted during the first weeks of the attacks, and Mort's determination inspired all around him. His promotion to Deputy of InterIntel made him the leader of an elite team of interagency counter-intelligence analysts. The unexpected call from President Cumberland erased any of Sue's hopes for Mort's retirement, but her husband found a renewed sense of purpose working with the best and brightest analysts at InterIntel.

☆ ☆ ☆

The call from Clayton Harcourt was expected. The confident voice and the direct approach gave Mort a good first impression of the tall and quiet man he was about to meet. Mort's office was very large by Washington standards. He enjoyed a view of the Potomac and the Mall, a perk more fitting for the head of the American Farmers Federation or some other powerful interest group. From his corner office, Mort could see the Washington Monument on one side. On the other side, he could see a partial view of the river. The corner office seemed plush for a public servant, but Mort was not an ordinary bureaucrat. He earned his pay through hard work and dedication. His motto was "a job well done is a job worth doing." As he was about to reach for the stack of reports in his in-basket, his assistant announced the arrival of Dr. Clayton Harcourt.

Mort walked out to the hallway and introduced himself with a firm handshake.

"Clayton, nice to meet you. Please come on in."

Mort liked Clayton instantly. The clear, pale eyes, the straight posture, the thin smile, all spoke volumes of the man's quiet professionalism. A bit older than Jeff, Mort estimated. The internal file listed a sharp intellect as only one of Clayton's assets. It was good to see this man come aboard at such a critical time.

"How was the trip on Air Force One?"

"Long, but the food was good."

Clayton never liked red-eye specials. One way he fought jet lag was to graze throughout the entire flight. A selection of fresh fruits and cheese had kept him going as he worked his way through the lengthy TOVAIR report.

Mort opened the wall cabinet behind his conference table and offered Clayton a giant blueberry muffin. Then, he reached for the pot of coffee and poured two cups.

"Here, have one of these. My wife baked them this morning, and I don't dare take them back home."

"I can use a cup of brew. The TOVAIR report kept me awake last night on the way up here. We seem to have more questions than answers at this point."

"What do you make of it?"

They sat at the end of the conference table, and Clayton got right down to business. Mort was eager to hear Clayton's assessment. Perhaps this fellow could see the missing links. Mack Cumberland was betting that if there was anyone who could find the right trail, Clayton Harcourt was it. This was a big bet. Win, lose, or draw, the end game was near. In three months, the American people would elect their next president and TOVAIR seemed interested in disrupting the political traditions of a free society.

"We do not seem to have an answer as to how the new financing mechanisms of this network are configured. We seem to be looking for answers in all the old familiar places – shell organizations, philanthropic organizations, money-laundering schemes through Western financial institutions, mutual fund companies, investment banks, hedge funds, and even the convoluted *halawas.*"

Clayton paused but did not bother explaining how these traditional Middle Eastern finance intermediaries functioned. He figured Mort knew they had served for centuries as informal channels to transfer funds.

"I think the clues are elsewhere."

Clayton pulled a printout from his folder. "Mr. Rourke, ..."

Mort cut in: "Hey, please just call me Mort."

Clayton liked Morton's casual tone because it reminded him of the carefree life he enjoyed out West.

"OK, Mort, take a look at this printout."

The institutional names were familiar. All the major investment banks around the globe – Citicorp, Deutsche Bank, and Morgan Stanley – filled the coded pages.

"Wait a minute; I thought you said we need to look elsewhere. These look like the usual suspects." Before Clayton could answer, Mort saw the columns showing underwriting amounts for each institution's sovereign debt issues and their respective national governments. He was now intrigued, and asked:

"You think these guys are involved in the international sovereign debt market?"

Clayton nodded. "It's more than that. I think they are using sovereign debt issues to raise funds and directly finance their activities under the cover of fiscal policy in countries with weak governmental institutions. We are talking about this entire list of countries across every continent. Rising national debt levels in each and every one of these countries has been possible through the increasing access of these governments to private market financing, notes and bonds."

Mort was quickly sorting out the pieces of the puzzle laid out in front of him, but the picture was not yet completely clear. Clayton sketched the main outline of his theory:

"Look at the sharp rise in government debt levels over the last two years for each one of these countries."

The list was alphabetical from Argentina to Zambia. The figures were in the billions of dollars for each entry. Morton glanced at the long list of figures, as Clayton continued:

"Many of these countries are defaulting on their debt payments, some are relying heavily on IMF bailouts, and some are calling for debt relief. Guess who pays? We do. And we can't question officials in any of these countries as to their lack of fiscal prudence."

Mort was beginning to understand Clayton's general argument, but he was unsure of the role of the IMF. He interrupted:

"I thought the IMF imposed specific conditions on these troubled governments. Am I wrong?"

Clayton explained that although the IMF sets specific policy guidelines for nations at the brink of bankruptcy, implementing those guidelines is very difficult.

"We try through IMF conditionality to bring some sense of fiscal restraint, some transparency, but our effectiveness is very limited. Corruption combined with national sovereignty makes for good bedfellows to cover illicit activities from prying eyes."

Mort took notes on a yellow pad, as Clayton pointed out the reasons it was so difficult to detect direct money transfers between governments:

"They figured this out. They can run money through private financial institutions only for so long. Private capital markets are transparent. So, I think they now run money through official channels. These transactions are opaque. And corrupt government officials provide ample cover."

Mort took a deep breath. He was not familiar with the workings of the international financial system and was not certain that he was asking the right questions.

"Are you assuming that all of these governments are in some way involved in a coordinated effort to finance TOVAIR? You think there are key players in each one of these governments who know how the money moves?"

Clayton helped himself to another cup of coffee and poured some for Mort.

"I suspect the effort is not coordinated. TOVAIR is a highly decentralized conglomerate, it's not a command and control outfit. The mission is well defined and understood through the entire network, namely to destroy democracies and market economies." He paused as if to pinpoint motives and then added:

"Political and economic freedom threatens TOVAIR's survival, so they are using weak democracies and emerging market economies as proxies to destroy us. The strategy has changed from the days when terrorists launched simultaneous attacks on innocent civilians. But, we need to consider that the threat of such attacks is not over."

Mort was still taking notes but he paused when Clayton got up and walked across the room and examined a large world map on the wall. Clayton traced his index finger slowly across five continents, stopping in selected countries as he spoke.

"TOVAIR probably identified key players in each of these countries. The majority sit at the top of the food chain without even suspecting they are prey themselves. Corrupt officials in the ministries of finance and other key executive agencies in charge of major governmental programs look the other way when official funds disappear. Bribes help. And underwriters of sovereign debt issues provide additional cover."

Mort realized the serious implications of Clayton's theory and shook his head.

"If you are right, our job gets tougher by the minute."

Clayton sat back and delivered the second part of his assessment.

"Yes, and there is more. I scanned your team's report outputs for the last six months. Not even a hint of these connections and the potential for civilian attacks on our own soil. The raw data is there, but no sign of any of this in the final reports."

Mort stopped taking notes and listened to each and every word. Clayton spoke with confidence.

"I see three possible scenarios. First, a programming flaw could be fixed relatively fast. Second, analysts are either rejecting or omitting variables leading to important clues. Third, the data we are getting from the field is not reliable. To start out, I recommend we look at the output of each team member. Is there any way to get a picture of individual and the combined metrics from the field?"

Mort's response came quickly. The possibility of a renewed wave of civilian attacks on U.S. soil haunted the Cumberland administration, and kept Mort on edge. InterIntel's central mission was to identify and eliminate terrorist threats before they had a chance to become actual acts of violence against American citizens and assets. The prospect of finding evidence of analysis tampering in his own shop did not make Mort happy. He resolved to address the problem without any delay.

"I'll have the techies do a run on the programming side today, and I'll review the chart flows for data analysis myself. Our team consists of forty-five analysts. I'll run an updated background check on all; we now have a program that grades their work, a sort of analysis of their individual and collective outputs. I should have something for you in the next couple of days."

Chapter 3
Partners of Convenience

Will Rogerson rubbed his eyes and finished entering the electronic buy order for a block of 500,000 shares of Total Oil, the French oil and gas producer. He still felt jet lagged from his London flight. The meeting with Francois Duvenoix had been stressful, particularly as he mentioned the call from his old partner, Clayton Harcourt. Francois was always a bit high strung but on this day, he seemed particularly prickly. Will did not even bother to say that Clayton wanted to join Eagle Investments. He knew what the answer would be, but he felt obligated to tell Francois about the call. He did not expect the violent reaction.

"What do you mean he called? I thought you two were no longer communicating. I thought I made it perfectly clear. Our partnership demands your complete loyalty. We bailed you out. In return, we only asked that you sever your ties to all former clients and partners. Is this too much to ask of you?"

The French accent was getting thicker, the voice a bit shrill. Will did not want to jeopardize his relationship with Duvenoix. What started out as a business partnership was now more than that. It had become a life-saver. The bailout came just days before Will faced bankruptcy. Duvenoix paid quarterly fees that kept him and his family afloat, enjoying the lavish lifestyle that almost cost him his marriage and his business.

Will appreciated his benefactor. Lately, however, the Frenchman had turned increasingly more demanding. Not just the insistence on higher investment returns but the pressure to engage in more risky international ventures. Absolute silence about their offshore transactions was becoming a matter of life or death. Devenoix's parting comments still chilled his spine.

"Don't forget my friend; your family's life is at risk. Some of my clients are less forgiving than I am. I trust our deal will hold. You keep quiet, and you'll have nothing to worry about."

Will Rogerson felt little comfort in those last words from his business partner. He checked the trade confirmations and was pleased with the execution price of this last purchase. He followed Duvenoix's instructions carefully and checked his personal fund transfer. His partner had kept his side of the bargain; Western Associates showed a deposit of $3 million posted yesterday, just at the time his plane landed at JFK. Will figured that amount represented about one percent of the total annual return on the investment portfolio he was now managing for Duvoix and his affiliated companies. Trading twenty-four hours a day was taking a toll on Will's nerves and a shot of Tanquerey helped to make the phone call he had dreaded since last week. Two rings, and then the familiar voice:

"Gone fishing. Please leave a message. I'll call you back."

"Hey, Clayton, Will here. Sorry buddy, afraid we won't be able to work it out. Partners are planning some restructuring. We are not taking on any new deals. Be glad to give you a few names in town for you to contact.... Let me know. Hope you caught a big one!"

Will was glad that Clayton had not answered the call. Somehow, he felt sick to his stomach thinking of how he had deceived his best friend, but it was too late to change the course of events. Will called his driver to let him know that he was on his way to the parking garage on the second floor. The limo was part of a deal made in Paris last year. Devenoix had hired the driver, Lenny, a clean-cut, quiet college kid from Marseille, now studying architecture at New York University. Will then called his wife to tell her he was on his way home. Before leaving his office, he typed the symbol TO. The after-market price of Total Oil was up two cents on high volume. Devenoix would be satisfied; few investment pros could match Will Rogerson's market timing skills.

✡ ✡ ✡

Tom Munroe climbed up the steps of the Foggy Bottom subway station, stepping out into the damp street. The evening rain was cooling the air, and he walked a few blocks to the south entrance of the State Department. It was late in the day, but he knew Alex Keynes III would be at his desk, particularly after receiving the phone call Tom had placed earlier in the afternoon. Tom flashed his security card, and the guard waved him through the metal detector gate.

He took the elevator to the third floor and could hear his own footsteps along the deserted corridor leading to Alex's office. Tom walked in as Alex was reaching for his raincoat.

"I thought you would not make it this evening."

The dry tone revealed Alex's annoyance. He was an arrogant bachelor whose sense of self-importance was not matched by his present dead-end desk job at State. The Cumberland administration had appointed a few Western "take-no prisoner" type cowboys to the top positions in the department, and these political hacks had managed to derail the careers of the most devoted liberals at State. Many Foreign Service officers had been recalled from their overseas assignments. Some had to give up their high diplomatic perches in exotic capitals. Some had been reassigned to the most mundane desks in Washington. It was definitely a political house cleaning of the first order, and Alex Keynes III had been one of the first targets of what in the hallways of State was known as Cumberland's Great Purge.

Keynes's tour in Beijing was cut short. He was upset at the imposition of having to return to Foggy Bottom, far away from the action and the contacts that propelled his career forward. Prior to China, he had served in the Soviet Union, India, Pakistan, Indonesia, and South Korea. In between these assignments, he did a tour in New York, at the UN mission. There he met the friends that to this day were like family to him. Some even promised a lucrative golden parachute to help Keynes retire anywhere in the world.

Some years later, Alex enjoyed a stint at the NSC, where he first met Tom Munroe, a former CIA operative who had moved up to a management position. While at the NSC, Tom and Alex bonded through a shared and secret admiration for centralized regimes and their command and control tactics. In such systems bureaucrats ruled, and both men lusted for more power than that granted by their career jobs.

"We had another crisis of confidence. Your 'friend' ordered a massive audit of our main analysis unit. He wants the tech guys to do a complete audit ASAP. So much for your reliable sources."

Tom's sarcasm flowed slowly like maple syrup on a cold winter morning. Alex walked past him toward the elevator. His tone was dry.

"Let's go for a walk."

They walked out of the building in silence and headed toward Virginia Avenue. Tom broke the silence.

"Morton Rourke is behind the latest request. I have no idea what triggered it but know that he has some big contact at the White House. Might even be the President. When we picked up Harcourt in Idaho, the old man spent some time alone with him. This morning Clayton paid Morton a visit. It doesn't smell good."

Alex had read Clayton's file. The connection between Mack Cumberland and Clayton's father was a nice cover for the one-on-one meeting. Was the President now using Harcourt as a cutout for his domestic agenda? Alex wondered, and quickly concluded that his question was of secondary concern. A more important question for Tom followed:

"What is Harcourt's official assignment?"

"He contacted his ex-partner at Eagle Investments, and then read the TOVAIR report on the way into town. Before we landed, he indicated that he needed some time to do some follow-up. That should keep him busy for a while. I asked for a report at the end of the week. Will Rogers will not be a problem. But Rourke could be another story."

"Rourke and Harcourt together," corrected Alex, and added curtly:

"Keep an eye on this and keep me posted." He did not give Tom a chance to respond. He hailed a cab just pulling out of the Watergate driveway, jumped in, and quickly disappeared into the night.

The reception was well underway by the time Sanford Gillman, the gregarious host, greeted Tom Munroe.

"Glad you could come, Tom."

The lavish Georgetown home was Washington's premier fundraising Mecca. Gillman was a certified member of "Gucci Gulf," an elite community of high-powered lobbyists who knew anyone and everyone, the movers and shakers capable of lifting or destroying careers. Money mattered within the Beltway; Gillman knew how to turn on the money spigot and nurture ambitions with the milk of politics. This evening's event was a fundraiser for Senator Priscilla

Parks. She was the Chairwoman of the Senate Commerce Committee and was a ranking member of the powerful Appropriations Committee, not a bad assignment for a rookie senator. Rumors about her desire to run for president had been swirling around the Capitol for months. Her repeated denials were barely credible. She was an ambitious demagogue who favored corporate tax increases, an expanding welfare state, and drastic reductions in military spending. Her opponents considered her an abrasive opportunist, elected to office through her husband's connections. Gregory Parks was a wealthy trial lawyer who despised corporate America. He had lined his pockets with hefty tobacco litigation fees. Gregory's friends were loyal Priscilla supporters. Through the junior senator, they could manipulate public policy. Now, with a weak nominee who could not win against the incumbent, they were ready to help her enter the presidential race.

Gillman led Tom towards the library, where a few guests gossiped about the latest marital tribulations of Senator Parks. The host poured Tom a drink. Arm in arm the two men walked towards the balcony overlooking the terraced garden. Tom did not care for Gillman's penchant for physical closeness but understood why he was fond of twisting arms, literally. When they could no longer be overheard, the lobbyist said:

"Tom, I made a transfer to the account yesterday. You should be able to access the funds any time. My client was pleased with your report. He expects you'll keep him posted about your State Department contact soon."

"I'll do my best."

Tom barely sipped his very dry martini. Earlier this evening had not been the right time to approach Alex about a new venture. Gillman's client was interested in knowing more about State's initiatives in the Middle East, and he would have to approach Alex another time. The latest deposit would come in handy now that the balloon payment on the beach house was coming due. Tom overlooked the fact that Gillman's "client" was a potentially lethal liaison. What mattered was that it delivered money as promised, every quarter. He was not too picky when it came to information. Tom considered the arrangement a low-risk venture to supplement his income and help his family. Pathway Consulting was a convenient vehicle to launder these funds, and Tom's daughter Pat was a loyal partner.

It was shortly after midnight when the last guest pulled away from the Georgetown driveway, and Gillman poured himself another drink. He walked into his cluttered office to finish the day's work. The e-mail message to Abdul Hakim was brief.

"Delivered your goods. Consultant will complete next report soon."

Gillman had met Hakim, an Egyptian entrepreneur, when they were both board members of Altell Inc., a now-defunct telecommunications firm. Their association over the years was mutually profitable. Hakim had multiple business interests around the world, and Gillman had powerful clients willing to contribute valuable insider information to benefit Hakim's ventures. Gillman's compensation from the Hakim account was hefty, but he figured Hakim's profits justified the payoff. Hakim had deep pockets and this was an instant source of attraction to Gillman, who disliked the man but enjoyed the profitable relationship. Hakim, a.k.a. Ahmed Assoud, not only had deep pockets; he had deep secrets.

Gillman could not put his finger on it, but suspected Hakim was involved in more than the telecommunications business. He figured Hakim was tied to the oil business as well. Those credentials were good for Gillman's fundraising schemes. Gillman liked his clients to have a diverse source of revenue – a diversified portfolio was a prudent bet against market cycles, and diversified clients were more secure clients. After sending the e-mail to Hakim, Gillman checked the daily performance of his online investment account statement and was pleased to see the account moving in the right direction. Up another three percent since last night's closing balance. He shut off the light and headed upstairs to rest for a few hours before a series of meetings scheduled early the next morning on Capitol Hill.

Chapter 4
Operation Zamzam

Thousands of miles away, the World Energy conference participants at the Cairo Hilton resort were taking a break between sessions during the first day of their week-long strategy retreat. Ahmed Assoud checked his e-mail messages on the way to the bathroom and was pleased to hear the news from Sanford Gillman. The American seldom delivered anything of significance but the investment in this relationship had the potential to yield hefty profits, financial and otherwise. Of particular interest was the possibility of Senator Parks becoming President Parks. This would open up new windows of opportunity to achieve TOVAIR's goals. Gillman could provide access to the center of American power in ways few others could.

As he relieved himself, Assoud made a mental note to send Gillman an invitation to meet him in London next month. It was critical at this time to have a face to face visit and lay the groundwork for the next phase of operation Zamzam, named after the famous spring flowing across Mecca and into the courtyard of the ancient temple, Ka'bah.

A water spring in the desert was a symbol of hope and life. Zamzam was the perfect metaphor for the revival of an Islamic empire that Assoud envisioned for the twenty-first century, an empire that would revitalize the Umma, the Islamic community and way of life. He believed that the quest of empire justified all violence and was only possible with the elimination of all infidels. He never bothered pondering the contradictions of his twisted logic. He knew that the tactics of the past were no longer viable. Attacks on unsuspecting civilian victims did not get the attention of Western governments. Even attacks with large numbers of casualties did not generate the American policy changes necessary to bring back an Islamic empire in all of its ninth century glory. Assoud was convinced that the only way to overcome America's power was to attack it from within. He no longer believed that sleeper cells of loyal Islamic fighters could destroy America and its Western allies.

The Americans in particular seemed resolved to fight back, and Assoud was certain that unless he could break their will to fight, their "war on terrorism" would continue unabated. His Islamic empire would remain an elusive dream. He was not willing to give up violence against civilians but thought that the main strategy of operation Zamzam would be to undermine the American power centers from within by pulling hard at the strings of corruption and greed that animated the main actors on America's political stage. The possible election of Parks would speed up the timetable for executing Zamzam.

Assoud was confident that Gillman was a powerful and gullible American, the perfect pawn to lead the way to the center of American power. Gillman would not suspect Assoud's true agenda. The power broker was greedy. As long as money flowed into his pocket, he would continue to deliver key information. Ahmed Assoud walked back into the conference room now filled with smoke. He hated the smell of cigarettes as much as he hated the West.

✲ ✲ ✲

Clayton's coffee was cold and tasted stale. He spent his second day in Washington poring over the latest raw data on TOVAIR. After a long day analyzing the latest raw intelligence in a windowless office, he felt fenced in. He looked forward to walking to his temporary studio apartment, provided by the Agency across the river. He stepped out of the lobby of the non-descript building just a few blocks from the State Department and noticed that on this particular evening Foggy Bottom had a musty smell, a typical city smell that made him long for wide open spaces. On his way towards the Georgetown Bridge, he noticed that Marshall's West End, a traditional English pub located in the basement of an old hotel, had been demolished. Clayton fondly remembered the aroma of freshly baked bread and clam chowder; the smell invited one to slow down and settle in for a hearty meal. It was a neighborhood kind of place. Clayton could relate to the owner, a fellow Coloradoan, who enjoyed river rafting.

Colorado seemed a far-away memory. Since Tom's unexpected call just three days ago, even his cabin in Idaho seemed to fade into the past. For now, a cramped, colorless government office filled with computer monitors and a Spartan apartment in Georgetown were home. He walked briskly, thinking of the day's puzzles that remained unsolved. He had more questions than answers at this time but was glad that the president had given him hope to finally learn more about Jack. He had not heard from Morton today and was surprised because he seemed to be a man of his word. Perhaps the review was taking longer than anticipated. He would wait another day and then check back; after all, the president wanted an action plan soon.

When he entered the apartment, the red light on the phone was blinking. The first message was forwarded from the cabin's number, a negative answer from Will Rogers. Tom probably knew the content of the message, and there was no immediate need to contact him. Will sounded troubled and Clayton thought that perhaps he would come up with an excuse to go see his old friend soon. Face to face, he might be able to find out what exactly Will Rogerson knew about Francois Duvenoix. Clayton was about to check the second message when his phone rang. It was Tom Munroe.

"Clayton, get ready for a long flight, my friend. Old Ahmed Assoud is at a World Energy conference in Cairo. This is a perfect opportunity for you to get reacquainted. I'll brief you on the way to the airport. I'll pick you up at 5:30 tomorrow morning."

The second message was from Morton. "Clayton, you were on to something. I am still working on the analysts' output reports and will be in the office until late today. Call me here or at home."

Clayton checked his watch. It was 10:30 pm and he figured that Morton might be at home by now but just in case, he dialed the office first. On the second ring, Morton answered. "Morton, I just got home. I'm returning your call and have news for you. Tom just called me. I'm to leave tomorrow at 5:30 am for Cairo. I have a sense Tom wants me out of town."

"You are probably right about that, particularly after what I am finding. We are not on a secure line. It will be best that we get together when you get back. Any idea when that will be?"

"I'm just checking on the Internet as we speak, and see that the Cairo conference at the Hilton ends on Monday, so I should be back by Tuesday." While Clayton spoke, Morton checked his son's travel schedule.

"Clayton, my son Jeff will be in Cairo Saturday. I'll have him contact you. Anything you need, you just let him know. I'm proud of that kid. I know you two will get along. Take care and carry on."

"Yes, sir."

Clayton hung up and wondered what evidence Morton had discovered. He was sure that Jeff's travel to Cairo was not coincidental. He knew that Morton understood the risks of his immediate mission. Jeff's presence was a prudent security measure, a standard operating procedure. For the most part, Clayton dismissed SOPs. This time, as he prepared to meet the enemy, he was grateful for the precautionary safety net.

✲ ✲ ✲

The Dulles Airport terminal was bustling with early morning commuters. Tom had dropped Clayton off at the United check-in counter after handing him a folder with his new passport, travel itinerary, and briefing papers. His new business card read *Clayton H. Harcourt III, CEO, Plano Energy Corporation, 2339 Caravan Way, Dallas, TX 76999*. He wondered if CEOs traveling with a worn-out duffle bag were considered eccentric. Well, this entire trip was unconventional, so why not play the part. He had not packed his fly rod for this journey because he recalled that the muddy Nile offered no angling adventures. Besides, this trip would be a different kind of fishing expedition.

According to Tom, Clayton was expected to establish a business relationship with Assoud that could lead to an inside look at vital TOVAIR operations. Tom's theory was that money and power motivated Assoud. A joint venture with a wealthy and well-connected American acquaintance would be irresistible to Ahmed Assoud, the CEO of Al-Aldinah.

The downside of Clayton's Cairo mission was that Assoud knew of his past CIA affiliation. But even this negative could be turned into a positive. Tom suggested that to remove any possible shred of suspicion, Clayton should claim that he left the CIA bitter and disappointed. He would have time to assess the situation in detail on his long flight to the Middle East. Clayton remained skeptical of Tom's tactical plan and was willing to improvise. Like an angler on a windy day, Clayton knew how to approach a mountain stream when elusive trout would refuse to take any fly patterns.

✲ ✲ ✲

The Egyptian customs official wanted to know what brought Mr. Harcourt to Cairo.

"I will be attending the OPEC conference at the Hilton."

"I see. Are you a businessman?" The inquiry seemed redundant since Clayton had handed his official conference invitation, his passport, and business card.

"Right."

"How long do you plan to stay in Cairo?"

"Three days."

"Plan any trip outside Cairo?"

"No."

The customs man stamped Clayton's passport and waved him through. Fortunately, Clayton had not checked his bag, so he was able to skip the long line of passengers waiting for their luggage and headed straight to the checkout point leading to the airport terminal.

He first noticed the angular face through the glass window separating the crowd gathered to welcome passengers. He was taller than most men around him, and his local attire was well worn. He blended into the crowd and followed every one of Clayton's steps. Clayton moved swiftly through the crowd towards the Hilton limousine counter and handed the attendant his ticket. He looked around but the man he had spotted a few minutes earlier was nowhere to be found.

Clayton wondered where he had seen the face before and could not quite pin down the place or circumstances. He remained alert in the way one does when stepping out into a busy intersection. After a ten minute wait, his ride arrived. He climbed into the limo; the only other passenger was the man he had spotted earlier. Clayton's instant reaction was to confront the stranger in local garb but before he could say anything, the man introduced himself.

"Clayton, I'm Jeff Rourke. Welcome to Cairo."

Chapter 5

In the Arena

Jeff Rourke's handshake was firm and he looked like the spitting image of his dad Morton. His demeanor exuded professional confidence and Clayton felt instantly at ease. "Good to meet you. Your dad said that you would be here tomorrow…"

"That was the original plan, but I thought it would be safer to touch base before you get to the Hilton." Jeff's tone was now grave, as he spoke in a calm and firm voice.

"We have had a task force in place tracking TOVAIR's operational plans. We have reason to believe that they are reaching a critical decision point. They are using the World Energy meeting as a ruse to bring together top people from around the world. A member of our task force, who got very close to the action was murdered last night."

Jeff paused to let Clayton digest the news. Clayton's thoughts were racing across the possible implications for his own mission. If Ahmed Assoud was naturally suspicious, the recent discovery of an inside informer would raise new red flags and it would be more difficult to break the ice. Tom's plan would be more difficult to implement. Jeff broke the silence.

"I'll stay very close to you. Others from our task force will be available for backup should you need it." As he spoke, Jeff handed Clayton pictures of three Delta Force colleagues assigned to Operation Eagle One.

"You may see these guys from time to time, ignore them. If you see them stay very alert because you will be in harm's way. If you need to get a hold of me here is my number. Call anytime." Clayton handed Jeff the pictures back and tucked the number in his shirt pocket.

"Not a good idea," said Jeff, pointing at Clayton's pocket. "Just memorize it. It's safer that way. Almost forgot to tell you, my dad said to let you know that you were right on target. He finished his review and will brief you when you get back to Washington."

Clayton's thin smile showed his appreciation and apprehension. "Thanks, that is, if I make it back. From the sound of recent developments around here, I'll have to watch my back. After so many years away from the field, I'm afraid I'm a bit rusty."

Jeff smiled. "Don't worry. We'll take care of your back. Plus, I'm sure your instincts will kick in and so will your training."

The limo slowed down and for the first time, Clayton noticed the palm trees lining the boulevard along the Nile. The sun was just coming up and the city was not yet awake. The driver pulled up to the entrance of a small hotel that looked more like an apartment building in a narrow cobblestone street off the main road. Before Jeff stepped out into the street, he turned to Clayton.

"Well, this is where I camp out. The Hilton is just a few blocks from here. Call me if you need anything. Be careful."

"Thanks again, Jeff."

The limo returned to the main road and Clayton spotted the entrance of the Hilton. He felt exhausted. Jet lag was just beginning to take effect, but he felt an extra jolt of energy as he stepped into the lobby and detected one of the three Delta men working on Operation Eagle One. He had a neatly trimmed reddish beard. He seemed utterly relaxed, sipping a cup of coffee and chatting in German with an attractive blonde. Clayton walked past the couple and handed his reservation to the young clerk behind the front desk, who flashed a friendly smile and gave Clayton his room key.

"Welcome to Cairo, Mr. Harcourt. Enjoy your stay with us."

✲ ✲ ✲

The eleventh-floor room had a good view of the Nile. The river softened the rugged edges of the city and meandered lazily across its center. The ribbon of rust-colored water sharpened the contrast of faded buildings packed tight against each other. Row after row of urban sprawl stretched as far as the eye could see. A pale cloud of yellow smoke and dust hung across the sky, reaching the edge of the desert, hardly visible at a distance. The slender minaret of a nearby mosque rose high above the ground and the sound of the muezzin's first call to daily prayer echoed across the rooftops. Clayton rubbed his tired eyes and checked the time. Six o'clock in the morning and it felt like late afternoon.

In two hours, the World Energy conference sessions would resume and he needed to get there early. He also needed to figure out how to approach Assoud. He remembered him as a prickly fellow with a short attention span. The approach would have to be direct and swift. His presentation would have to be smooth and natural; just like the presentation of an artificial caddis fly in the midst of a furious hatch. He would have to set the hook quickly and then maintain enough tension to reel in his prey.

The encounter with Morton's son on the drive from the airport had been brief. Clayton appreciated Jeff's professionalism and stark warning. Before leaving his room, Clayton flushed Jeff's cell phone number down the toilet and repeated the number to himself one more time. He tucked his cell phone into his briefcase and rode the elevator down to the mezzanine, right above the lobby. A group of conference participants were mingling and drinking coffee from small glass mugs. Clayton leaned over the balcony to get a closer look at the gathering below. He noticed a small group mingling around a graying middle-aged man of slight built dressed in a charcoal grey suit. When the man turned his head to greet another man approaching the small group, Clayton instantly recognized the face.

✲ ✲ ✲

Ahmed Assoud had aged a bit since his younger days at the US embassy in Karachi but the large scar on the left cheek and the thick moustache were still distinctive. The group began to move toward the staircase leading up to the mezzanine and Clayton entered the main conference hall, where the first speaker of the day was checking his notes at the podium. Dr. Rashid Binari was a prominent Indian scholar from the Center for Indian Studies at Beijing University. His topic was *"Collaborative Agendas: The Marriage of China and India's Energy and Computer Software Industries."*

Clayton sat down at a table near the back of the room, where he could observe the entrance and most participants as they came into the room. The group of men who had been talking to Ahmed Assoud entered and sat together at a reserved table. Assoud was not among them. Clayton checked the program and noticed that the general session would run until noon. During the afternoon, the conference would break up into smaller workshops. One of those workshops listed Assoud as a panel discussant. The speaker was testing his microphone when out of the corner of his eye, Clayton noticed Assoud strolling into the room and tucking a cell phone into his pocket. He sat by himself just a few feet away from Clayton. When the lights dimmed and the chatter of the crowd settled, the speaker began his Power Point presentation.

Dr. Binari argued for continued collaboration between China's growing oil industry and India's robust computer software manufacturers. He started out by presenting evidence of the close trade ties between the two countries for the past twenty years had resulted in profitable joint ventures in the fields of renewable energy development and ocean science and technology. He argued that China's natural resources and India's technology created a powerful partnership capable of turning China and India into the most powerful energy suppliers of the twenty-first century.

On his flight to Cairo, Clayton had read that Saudi Arabia was engaging in secret talks to join the Chinese-Indian energy partnership in an attempt to sever its ties to OPEC nations and become instead a member of the most powerful energy alliance in the world. As the Q & A session got underway, Assoud slipped out of the room. Clayton followed him.

"Ahmed, so good to see you! I just noticed you walking out and I wanted to say hello." Clayton's small smile was barely noticeable. Ahmed Assoud looked startled.

"Well, long time no see, my friend. What a pleasant surprise. What brings you to Cairo?"

This was the only chance Clayton had to make his pitch. He handed Assoud his business card and replied, while checking his cell phone for messages.

"The chance to do business. In Wall Street, I made some great contacts and now I'm working on a large deal. A client is looking to put some big money to work, and there are some interested parties attending this conference."

The large scar seemed to stretch a bit as Ahmed pursed his lips and whispered, "You are in the right place, my friend. This is the place to make deals."

Then in a lighter tone, he continued, "Let's catch up later today. After my panel discussion, I'll have a few minutes to chat. I'll meet you at the bar downstairs."

Clayton nodded and went back into the conference room, where an animated speaker was starting his presentation with a joke in a very thick French accent.

"So, zee Frenchman asks to zee Englishman: Why don't you like Americans? And zee Englishman saiz: Just like during WWII, because zey over drink, zey over eat, zey are over sexed, and zey are over here."

Loud laughter erupted across the room. When the noise subsided, Pierre Theault proceeded to lecture and gloat about the success of the United Nations Security Council in isolating the United States and defeating its attempt to secure votes for its military presence in the Middle East. The rest of the morning yielded more anti-American rhetoric. Clayton was relieved when the afternoon sessions began.

✡ ✡ ✡

Ahmed Assoud was a deft panel discussant. He critiqued all four panelists presenting evidence for each of his claims and summing up the strong points without siding with any of the speakers. Clayton complemented him as they sat at a small table in the elegant hotel bar. Shortly after ordering drinks, Clayton noticed the couple he had spotted earlier upon his arrival, sitting at a nearby booth.

Assoud wanted to know what kind of business opportunities Clayton's client was interested in pursuing. Clayton explained that his client, a very wealthy corporate CEO, was looking to diversify his private foundation portfolio and was interested in a Middle Eastern joint venture. Assoud leaned forward raising his bushy eyebrows.

"Why the Middle East?" He did not seem very interested in hearing the answer, as he sat back, called the waiter, and ordered a second round of drinks. Assoud was quite intrigued by the possibility of expanding his network of highly placed and unsuspecting assets in America. VIPs who had access to funds and could influence decision makers were the ideal target for implementing TOVAIR's nefarious agenda. He wanted to know more. But this was not the time to show his eagerness.

Clayton looked around the room, as if to assess who might be within hearing distance. He noticed the man with the red beard and the blond woman. They were holding hands and seemed oblivious to their surroundings. Jeff Rourke had his team in place. Clayton leaned forward and whispered across the table, forcing Assoud to lean forward.

"My client already has substantial commitments around the globe and feels that the Middle East is an ideal market to place some large bets. Most American and European investors are moving out of the region because they feel the risks exceed the rewards. My client's contrarian views have yielded hefty returns in the past and he expects the same can happen here. He spent time in this region early in his career with Exxon and loves the culture and people. He wants to make socially responsible investments in the region. He believes in social justice. He is willing to put a billion dollars to work here."

Clayton paused. He had stretched the story far beyond the deceit hatched in Langley. The briefing papers suggested dangling a million dollars to lure Assoud. Clayton sensed the need for a flashy close because he knew Assoud was a greedy customer.

Assoud closed his eyes and thought that the story sounded too good to be true. He told himself that a wealthy American with a progressive agenda, deep pockets, and an established foundation to channel money to the Middle East was a big prize for his existing network. At the same time, he reminded himself that he would verify Clayton's story before any commitments. He would check up on Plano Energy Corporation this evening. He knew Clayton had left the CIA to join a private firm on Wall Street and remembered Clayton's sound business acumen. Assoud was reluctant to show interest in Clayton's client because his first instinct was to mistrust any American.

Before joining the Jihad against the West, Assoud's dealings with Clayton had been useful. He remembered Clayton's dissatisfaction with the government bureaucracy. No doubt, money had attracted him to the private sector. If money was the motive for a career change, greed could be the motive for career advancement now. Clayton might once again be useful; this time he might become a pawn to attain TOVAIR's goals. Assoud wanted to know more about Clayton's client network. Feigning indifference, he commented, "Your client sounds like a good Samaritan. I am sure you will find good contacts here. Enough business talk for now. How long will you stay in Cairo? Perhaps we can get together again before you leave?"

Without hesitation Clayton accepted Assoud's invitation to attend a private reception to be hosted in honor of the Saudi oil minister, a personal friend of Assoud, the following day. After his meeting with Assoud, Clayton skipped the conference dinner and headed straight to his room. As he entered the elevator and before he had a chance to push the eleventh-floor button, a tall man with a black Western hat and faded cowboy boots entered the elevator. He looked at Clayton and grinned, barely moving his thin lips.

"Howdy."

Clayton instantly recognized another familiar face from the set of photos Jeff had shared on the ride from the airport. This Delta Force team member rode silently to the tenth floor and stepped off the elevator with caution. He looked like the kind of man who leaves no tracks on a fresh field of snow. Clayton continued up to the next floor and began to feel uneasy as he approached his room. He turned the key slowly and noticed that the lights in the bathroom were on, just as he had left them. The faint smell of cheap cologne revealed that an intruder had either just departed or was still hiding in the room. Clayton approached the bathroom with extra caution, trying hard to remember the karate moves he had mastered so long ago. He was relieved that for now, at least, he did not have to put his martial skills to the test.

Someone had gone over his belongings hastily, as one of Clayton's folded t-shirts stuck out of the outer pocket of his carry-on bag and his laptop computer case was unzipped. The intrusion did not surprise Clayton, but the sloppy execution did. He had left paperwork about the fictitious Plano Energy Corporation on the desk and noticed that the company brochure with a prominent client list was missing.

"They took the bait; now we'll have to wait and see if they run with it."

Clayton walked out on the balcony and gazed across the cloud of thick dust enveloping the city. A languid sunset unrolled puffy pink clouds across the horizon and at a distance a mosque called the faithful to prayer. Clayton felt exhausted but reminded himself that his workday was not yet over. He had to e-mail Tom and update him on the day's progress. He would leave out the details and just send a cryptic message.

"Our client seems somewhat interested in proposal. We will continue discussion tomorrow and will keep you posted."

Tom's reply was immediate.

"Somewhat interested is not good enough. Sell hard."

A coded message from Morton, sent earlier that morning, was much friendlier.

"I'm glad to hear my boy made contact. Before you leave Cairo, I'll send you an attachment with all of my findings, so you can study on your way home.

Still trying to get to the bottom line and will need your help. See you soon, Mort."

Clayton barely ate the club sandwich he had ordered through room service and fell asleep listening to the BBC newscast.

✲ ✲ ✲

Assoud kissed his friend Abduhl Sar-al Diab, the Saudi oil minister, who was also his guest of honor, on both cheeks and welcomed his entourage aboard the Salinah, the extravagant yacht Assoud had commissioned and named after his first wife. The guests arrived promptly between five and six o'clock, as the party was to sail down the Nile for a reception and dinner before returning to the yacht club just minutes away from the Hilton. Clayton arrived shortly before the short cruise began and walked over to the bar. To his surprise, the bartender looked quite familiar, a short stocky fellow with intense black eyes, a thin mustache and a crooked smile. He looked Italian. His crisp white shirt showed his name, Tony, embroidered in gold. He was the third member of Jeff's Delta team Clayton had spotted since his arrival.

"What may I get for you, sir?"

Clayton grinned and asked for a club soda with a twist of lime. A firm hand squeezed his shoulder. When he turned around, there stood the host of the party with a wide smile, patting Clayton on the back.

"Welcome. So glad you could join our little party. Come, let me introduce you to some friends."

With that, Assoud waved at a small group of men standing on the upper deck to come down.

"Fellows, here is an old friend of mine I want you to meet. This is Clayton Harcourt, CEO of Plano Energy Corporation. He is here on business, big business."

"Francois Duvenoix," said the Frenchman, extending his hand and piercing Clayton with suspicious eyes. A German and an Irishman introduced themselves. Assoud advised Clayton to visit with these men because they could be good business contacts for the future. After the introductions, Assoud moved on to greet other guests. Francois Duvenoix wondered whether to tell Assoud about the conversation he had with Will Rogerson in London just a few days ago. If in fact Clayton Harcourt was an "old friend," maybe Assoud was using him to check up on Will Rogerson and through him check on his own loyalty to TOVAIR. On the other hand, if Clayton was not who he claimed he was, the earlier call to Will was perhaps a ruse to snoop on TOVAIR's business – after all the man had worked for the CIA.

Duvenoix calculated that to warn Assoud in vain would result in some kind of punishment, a cut in pay or worse, perhaps physical torture. On the other hand, not warning Assoud of a possible ploy against TOVAIR would result in death. The favored kind of punishment for Western traitors, a beheading, was Duvenoix's recurring nightmare. Fear sharpened his mind and speeded up his decision to act. If his suspicion about Clayton Harcourt was accurate, Duvenoix figured he stood a good chance to climb up the ladder of Assoud's organization. He decided to talk to Assoud without delay about his doubts.

☆ ☆ ☆

Aisha Al Ramzi was a sophisticated woman of regal beauty. Assoud's youngest daughter had been educated at Oxford, was married to Egypt's president, and she was one of her father's most trusted advisors. Aboard the Salinah, she played the role of gracious hostess whenever her father called on her to listen, negotiate, or persuade. Assoud's three wives were seldom seen in public but Aisha was his strongest public relations weapon. She was soft spoken with an unassuming demeanor that barely covered up her steely determination. Like the gauzy veil she wore this evening casually covering her jet-black hair and narrow shoulders, her thirst for power was hardly concealed by her translucent skin. She approached Clayton, who was walking towards the dinning room, and took his arm. Looking calmly into his eyes, she introduced herself.

"Would you mind being my dinner escort tonight, Mr. Harcourt? My husband is out of town and my father trusts you."

She paused, pursed her lips, and then eased into a mischievous smile. Clayton realized the woman pressing her body close to his was the worldly Aisha Al Ramzi, philanthropist, wife of a president, and daughter of a terrorist.

"I will be honored, Mrs. Al Ramzi."

"Sorry, I did not introduce myself properly. Please call me Aisha. May I call you Clayton?"

He nodded as they walked into the dinning room, where most of the guests were already seated. The host was rising from his chair next to the guest of honor. Assoud smiled broadly, as he saw his daughter enter the room with Clayton. He raised his wine glass and offered a toast.

"Welcome to the Salinah, my dear friends. My daughter and I are honored to have you join us for this very special occasion. Tonight, we celebrate friendship. No friendship has been more important to me than that of my dear friend, Abduhl Sar-al Diab. May we continue to work together to achieve a perfect world."

Before the first course was served, Aisha leaned closer to Clayton. Her voice was a soft whisper.

"Father tells me that you are looking for investment opportunities. He is very impressed with your accomplishments. I am interested in learning more about what kinds of opportunities you are pursuing in our part of the world. Perhaps I can be of help."

Clayton sipped his wine slowly and measured his reply. He explained that his client was interested in putting money to work in socially responsible projects in this region. "He might consider projects in education, health care, community development."

Aisha listened attentively. The prospect of raising money in the West for legitimate causes that could in effect funnel funds to other projects was intriguing.

"As you know, I am very interested in improving the delivery of education and health care in our country and region. I am constantly looking for private funding opportunities to relieve the needs of our people. Here in Egypt, our government is not able to provide a safety net for the poorest of our urban and rural populations. My husband is a firm believer that we will need to establish partnerships with international organizations to improve standards of living. I believe that private foundations could be another effective source of funding for building schools and teaching our children to read and write. Private foundations could also become involved in establishing rural clinics, training doctors, and partnering with our government to deliver medicines to remote areas. Would your client agree to fund such projects? And if he would, what strings would he attach?"

Clayton was pleased to hear these questions and like a skilled angler, he readied himself to set the hook and reel in his prey. Just a few days ago, at Dulles, while waiting for his Cairo flight, he had read a *New York Times* article announcing that Egyptian President Al Ramzi had sent his wife Aisha to the United Nations to make a pitch for education and health care funding. The article also mentioned that she had been appointed to a UN commission for promoting welfare programs in the Middle East.

"My client is ready to invest a billion dollars. He would want to receive a brief proposal specifying the goals and scope of the projects, who would benefit, estimated cost, and length of time necessary to achieve goals. That's all. No strings attached."

Clayton paused briefly to give Aisha time to consider the simple plan. "He is interested in projects that help more than one country. He wants to spread his wealth wide in this region."

Aisha fixed her almond eyes on Clayton in a way that made him quite uncomfortable. She was sensuous and cunning. Her skin was as clear as the white porcelain tea cup she placed back on the saucer after moistening her lips to savor the sweet Bakklavah on her dessert plate. She leaned closer, and Clayton could smell her perfume. It reminded him of a forest right after a hard rain shower. She touched his leg.

"When will I have a chance to meet this generous client of yours?"

Clayton instinctively wanted to pull away from this woman. He was relieved when her veil slid off her shoulders and she reached up to drape it loosely across her back. In that same moment, Clayton pushed his chair away from her and cleared his throat. His mouth felt dry and he sipped some water while she waited for his reply.

"I am afraid you will not have a chance to meet him soon. He is a very private man and wants his identity to remain anonymous. He will personally review your proposal, I assure you."

Aisha seemed disappointed at Clayton's reply and cool retreat. Clayton sensed it was time to soften his demeanor. He smiled and looked into her eyes.

"And should he choose to fund your projects, I will personally appeal to him to meet with you. You never know, he might make an exception."

Aisha smiled back and brushed her leg against Clayton. He felt a warm rush across his entire body and decided it was time to get some fresh air on the upper deck.

Aisha spoke again, as if she was reading his mind. "Clayton, I like it when men make exceptions."

He ignored the advance. "Can I tell my client that you are interested in seeking funding from his foundation?"

Before Aisha could answer, her father approached them and putting one arm around his daughter, said to Clayton, "Well, I see you are seducing my daughter, you better be careful!" He paused and grinned. "Just kidding you my friend. Isn't she beautiful? I should never have let her leave the house. My little girl has big responsibilities in her husband's land. She will play a very important role in the world. You should tell her about your client, Clayton."

Clayton was about to answer, but Aisha replied to her father's suggestion. "Father, we were just talking about Clayton's client. I am very interested in finding ways to identify projects to match the objectives of this most generous donor." Aisha seemed subdued in the presence of her father and avoided looking at Clayton. Assoud patted her on the back and turned to Clayton.

"I told you that this was the right place to find interested parties for your client. You are very fortunate, my friend. It seems as if you have my daughter's full attention this evening." Assoud tapped Clayton on the shoulder and fixed his eyes on him. The smile was icy cold.

"The First Lady has contacts throughout this region and I recommend that you give her proposal careful consideration."

Assoud's warning sounded like a fire alarm. Clayton was certain that the daughter was following her father's wishes and he realized that her advances posed unexpected danger in his mission. Without waiting for Clayton's reply, Assoud moved towards another table, where Francois Duvenoix was engaged in an intense debate with a couple of Saudi officials and a Chinese woman. When Duvenoix saw Assoud, he excused himself and walked towards the host. Clayton noticed that the two men spoke in hushed tones and then walked out of the dining room. Assoud looked very upset.

Chapter 6
Mission in Peril

The evening was calm as the Salinah docked near the center of town. Some guests were mingling in small groups and others were disembarking. Tony, the bartender, was clearing the tables on the main deck when he noticed the two men climbing the stairs to the top deck. Clayton was watching the city lights by himself, after accepting Aisha's invitation to remain on board for a business talk with her father and other business associates. She had hinted that after the business meeting she would welcome his company.

"I do not like sleeping alone," she told him.

Clayton did not hear the slow steps behind him but the blow was swift; it seemed to have come from nowhere. He felt a sharp pain on his left temple and his ear was still ringing when he attempted to turn around and hit his assailant. A second blow came from another man pointing a shiny blade at Clayton's throat. Clayton kicked the second attacker in the groin and pushed him hard. In that very instant the first attacker slumped over, bleeding profusely from his mouth. He had been shot through the head at close range. Clayton swung around just in time. A second silent shot hit the second attacker, who was crawling back towards him holding the knife that only seconds ago was so close to ending Clayton's life.

Before Clayton had time to realize what had happened, a sturdy man emerged from the shadows.

Clayton was ready to attack him when he heard a clipped East Coast accent.

"Let's get out of here. Follow me."

Tony jumped into the dark Nile and Clayton did not hesitate to follow him into the river. The men swam about 300 yards. They could hear the commotion aboard Assoud's yacht. When they reached the shoreline, they sneaked through some brush and past a few old wooden boats in disrepair, Clayton collapsed. He felt a sharp pain on his right side and realized that he had sustained a deep cut under his right arm.

"C'mon. We need to keep going. It's not safe yet."

Tony prodded Clayton to get up and keep moving. The two men moved quickly towards a sedan parked in a dark alley near a dilapidated warehouse. Tony motioned Clayton to stay behind, while he moved closer to the vehicle. The driver seemed asleep but as Tony approached, he straightened up and looked at his watch. Tony recognized the signal. He opened the back door of the car and motioned Clayton to get in and lay on the back seat. He jumped in the passenger's side and they sped off.

"A close call?" asked the driver. Clayton recognized Jeff's voice and he wanted to answer but his mouth was dry and his tongue felt like lead. He felt dizzy and knew he was passing out. Tony answered for him.

"Yep, it sure was. Clayton got cut but we can take care of that on the way out of town. I think the dragon lady put something in his drink. We better get to your place in a hurry."

✲ ✲ ✲

Susan Rourke liked to serve breakfast in her bright and sunny kitchen. It was Saturday morning and Morton was planning to spend a few hours at work, so a hearty breakfast was in order since he would probably skip lunch. Morton seemed concerned this morning. Susan knew that work consumed most of his waking hours but she never asked any questions. She was worried about Jeff because she had not heard from him in over a week and knew that her son was often in harm's way somewhere in the Middle East. She knew that Jeff often communicated with Mort through work and as Morton put the *Washington Post* down before tackling a short stack of buttermilk pancakes, she inquired:

"Honey, have you heard from Jeff this week?"

He smiled as if to put her at ease, and said, "That boy is busy. He e-mailed me yesterday and said everything is fine. He said to give you a big hug, so you'll get one right after I finish breakfast."

Susan was relieved. She suspected that her husband was embellishing her son's message but she looked forward to her husband's big bear hug. She did not want him to work as hard as he did but she was so very proud of him.

Morton gave Susan the promised hug and left for the office shortly after 7 a.m. As he pulled out of his driveway, his cell phone rang. The White House switchboard operator told Morton to hold for the President of the United States. Mack Cumberland liked to get up before sunrise. He claimed that by getting up before anybody else he could be sure that at least for a couple of hours nobody would mess up his day. He had received Morton's message just a couple of hours ago and wanted to get more details about the attempt on Clayton Harcourt's life.

"Good morning Mort, got your message. Tell me more."

"Good morning Mr. President. Clayton is recovering quickly, sir. He is at a safe house and the Delta team is taking good care of him. I spoke to him briefly on the phone this morning and he has received instructions from Tom to leave Cairo ASAP and fly to Riyadh. He seems eager to proceed with the mission."

He paused and added, "Sir, with your permission, I would like to get Clayton back to DC. He is right on target on his InterIntel assessment, and there is too much risk for him in the region now."

The president told Morton to talk to Clayton again and reevaluate all options. "I trust, you and Clayton will come up with the best way to move forward."

* * *

Clayton woke up with a headache but a second cup of coffee helped him get his bearings. The safe house was hot, but the ceiling fan above his bed kept him somewhat comfortable through the night. During daytime, the desert heat hung around like a pesky bug. Jeff walked in the room with a big smile and handed Clayton a size 12 Royal Wulff fly.

"Guess you were planning on landing a big fish! I found this in your shirt pocket."

Clayton sat up and inspected his favorite fly. "Yeah, like the Boy Scouts, I like to be prepared." He then told Jeff about his fly-fishing passion.

"Angling is not much different from the craft of intelligence gathering. When you fly-fish you need to stay focused; you can't be thinking of anything else. You have to concentrate on multiple factors, like water temperature, bugs, reading the water, presenting the fly naturally, and rolling out your line with the perfect cast. Deception is part of the game. You have to deliver a stealth performance."

Jeff seemed like a little kid listening to fireside stories at camp. He shared some fishing stories of his own. He recalled that his dad would take him and his twin sisters fishing. All four would pile into a little rubber dingy and he would put worms on the girls' hooks because they were too finicky to touch the squirmy creatures. After recounting his childhood fishing adventures, Jeff paused as if to relish the memories and then he became serious.

"Heck, now I can even eat worms, if need be. Around here, scorpions are a more likely fare. When we get home, maybe you can teach me how to fly-fish." Clayton enjoyed listening to Jeff's stories. He grinned as he held the fly against the light. The white upright wings looked scruffy and reminded him of his favorite creek, now so far away.

"You saved my life. The least I can do is to show you how to put one of these babies in the water."

Clayton was feeling better and getting ready to leave for Riyadh when his cell phone rang. Morton tried to persuade him to return to Washington, pointing out the impending danger. Clayton insisted that it was important for him to walk through TOVAIR's labyrinth of deceit. He convinced Morton that he could be more helpful by staying in the region than by returning to D.C.

✲ ✲ ✲

While Clayton was in Cairo, Morton had discovered that there were no programming flaws at Inter-Intel. But two teams of analysts working under Tom's supervision were systematically omitting variables in their analysis, which suggested that either they or Tom were manipulating the data in some way.

Morton also ran a cluster analysis of various sets of raw intelligence collected directly from the field in Saudi Arabia, Iran, Egypt, and Syria, and found that Saudi sources repeatedly generated contradictory data that was often not reliable. Clayton used this last piece of evidence to support his claim that the trip to Riyadh was imperative. He would need to have Jeff's team backing him up but he was confident that they could work together to unravel TOVAIR's plans.

Morton reluctantly gave his approval for Clayton and the Delta team to proceed to Riyadh. On the one hand, he feared that exposing Clayton to the hazards of an operation in the field would risk losing a vital asset against the enemy. On the other hand, he accepted Clayton's argument; Morton was confident that Jeff and his team would be up to the challenge of infiltrating TOVAIR at the highest levels of the organization.

✡ ✡ ✡

The Delta team flew out of Cairo shortly before midnight, and six hours later Clayton boarded a commercial flight to Riyadh. The sun was rising as the aircraft rose above thin clouds and Clayton was glad to lose sight of the city, where only a few hours ago he had felt the first deadly blow to his head. The cut below his right arm was still sore but his head felt clear. He decided to use his airborne time to map out his next moves. He was determined to dig deep into the terrorist network threatening his life and that of countless innocent civilians throughout the free world.

The mission was personal now, and he felt a deep sense of duty. Clayton did not feel a shred of personal revenge after the attack. He was ready to stop TOVAIR from killing with impunity. Assoud aimed to destroy what Clayton's father and grandfather had fought to preserve. Jack had given his life for the principles he believed in and for the country he so loved. Now, the son he never had a chance to hold felt a rush of adrenalin thinking that this was his chance to live up to his father's sacrifice.

✡ ✡ ✡

Anthony Markowitz had joined the Navy right after graduating from high school in Mickelton, New Jersey. He was a man of few words, a Desert Storm veteran who was proud to serve his country. He was fluent in Arabic and Farsi and was now a member of the elite Delta team. His commander, Jeff Rourke, liked to call him Tony the Terrible. Tony had a creative streak. He liked to draw and to paint with watercolors. He carried a small sketching tablet everywhere he went and doodled because it helped him solve operational problems. Tony also carried a very sharp pocketknife, a 22-caliber pistol, and a piece of wire at all times.

Operational problems in Riyadh were knotty, and Tony had little time to doodle. He was the advance man for the Delta team. He had set up the safe house in the outskirts of the city on a previous trip. He went out to purchase supplies to carry back to the hideout before Clayton's arrival.

The street market was crowded, but Tony noticed a familiar face – the man who had hired him to serve as a bartender on the Salinah. Tony decided it was best to leave right away without supplies. Tony moved fast and reached a dusty alley where he took cover behind a broken stone fence and a large pile of moldy garbage. The alley was deserted and Tony was about to sprint towards the safe house, when he saw the man turn the corner and walk in his direction. Tony spun around, took cover again, and waited.

The wire cut the man's throat at the very instant that Tony wrapped it tight around his neck and squeezed hard. Tony wiped the wire clean and returned to the safe house several hours later. He put his feet on the small kitchen table and began to sketch the profile of a small child he had seen hiding behind a torn building earlier that morning on his way to the market.

Clayton arrived at the Riyadh airport and was surprised not to find Jeff at the designated spot. Instead, Clayton spotted another member of the Delta team, the tall man with the faded cowboy boots whom Clayton had seen at the Hilton in Cairo.

"Howdy," he said, and told Clayton to meet him outside the terminal. They drove around the city and Clayton made notes as they passed by the Oil Ministry. Clayton was convinced that Assoud's friend, the guest of honor at the infamous river party, was linked to TOVAIR, and he had sketched a plan to dig out information through a mole now working at a low-level job in the Minister's office. Clayton arrived at the safe house after dark, and Jeff handed him a fax from Washington.

"Abort mission. We need to break all communication. If you pursue target, you will operate solo."

Jeff briefed Clayton about Tony's encounter earlier in the day and suggested that it was too dangerous to stay in Riyadh. Washington was recommending retreat, but Jeff had operational discretion. The team had an option to continue the mission. The tension in the room was palpable. The professionals sitting around the kitchen table looked at their commander, confident of his answer. Jeff turned to Clayton and said:

"As far as we are concerned, we are willing to stay and see this mission through. As for you, it's your decision. If you stay, you'll be part of our team. The situation here is far too risky to operate independently."

Clayton did not hesitate to respond. "Count me in." Then, looking at Tony, who was now busy sketching a crowded street market scene, he added, "I've seen your work close up. I think that together we can disrupt TOVAIR's plans."

Clayton set his notes on the table, and told the Delta team about his plan to "dig around" the Oil Ministry for clues. Jeff agreed that the Saudi Oil Minister, Abduhl Sar-al Dib, was a likely candidate to have close ties to TOVAIR. But Jeff was not confident that the mole, a young Saudi engineer whose mother was American, would be of much help on this dangerous mission. The man did not have access to the Minister's office and had reported that the security detail around the Minister's top floor had doubled in recent weeks. There was another problem. The mole's case officer in Riyadh suspected that the young man reported to someone else, maybe even in Washington. Clayton suggested a meeting with the engineer, so that Tony could sketch the layout of the building and the team could learn more about possible entry points to the building, security schedules, and other logistical details necessary to plan a night assault. The tension around the table eased as the team mapped out the finer points of their mission.

☆ ☆ ☆

Susan Rourke inspected her late summer blooms with an expert eye and the relaxed poise of a master gardener. Bright orange daylilies lined the border of her back yard. She walked slowly among large tufts of Russian sage, royal blue butterfly bushes, and healthy clumps of English thyme to catch every scent, discover every new bud, and clip off every wilted blossom along her garden path. Susan pampered her asters, yarrows, and crape myrtles as much as she spoiled her grandchildren. Her garden was a peaceful sanctuary, a quiet place to rest the soul and touch nature intimately. She liked to get her hands dirty. She mixed her own potting soil with peat moss and nutrients to give her plants a loose and airy home, so they could set deep roots and flourish.

Summer rain brought the promise of spectacular late blooms. April showers had been abundant and every green shade seemed more intense and vibrant. After deadheading her tall cardinal flowers, Susan sat on her wooden bench under the willow oak tree. On this cloudy morning, she was concerned about her son Jeff. Normally she would get a note from him every couple of weeks but she had not heard a word for over a month. Morton's daily reassurances were wearing thin; earlier this morning he had barely succeeded in covering up his own concern before leaving for work. Morton never delved into the details of Jeff's job but the familiar cryptic account implied that Jeff was once again leading a dangerous mission. Susan knew that in times of peril, her son's life could be as fleeting as the brief blooms of her beloved daylilies. The garden gave Susan strength. She prayed for her son's safe return and continued her morning stroll, snapping off a dead oak branch here and trimming off some withering strands of creeping purple thyme there.

✲ ✲ ✲

Jeff studied the young man from a safe distance, as the young engineer walked out of the coffee shop. Khalid Hassan was a slight man with a stooped back that made him look older than he was. He had been a sickly child and his mother, an American heiress to a chemical fortune, was overly protective. When she married her Saudi husband, her family disinherited her. Shortly after her wedding, her husband took in another wife and after the birth of her only son, Khalid, she became a recluse constantly complaining about her misfortune.

Khalid grew up hating his father and suffocating under his mother's tight control. He received a degree in chemical engineering from MIT not because he was a bright student but because of his father's connections. The Saudi prince, a distant relative of the ruling monarch, resented his American wife but was determined to keep Khalid from soiling the family name.

Jeff had never met Khalid because the young engineer's former controller was a CIA operative who was very protective of his sources and resented the wide range of operations assigned to the Delta team. In the global war against terror, turf battles among the various branches of the military were subsiding as evidenced by Jeff's highly diversified Delta team. For many intelligence officers both in the field and in Washington, the territorial imperative prevailed. Whenever their superiors instructed them to cooperate with members of other services, they put up much resistance. Jeff knew that contacting the mole's controller would be of little use. He also knew that he could not call on the White House to twist Khalid's controller's arm. He had to reach Khalid outside the usual channels of command.

Jeff approached Khalid. Khalid had stopped at a corner kiosk to purchase a newspaper, just like he did every day before walking to his mother's apartment. His routine never changed. He would leave his office, stop by the coffee shop, buy a newspaper, and visit his mother before going to his own apartment. The hunched young man felt tiny drops of sweat roll over his eyebrows, as he turned around to look at the man holding his arm with an iron grip. His fingertips felt numb. Jeff's voice was calm as he instructed Khalid to follow him or be ready to die.

Khalid was cooperative but visibly shaken by the threats he received from the man who lured him away from the newsstand and into a car that sped away. Once Jeff shoved Khalid into the car, the stranger's tone changed.

"Get down." Without much ceremony, Jeff covered Khalid's head with a coarse burlap bag that prickled the skin like a hundred needles stinging at once. When he arrived at the safe house Jeff covered Khalid's eyes with a thick black cloth and guided him into a stuffy room, where the questions began. Khalid accepted a cup of tea and was relieved to hear a friendly voice assuring him that all would be okay if he cooperated.

Clayton had written some questions in advance. He probed Khalid's knowledge and memory time and time again, hitting on the same issues, sometimes changing a word or two to check his credibility. At last, the questions ended. The same voice that had offered him the first cup of tea several hours ago, offered Khalid another drink. Shortly after Tony handed him a glass of water that tasted like metal, Khalid dozed off. He felt into a deep slumber for the rest of the night.

Chapter 7

Break In

After the informant passed out, Jeff's team moved swiftly. The interrogation of Khalid Hassan had yielded valuable information about the layout of the Saudi Oil Ministry, the exact location of the Minister's office, and the new security schedule. According to Jeff's plan, they had seven hours of darkness to slip into the Ministry, locate the Minister's office and more importantly his safe, break into it, and retrieve the incriminating documents that would give them a glimpse into TOVAIR's secrets.

Clayton was to remain at the safe house to watch Khalid and repeat the dose of barbiturates if he should wake up before the Delta men returned. If the team failed to return shortly before daybreak, Clayton was to follow a planned escape route. Each team member, disguised under a white and black *kaffiyeh*, focused on the tight schedule and the intricate operation ahead. The plan called for the men to split up into two small teams. Jeff would join Sean O'Brady, a fiery Irish redhead. Sean was skilled in explosives and charmed women, but he was a loner. Tony would join Rob Smith, a non-assuming Texan who favored faded Tony Lamas and was fast both on his feet and with his weapons. Shortly before ten o'clock, Jeff and his men left the safe house one by one.

The first phase of Operation Lightning went smoothly. The men convened in a quiet corridor on the third floor of the Oil Ministry after entering the building separately. Each had evaded notice, thanks to intelligence gathered through Khalid. The Delta men gained some precious time when incompetent and low-paid night watchers heavily guarding the two main entrances to the building neglected to watch over the less-known service entrance on the south side of the building. When they reached the third floor, Jeff and Sean waited until the guard went to the bathroom and then crossed the hallway and slipped into Minister Sar-al Diab's suite of private and official offices. Tony and Rob positioned themselves in a small office right across from the third-floor guard station. Their job was to cover Jeff and Sean while they located the safe and retrieved documents in the Minister's private office. Operation Lightning was working as planned until Sean attempted to force his way into the Minister's locked private office, triggering an alarm that rang through the corridors of the entire building.

Tony saw the sleepy guard spring up and run down the hall towards the Minister's offices. Almost instinctively, Tony followed him like a tiger catching up to its prey after stalking it. With a steady hand, Tony applied a tight tourniquet to the guard's neck, blocking his blood flow and shortening the man's life span. Meantime, Rob was skillfully disabling the third-floor alarm hoping that in cutting the wires there, the entire system would shut off. The alarm ceased ringing, and the corridor on the third floor became eerily quiet.

Tony picked up the guard's radio receiver and heard the panicked voice of another guard yelling. "Hello, can you hear me? What is happening up there?"

Tony responded in his best Arabic. "Nothing, my friend. I just checked the Minister's offices and all is normal. I missed the combination and that triggered the alarm but I just shut it off and all is fine."

"Are you sure? I can send someone up there to check again."

"Don't bother, it's almost time for your break. Enjoy it. I have an hour before mine and I'll call you if I need anything. Sorry for the false alarm."

Tony heard the other guard click off and wondered whether his story would keep other guards at bay. While speaking to the guard downstairs over the two-way radio, Tony dragged the limp body of the dead guard into a small office across the hall way. He rejoined Rob and they waited in silence ready to face any intruders from other parts of the building.

✲ ✲ ✲

Tom Munroe walked across the hallway to his office after meeting with his boss, the Director of Inter-Intel, and slumped into his desk chair. The news was not good. Just earlier that day, he had received a call from Morton Rourke instructing him not to contact Clayton. A top-secret cable from the Riyadh embassy informed him that Khalid Hasan was missing. Now, the Director topped the bad news with a request to meet with the Inspector General.

"The IG just has some questions for you regarding the latest audit; I want you to meet with him as soon as possible." Hearing his boss's instructions triggered Tom's headache, and he began to feel sick to his stomach. The news from the field was benign compared to the possibility of an IG investigation into InterIntel's reports. What could the IG be looking for?

Certainly this inquiry had nothing to do with the slush fund he had built up through Pathway Consulting. There was no possible way the IG could suspect the payments he was receiving through Sanford Gillman. Tom played out other possible scenarios in his mind. One question kept resonating in his sore head. "*What had triggered this investigation?*" He dismissed the possibility that his relationship to Alex Keynes III at State was now coming under the IG's scrutiny.

Tom's dealings with Alex were discreet. Although Alex was a temperamental character, particularly since his forced return to Washington, he had no motive to stir up the IG. The more Tom thought about motives, the more he leaned towards thinking that Morton Rourke had a personal reason to displace him. Morton's call earlier that morning was highly suspect. He had invoked the old staple, "need to know," when Tom asked why he could not contact Clayton. Morton only said that he was just following orders. It was clear that the order had come from above but when he asked the Director of InterIntel, he too seemed to join the circle of silence. His boss claimed that the order to not contact Clayton came from the "top." Tom suspected that the White House was directly involved in a field operation involving Clayton.

Alone in his office, Tom wondered aloud, "Why would the White House want to cut me off from the action?"

He had initially worried that the IG would look into his manipulation of intelligence coming in from the field, but Tom's fears soon subsided as he began to focus on the motives for the IG's inquiry. He now felt like a target of the infamous "Cumberland Purge" and he placed a call to a trusted friend who had been at the receiving end of the president's initiative to sweep the bureaucracy clean. The news would be a good excuse to set up a time to visit with Alex, and gather valuable information to pass on to Gillman's anonymous client.

Alex Keynes III took Tom's call. He impatiently listened to Tom's complaint about an impending IG investigation and his suspicions about the White House. When Tom finished his story, Alex reminded him that while politicians came and left Washington, the real power to get things done and to stop things from happening was in the hands of professionals like themselves.

"This too shall pass," said Alex confidently, while tapping his desk with a fountain pen bearing his initials.

When Tom asked when they could meet to discuss "other matters," Alex cut the conversation short, and hung up the phone. "How stupid could he be? He should know better!"

Alex Keynes III was irritated to hear from Tom. The call convinced Alex that he needed to distance himself from a man who no longer helped him advance his own career. Alex needed allies in Washington. Tom was becoming a liability, particularly now that he was under the IG's microscope. The relationship had been mutually beneficial up to the time when Tom was appointed Deputy Director of InterIntel. Somehow, from that point forward Tom Munroe seemed to take more than he gave, and Alex did not appreciate that state of affairs.

✲ ✲ ✲

Mack Cumberland sat in his private study with his feet propped on the desk and scanned the thick briefing book on his lap. He was expecting Morton Rourke to walk in any moment and was ready to ask him for an update on Operation Lightning. The president's reelection campaign was underway, and he was scheduled to leave for a week long series of fundraising events from coast to coast. His likely opponent, Senator Priscilla Parks, had just announced her candidacy as an "Independent." She was lagging by 15 points in the latest poll. Although his advisors had studied the trend of narrowing margins in the final months of presidential campaigns, they remained optimistic that victory was within reach.

The president remained skeptical. The election was five months away, a lifetime for presidential campaigns. Much could change between now and

Election Day. The President liked to focus his attention on foreign policy issues and did not let the demands of reelection dilute his zeal to end the global war against terror. Two of his predecessors had attempted to get their arms around the complex problem of extremist fundamentalists with limited results. Both had been one-term presidents. Mack Cumberland was determined to be re-elected and finish the job on his own watch.

"Good afternoon Mr. President." Morton extended his hand as he walked towards the president, who plopped his bare feet on the oriental carpet and got up to greet the veteran soldier with a warm smile.

"Good to see you, Mort. Please take a seat. How about some coffee?"

The two men walked past the open window overlooking the Rose Garden. A slight breeze carried the signature of the last cherry blossoms of the season; the sweet smell drifted across the room.

Mack Cumberland leaned back against his favorite chair and asked Morton, "What is the latest on OL?"

Morton Rourke knew the president liked succinct reports, so he gave Cumberland a brief update. "Mr. President, the Delta team is implementing its plan as we speak. So far, no news is good news. They communicated with the rest of the men now waiting for them in Amman. Six team members are standing by in Jordan to execute a rescue operation, if needed. The team in Riyadh has an SOP escape plan in place and will contact the group in Jordan as soon as they complete their mission."

"Is Clayton with the Riyahd team?" The president's question surprised Morton because the Commander in Chief seldom asked for operational details of this nature.

"Yes, sir."

Mack Cumberland leaned forward and cradled his pipe in his right hand. He spoke softly, as if sharing a secret with a trusted old friend. "Clayton's father, Jack, was in my unit. We were young kids. I did not really understand what it meant for him to expect the arrival of his first son, while wading into the swamps of Vietnam."

The president's eyes narrowed. He was searching his memory for details now distant but still vivid with a new battle under way. "Hell, we were fighting and the last thing on our minds was a newborn baby. Men were dying all around us. Jack kept talking about his kid. We didn't understand. We still did not understand when his buddy carried Jack's shattered body into camp after a nasty Vietcong ambush. Jack died that night clutching a picture of his baby son."

The president paused. Morton understood how emotions bottled up for decades unleashed images captured long ago, and now he understood why the president asked about Clayton.

"I promised Clayton that I would tell him about his dad and that war some day. Hopefully, I will not be too late."

"Mr. President, I know you will have a chance to live up to your promise."

Mack Cumberland nodded and lit his pipe to conceal the moisture building up in his eyes.

✡ ✡ ✡

Clayton had rehearsed the steps for his own escape in case the operation failed, and was ready to execute every one of them. He checked his watch and calculated a five-hour wait before Jeff would be back from the Oil Ministry. He looked across the room to make certain that Khalid was still asleep and sat down on the floor of the empty room. Clayton expected to find some clues to TOVAIR's financial maze among the documents Jeff and his team aimed to locate. He was certain that the terrorist network was shifting its offensive against the West, and that it was building a vast system of seemingly official transactions to finance its operations. But that was not all. Clayton had a hunch that parallel to developing new obscure financing sources – perhaps through sovereign debt markets – TOVAIR was actively engaged in financing schemes to throw sand into the wheels of Western capitalism.

"The rapid proliferation of hedge funds might be something for me to check," he reasoned. Clayton made a mental note to study SEC reports once back in Washington. He thought that it might be useful to identify unusual hedge fund transaction patterns designed to destabilize financial markets and unravel the tepid economic recovery of the global economy. Hedge funds moved money across national borders with great ease and traded in derivative markets, where transparency was an unknown commodity.

Compliance with global financial regulations was shaky in many parts of the world, and China was notorious for its lax enforcement of securities laws, making Peking an ideal haven to launder money and cause financial havoc.

Clayton made a note to examine Chinese private capital flows and to review the nexus between those flows and the flow of private funds across the borders of India and Saudi Arabia. As he thought more about the Saudi-Sino-Indian alliance, he realized that the Saudis were a convenient short-term partner for China. After all, the Chinese government had fought Islamic insurgents within its own borders in the recent past. Why would the Chinese embrace a partner who in part was responsible for terrorist acts within China itself?

Clayton speculated that China would strangle Saudi Arabia and gain control over its vast oil supplies. As for right now, Saudi Arabia needed China more than China needed Saudi Arabia.

"Why didn't I see this sooner? China will never be able to curb its demand for oil with its own supplies," said Clayton in a low voice and then shook his head as if annoyed for speaking aloud to himself.

Across the room, Khalid twitched in his sleep and turned over. Clayton got up and readied a syringe just in case the fellow worked his way out of his resting position. Clayton's train of thought reversed direction. He shifted his attention from speculative musing to empirical facts. He recalled the symbolism of the first terrorist attacks on US soil a few years back and concluded that TOVAIR's plans to shift from civilian to corporate and financial targets had been hatched long ago. After all, Islamic fundamentalists did not think in terms of years or decades but rather in terms of centuries.

The initial attacks on the most prominent American icons of military and financial might were a ruse. The murder of innocent civilians provoked, as intended, a military response of relentless force. For America's enemies, the attacks were simply a sly maneuver to distract America in the short run while the more important targets, the American economy and American political institutions unraveled over time. The enemy's strategy was to undermine public confidence and create incentives to trigger economic crises, big and small; the goal was to tear down the pillars of American success, the market economy and its democratic institutions.

"It's the economy, stupid!" Clayton told himself.

Ballooning American deficits to finance a war across the globe crowded out private investments, while unemployment skyrocketed. Since the first attacks, the American economy had slid into a funk, punctuated by short bouts of optimism. Clayton realized the unintended consequences of the enemy's deceit.

"We have been chasing sources capable of funding terrorist operations – operations often intercepted by effective counter-terrorist measures before they are executed – while we have ignored chasing mainstream financial transactions directed by TOVAIR with the sole purpose of destroying America from within."

Beyond its financial motives, TOVAIR had political designs on the West. How would TOVAIR manipulate financial markets for political gain? Would it go as far as attempting to influence the presidential campaign? Clayton remembered the scandal many years ago, when the Chinese had funneled illegal contributions into the coffers of a presidential candidate. Why would TOVAIR not attempt to pull off the same caper now? Who would be the target? President Cumberland? He dismissed the possibility. What about his opponent, Senator Parks? She was a more likely target; he would bring this to Morton's attention.

Clayton felt exhausted but knew that sleep would have to wait. He poured himself a cup of strong coffee and walked over to check on Khalid. The man was completely out. "Tony did a nice job on him," thought Clayton as he checked his watch one more time. It was just about 3 am. In two hours, the Delta team would be on its way to the Kuwaiti border.

✡ ✡ ✡

After entering the Minister's private office, Jeff and Sean searched the entire room and found a small safe concealed behind a bookcase. After several attempts, Sean guessed the right combination, turned to Jeff, and signaled OK. Sean smiled broadly, relieved that he did not have to move to plan B to open the safe. Jeff retrieved numerous files and downloaded them to his cell phone. Within seconds, the files popped into view at InterIntel headquarters and on Clayton's laptop screen. The Minister's private office was adjacent to a larger public office, where he received foreign dignitaries and conducted most of his daily business.

On their way out, Sean and Jeff inspected the extravagant room. A large, half-moon shaped desk dominated the room. Embedded in its sleek mahogany top, several computer monitors flashed real-time market transactions across the globe. Behind the desk, across a glass wall, there were five large computer screens labeled Currency Markets, Equity Markets, Options and Futures Markets, Corporate Bond Markets, and Sovereign Debt Markets.

These terminals tracked the performance of selected asset classes around the world and made the office look like a battle command center. Two neat stacks of computer printouts sat on a marble coffee table across the room. Jeff picked them up.

The third-floor hallway was clear and the two men hurried down the staircase towards the planned exit gate, in the basement of the building. There they found Tony and Rob breaking the lock to the Ministry's car pool garage. Soon thereafter, an official van drove slowly up to the garage exit, and the driver handed his ID to the armed guard. The guard looked sleepy at the end of his shift.

"Perfect timing," thought the driver.

The guard read the name "Khalid Hassan, Engineer, Department A." Without looking at the van or the driver, he handed the ID back and waved the van through. The first early morning light was about to make a spectacular entrance over Riyadh's eastern horizon.

Later that afternoon, another guard at the Kuwaiti border verified the passengers' identities and waved the five men through. Within an hour, Clayton and the Delta team were airborne. On the way to Amman, Clayton scanned the documents Jeff and his men had retrieved and realized that his hunch was right on target.

✲ ✲ ✲

The Saudi Oil Minister was more than Ahmed Assoud's close friend. Detailed accounts of fund transfers from the official Oil Stabilization Fund to Al-Aldinah provided evidence of a direct link between the Saudi government and TOVAIR's front organization.

Saudi Arabia had established this fund to smooth out wide swings in international oil prices and create a steady source of foreign exchange earnings for the kingdom. Large oil revenue deposits during times of high oil prices provided a cushion for leaner times. When world oil prices dropped, the Saudis drew funds from the Oil Stabilization reserves to maintain spending levels. Instead of funding government services, the fund's reserves moved directly to an "operations account" at Al-Aldinah.

Clayton had a photographic memory. He remembered the exact trend in international oil prices for the last two years and noted that as prices dropped, deposits to the Oil Stabilization Fund continued to climb. More significantly, detailed footnotes clarified the source of these cash infusions.

Underwriting fees, debt-equity swaps, and interest from debt issued by the governments of Argentina, Indonesia, Egypt, and many more nations. The record of countries and financial transactions was extensive; the amounts involved in these deals reached trillions of dollars. Clayton scanned the long list of less developed countries. The evidence linking TOVAIR to the ballooning debt-service obligations of these nations was becoming obvious.

"Any luck so far?" Jeff asked Clayton as they were about to land in Jordan's capital. Clayton nodded and pointed to an Excel printout stamped "PERSONAL."

"Here is an indication that we may have found some valuable nuggets; maybe we'll even be able to connect some dots. I still need to review the printouts you picked up in the trading room on your way out."

After landing, Jeff reminded Clayton of his promise to take him fly-fishing. Clayton smiled.

"You bet, a deal is a deal. I'll take you to the Henry's Fork of the Snake River."

Jeff smiled back: "Good, I look forward to it." He picked up his gear and along with the men of Operation Lightning got ready to join the rest of the team now waiting for him ready to board the Blackhawk.

Jeff's Delta team was ten men strong and they had just received instructions to head back to Saudi Arabia. Jeff and Clayton, men of few words, looked people straight in the eye, and bid farewell.

"Well, it's been great working with you, Clayton." Clayton felt like he had just met a friend for life.

"Same here, Jeff. Until we meet again on the Henry's Fork, take care of yourself." Jeff waved as he walked toward his men.

"Will do."

Chapter 8
Enemy Trap

Clayton waved back and watched the Delta team board the chopper. He walked into the terminal to catch his flight to London, and felt privileged to have known these men. He had not quite found the words to thank them for saving his life. Somehow, he knew that if he had said anything of the sort, each and every one would have shrugged his shoulders and said, "I'm just doing my job."

Clayton had forged a special bond with these men in a short time. He trusted them with his life, as they trusted one another with theirs. He observed them operate as one well-oiled engine, all its moving parts complementing each other in perfect unison. He admired their bravery and ease in coping with danger. He knew little about their personal lives, yet he knew much about their self-discipline, commitment, and sense of duty. That was enough. These men had a steady moral compass, a core set of values. They did not waver. They did not yield. They moved from job to job with confidence and without question or pretense. They were capable of saving and taking a life all in the same breath. They were innovative and fiercely independent, yet they worked together in seamless harmony. They seemed to be able to finish each other's sentences without exchanging a single word. They were fluent in several languages, mastered the idiosyncrasies of local dialects, and could switch identities with ease. They could talk, shoot, or knife their way out of thorny situations. They were complex men who lived each day applying their skills with the same attention to detail that sculptors devote to turning cold stone into a work of art. The Delta men aroused a tinge of envy in Clayton, because they lived on the same sharp edge that his father, Jack Harcourt, had known so well.

✲ ✲ ✲

The London Heathrow airport was teeming with heavily armed security guards. Cranky travelers, stranded for two days, clogged up the terminals and blamed an air controller's strike for their misery. Clayton elbowed his way to the counter, and learned that all flights were cancelled indefinitely. Stranded in a crowded airport was not his idea of a good night's rest after a long journey. He decided to take the Tube to a quiet place he knew not far from the airport.

"Welcome back, Mr. Harcourt. How good to see you!"

Mrs. Barton sat at her tidy desk and beamed behind a crystal bowl brimming with fresh cut flowers. She owned the two-story bed and breakfast and took great pride in knowing her guests by name. The portly grandmother liked to pamper customers with her epicurean creations and the understated elegance of her eighteenth century home. She was delighted to see Clayton, and before he had a chance to settle down for the night, she brought tea and squares of buttery shortbread up to his room.

Clayton was exhausted but was unable to sleep. He felt too tired to review the large stack of printouts from the Saudi Oil Ministry. Instead, he visualized wading into a cold stream and hearing the gurgle of slow moving water all around him. He then pictured himself casting and hearing the whoosh of the line unrolling overhead. He visualized the exact place where he had caught his first Atlantic salmon. It was a picturesque ribbon of water up in the Scottish Highlands. He remembered the smell of ocean mist and the jagged cliffs nearby. Clayton hoped to return some day to the place where his ancestors had built stone walls. They had carved the countryside into a myriad of plots that looked like the fitting pieces of a puzzle. Clayton fell asleep thinking about puzzles.

✲ ✲ ✲

Morton Rourke poured himself another cup of coffee and reread the e-mail from his son: "We made it. The angler is on his way home." Good news. He would wait to hear from Clayton before he placed a call to update president Cumberland on Operation Lightning. But first, Morton called his wife.

"Hi Honey, I just wanted you to know that Jeff sends you a big hug."

Susan smiled and told her husband that she loved him. Morton was about to call his assistant when his phone rang. Clayton was calling from London.

"Morton, I have just discovered an important link. I would like to stay here for a few days to get a hold of Francois Duvenoix."

Morton did not hesitate: "Out of the question. The man is too close to the top, you cannot do this on your own."

Clayton insisted: "Trust me. I have a plan that might work. At least give me a few hours to see if I can pull it off. If I cannot recruit the person I need to get to Duvenoix, I will not pursue it. I promise."

Morton nodded. "Okay. You've got two hours. By the way, you need to know – we put Tom Munroe on administrative leave while the IG conducts an investigation. More on this, when you get home."

"When I get home, I promised Jeff to take him fly fishing out West, in God's country." Morton smiled, glad that his son and Clayton had gotten to know each other.

✲ ✲ ✲

Will Rogerson was watching the congressional testimony of the Federal Reserve Chairman on C-Span. The equity markets were trading higher since the announcement that the Fed would lower the discount rate by 50 basis points. Bond traders were happy and so were equity jocks, but Will Rogerson was not a happy camper. He was long the November crude oil futures contract, and oil prices were dropping like a ton of bricks. It was time to act.

The phone rang as Will was calculating his next move to reverse recent losses. Annoyed at the untimely interruption, he answered with his usual greeting.

"Yes?" He recognized Clayton's grave tone:

"Will. I'm calling you from London and I need your help. This is a matter of life or death. Please listen carefully." Clayton told Will the motive for his call from Driggs. He told Will that he never doubted his innocence. He trusted that Will did not know about the true motives and business affiliations of his French partner, Francois Devenoix. Will remained silent, and then he dared to ask:

"You're working for the Feds?"

Clayton knew his childhood friend was a decent man, and counted on the values they shared growing up to bridge the distance between them. "The truth shall set you free," Clayton's grandfather used to say whenever the young lad attempted to pull off a fib on the old man. Clayton answered without hesitation.

"Yes. But I cannot do this job alone. I've made a reservation for you to leave New York this evening. Please come to London and help me out."

Will hesitated. He told Clayton that he sensed he was under surveillance, and that he feared for his life.

Clayton retorted, "If you do not come to London, your children will be harmed. We are not dealing with the PTA. We are not dealing with commodity traders. These people kill for a living." Then, he closed on a calmer tone.

"Will, we have known each other our entire lives. You are like a brother to me. Trust me on this one. I know you are worried; I sensed that when I called you from Idaho. Now, is not the time to back down. We must act. I'll fill you in on the details of what we need to do when you get here. Do we have a deal?"

✲ ✲ ✲

Lyn Chang stretched her arms above her head and closed her eyes as she soaked in the bathtub. She had arrived in London later than expected and was relaxing before her scheduled interview with Total Oil executives later that afternoon. She stepped out of the tub dripping wet and walked to the open window facing Mrs. Barton's cottage garden. Lyn appreciated the artful English attitude towards mixing and matching plants and flowers. English gardens seemed chaotic but produced a lush combination of colors and smells unlike the more orderly Asian gardens. Lyn Chang liked the unruly nature of English gardens because they resembled her own secret preferences.

Growing up in Hong Kong, she had an appreciation for Confucian values. Whenever she had a chance, however, she defied tradition and chose the less traveled road. She came to London frequently. This crowded garden was a welcoming refuge from her risky ventures. Lyn's business card suggested that she was a writer for the *China Energy Monitor*, a weekly publication sponsored by major Asian, African, Middle Eastern, and European oil companies. Yet her work was not limited to research and writing. After getting dressed, Lyn brushed her long hair and pulled it back into a French chignon, accentuating her high cheekbones and her striking features. Satisfied that she had accomplished a sophisticated corporate look, she picked up her briefcase and headed out of her room.

She caught a glimpse of the tall American as he climbed the stairs. He was rugged and athletic. She slowed her pace, smiled, and tilted her head as if smitten by his good looks. She was a good actress.

"Good day, have we met before?"

Clayton detected a seductive tone behind her confident demeanor and smiled back. His was a cautious smile.

"I don't believe so." Clayton strained to remember where he had seen Lyn Chang before. Her face looked familiar. He could not remember. She was an intriguing woman. "Best to remain alert," Clayton reminded himself.

Clayton called the airport for an update on flight arrivals and learned that final negotiations were still underway to end the strike. Will's flight would be delayed another day, at best. The delay was a chance to continue his search for clues and polish his plan to uncover more TOVAIR secrets. The Saudi documents provided clear evidence that TOVAIR was directly engaged in creative fund transfers across the globe.

It was possible that hedge funds provided a safe haven for these transfers. That could explain the proliferation of hedge funds in every major capital market. TOVAIR also had become a major underwriter and buyer of sovereign debt from Argentina to Zambia. A complex web of multinational joint ventures, mergers, and acquisitions generated what seemed to be legitimate global funding sources for TOVAIR.

The terrorist network collected underwriting fees from these governments through multiple financial institutions. Many inconspicuous and familiar names appeared on the Saudi printouts. These were well-known insurance companies, banks, and brokerage firms.

Friendly neighborhood bankers across the globe were probably oblivious to the fact that TOVAIR controlled their parent companies. Canadian, European, Latin American, and Asian conglomerates were unsuspecting fronts for transactions designed to fund nefarious operations against Western governments and their citizens. Furthermore, TOVAIR was the largest buyer of sovereign debt issued by developing countries across the globe. The semi-annual payments provided a handy source of cash to fund TOVAIR's priorities.

The network circumvented default risk in a clever plot to make the victims pay for the crime. The International Monetary Fund guaranteed sovereign high yield debt under new rules approved by the majority of its members and opposed only by the United States, Australia, New Zealand, and the United Kingdom. These rules made it easier for TOVAIR to manipulate sovereign debt markets with impunity. Clayton concluded that the IMF guarantees were a moral hazard, an expensive insurance policy, courtesy of the taxpayers in countries that opposed IMF bail-outs of bankrupt governments. These countries were key TOVAIR targets.

Clayton had skipped lunch to study the data and he remained puzzled about multiple entries labeled "personal transfers" to a Swiss bank account under the initials S.G. This was a tempting morsel. The fund transfers ranged between $500,000 and $30 million. "S.G." seemed to be a large operation. Who was S.G. and what was his mission? Those nagging questions kept popping into Clayton's mind as he read and re-read the documents scattered on his bed. It was late in the evening when Clayton decided to take a break and get a bite to eat at the pub around the corner from Mrs. Barton's place.

✡ ✡ ✡

Morton checked his e-mail one more time before meeting with the IG to go over Tom Munroe's file. Clayton had sent an update on the Saudi documents, and was asking for any information on a Swiss bank account under the initials "S.G." The Swiss were notorious for keeping a tight lid on confidential client information. The multiple transfers amounted to over $100 million just in the past two years, and Clayton suggested S.G. could be some influential figure in the United Kingdom or even in the United States. Clayton's hunches proved right on target so far, and Morton picked up the phone and dialed the private number of a banker in Geneva to inquire about "Mr. S.G."

The IG walked in just as Morton hung up the phone. Either Tom Munroe was tweaking raw intelligence reports coming in from several field offices around the globe or someone in his staff was modifying the field reports. The reports from Riyadh were particularly intriguing because a source in the Oil Ministry seemed to be reporting directly to a Washington DC case officer, a highly unusual situation. E-mail traffic from Tom's personal home computer seemed to match a communication link to the source's home computer in Riyadh.

"We'll be looking further into this finding," said the IG, pushing his reading glasses up his nose. Furthermore, he reported that Tom's teams downplayed or ignored Saudi reports from other sources in their final intelligence estimates. Tom and his subordinates were now undergoing lie detector tests. The IG left after promising Morton a complete report by the end of the week.

✲ ✲ ✲

Lyn Chang was beginning to feel jet lagged after a productive meeting at Total Oil's executive headquarters. She had planned to write her report that evening but decided to have a quick meal before getting back to her room. When Clayton walked into the pub, she decided the report would have to wait. He noticed her sitting alone, walked up to her table, and with the most charming smile, he said:

"Hello stranger, mind if I join you?"

He did not wait for her reply and sat down.

"Please do. I'm Lyn. Did I miss your name?"

"No, I don't believe I told you. I'm Clayton. We have to stop meeting like this." She was devastatingly beautiful.

"I kind of like it. Meeting you like this, I mean." After a brief pause, she continued: "I've never seen you before at Mrs. Barton's, and I usually stay there when I come to London." She told him she was born in Hong Kong, and was now living in Canada.

He told her that he had only been to Hong Kong once and would like to go back to see more of the islands surrounding Kowloon. She noticed his green eyes. They looked intense and translucent, like polished jade.

Walking back to Mrs. Barton's place, Clayton asked casually, "What brings you to London?"

"Business. I write for a trade magazine." She seemed to follow his lead, and replied to his brief questions with short answers. He probed again.

"Interesting. What kind of trade magazine?" She hesitated, and then replied, "Energy."

"Interesting," he noted, and they walked in silence the rest of the way.

She invited him to join her for a cup of tea. Breaking his own rule to decline invitations from strangers, Clayton followed Lyn into her suite. When she unfastened her hair and slipped out of her silk dress, Clayton knew he was in trouble. Lyn Chang had a firm body. Later that night, Clayton tiptoed across Lyn's room and on his way out, he glanced at the folder on her coffee table. The title read, "Total Oil Progress Report."

"Interesting," he told himself and quickly scanned the document before downloading it to his cell phone.

✡ ✡ ✡

Flight 505 arriving from New York was finally landing at Heathrow. Clayton was finishing his coffee and reading the *London Financial Times* while waiting for Will Rogerson. The childhood friends shook hands and made small talk while they drove to Mrs. Barton's place.

"Welcome, Mr. Rogerson!"

The friendly innkeeper handed Clayton the keys to Will's room and with a conspiratorial air, she leaned across her desk and reported:

"Ms. Chang said to tell you 'Farewell.' She checked out earlier this morning. A lovely girl, isn't she Mr. Harcourt?"

"Indeed."

Will turned to Clayton and told Mrs. Barton: "Well, he's up to his old tricks. Girls always swarm around this boy like bees around the honeycomb."

Mrs. Barton giggled as the two Americans climbed the grand staircase. They seemed to rekindle their boyhood friendship when Clayton reminded Will: "Women are a great deal of trouble. I plead innocent."

They laughed as they recalled their younger days. The bond between them seemed less strained. Joking their way around the more weighty matters that brought them together in London eased the tension.

Clayton and Will settled into the Queen Anne chairs in Mrs. Barton's library on the second floor overlooking her garden. After recalling carefree times growing up in the "Wild West," Clayton eased the conversation towards a more difficult topic.

"What is your relationship with Francois Duvenoix?"

Will recounted the course of his business dealings with the French Algerian and the initial reason for partnering with him; a bankruptcy would have been devastating to his family. He was trying to protect them, he explained. At the same time, he was afraid to share his financial crisis even with his best friend, his partner at the time.

"I cooked the books," he confessed. "Clayton, the profits you saw...." Will hesitated, and then continued, "Those profits were just figments of my imagination. I lied to you, to my wife, and to the IRS. I was in deep trouble." His hands were shaking. Ashamed of the past and uncertain of how his confession would affect his future, Will blurted out: "When Duvenoix offered his first cash infusion, I made good on what I owed you. I returned your share of the profits. I was terrified that you would find out." His jaw tensed up, and he looked his friend straight in the eye.

"I'm sorry. That's why I came. I owed you an explanation and an apology. I broke our trust and now I'm ready to do whatever you need me to do."

Clayton realized that the plans for an early retirement that he and Linda had mapped out had just been dreams. He set his anger aside and said:

"We all make mistakes, Will. Looking back does not solve the problem in front of us." He paused and looked at the shadow of the friend burdened by past mistakes. Deceit had drained their friendship, and only trust could bring them back together. Clayton trusted his own instincts and decided to give Will a second chance.

"You need to contact Duvenoix. You'll call today and ask to see him right away. Tell him that the SEC snooped around your office and you flew here to seek his advice. You'll insist that he come here."

Will considered the request.

"That will not work. He won't come. He's totally paranoid about security." Clayton pulled one of the Saudi printouts out of his pocket and handed it to Will.

"Tell him that a friend of yours e-mailed you copies of some Saudi souvenirs he took back to the United States after a visit to Riyadh. He'll come."

Clayton explained that Francois Duvenoix probably had heard about the missing documents and knew that they implicated him in the innermost secrets of TOVAIR's operations.

"Tell him that you will give him these copies in exchange for his advice. And remind him that he is to come alone, without a trailing security detail."

✲ ✲ ✲

Francois Duvenoix hung up the phone and immediately called his security chief to instruct him to set up a tight surveillance team surrounding "The Breakers," a bed and breakfast located at 14 Fox Hunt Hill. He then instructed his driver to drop him off at that address and wait for him at the park nearby. After finishing his meeting, he would walk across the park to ride back to his office on the Strand.

When Will Rogerson opened the door to greet his business partner with a tentative smile, Duvenoix stepped into the room, and soon felt the end of a 22-caliber pistol behind his head.

"Welcome, Francois. Get on your knees. Down. Now. Put your hands behind your back. Don't move or I'll blow your head off." He did not recognize the voice but it sounded calm and determined. He had no doubt that the man breathing down his neck meant what he said.

Will spun around and tied some wire tight around Duvenoix's wrists and ankles. The wire seemed to cut right through his skin. Only when he felt a slight relief of pressure from the gun pressed against the back of his head did the Algerian look up. Will was now holding the gun. The tall man who had held the gun to his head behind his back now stood in front of him, looking at him with cold green eyes. Duvenoix recognized the face. The tall American was clad in blue jeans and a white t-shirt that read: "I fish, therefore I lie."

Clayton got right to the point: "Francois, my friend here tells me that you are an important business man. I have some information you want, and you have some information I want. So this transaction should take no time at all."

Clayton pulled up a chair and sat down. He wrapped his arms around the back of the chair and stretched out his legs, letting the soles of his boots face Duvenoix. Disgusted by the subtle insult, Duvenoix attempted to move his small, contorted frame to avoid the offending sight. He felt the gun pressing harder against his skull.

"I recommend you sit still." Will's voice seemed less calm than the man in front of him. Francois Duvenoix felt a drop of cold sweat run down his spine.

"I'm Clayton Harcourt, and I believe we met before at a mutual friend's party. Now, I suggest you cooperate and you'll be back to your office in a New York minute."

The commanding voice was colder than the ice under his feet during one of his early stays in a TOVAIR training camp along the Afghan-Pakistani border some years ago. One thought crossed his mind: "Okay, let's make a deal and then I will kill you." His tone was conciliatory.

"What is it that you have that I want so badly?"

Clayton pointed to the open briefcase filled with the incriminating documents.

"Those documents belonged to Abduhl Sar-al Diab; now they belong to me. You want them because your name appears in a number of places."

Clayton leaned forward like a poker player thinking hard about his next move and giving all the wrong signals to the right players. He grabbed the briefcase to give Duvenoix a close-up of the documents. Some of the documents tumbled and landed on the floor. Like a stack of poker chips towering in front of a tough opponent, the printouts drove Duvenoix to play his hand.

"A million dollars. I'll pay you cash."

Clayton shook his head and Duvenoix doubled the offer before Clayton had a chance to tell him that money was not the object.

"All I want is one simple set of words." As he spoke, Clayton got up, grabbed his laptop, and returned to the chair in front of Francois.

"What is the password to all of your TOVAIR files, that's all I want."

"You won't get that." Duvenoix was sweating profusely. Clayton turned up the heat.

"Okay, you'll give the password to some Israeli friends of mine staying in this lovely home. And if they are not persuasive enough, they have some Turkish friends who would like to meet you."

Clayton got up and reached for a syringe lying on the desk behind him, and walking towards a trembling Duvenoix, said: "Don't worry, you should not feel much pain, this will help you relax."

"Wait," the French Algerian screeched, "maybe we can work something out."

Clayton was firm. He would not budge. "The password."

Duvenoix felt stark naked. He played his last card, and pleaded for Clayton to be reasonable. He argued that he did not have access to any TOVAIR files. He said that Assoud kept a tight control over all operations using his European alias, Abdul Hakim, an Egyptian identity he used to run all operations from his Paris headquarters.

"I'm just a little peon, how do you say? I just push pencils. Do you understand?"

"I understand that you are lying and I'm running out of time and patience." Clayton was determined to get what he wanted. Will held the gun steady. He had never seen Francois Duvenoix shrink with fear and become smaller with each word spoken.

"Coward," thought Will, "this bully was nothing but a coward all along, and I allowed my own fears to play into his heavy hand. This little man is just another fanatic full of hatred and deceit."

Will tightened his grip around the pistol, and Duvenoix felt the thrust against the back of his head. Clayton held the syringe in one hand and pressed the bottom of the palm of his other hand right below Duvenoix's nose. He gradually applied upward pressure, causing great pain in very little time. He was ready to push harder, risking Duvenoix's extinction, when he heard a faint mutter. Clayton eased the pressure.

"Speak up, I can't hear you."

Duvenoix took a deep breath and in a broken voice repeated the password: "Ajnadayn."

Clayton recognized the name. Ajnadayn was the name of the town in Palestine where in the spring of 634 a great Islamic battle took place. Muslim armies conquered the Byzantine town at the dawn of the Arab empire. Clayton logged on to his laptop and typed in the password. Several files coded with a combination of letters and numbers appeared on the screen. Clayton scanned the files at random and once opened, each one seemed to be encrypted. He was not surprised to see these security layers protecting TOVAIR's secrets. He zipped all files and sent them directly to Morton for analysis. He attached a cryptic message.

"We netted a nice rainbow." He also copied the files to his hard drive and made an extra disk copy, just in case.

"Well," Clayton said, looking straight at Duvenoix, "you keep secrets well protected. Help me understand your role in the chain of command."

Duvenoix felt queasy. His mouth felt like sand paper and a sharp pain right between his eyebrows was beginning to feel like a corkscrew twisting slowly up into his brain. "This barbarian was ready to kill me," he thought to himself, avoiding Clayton's stare, "but I will live to kill him." In a raspy voice, he pleaded for time to clear his head.

"Water, please."

Clayton asked Will to get Duvenoix a glass of water, and the Algerian was relieved to get the gun off his head. With his hands still tied behind his back, Duvenoix drank up the entire glass.

"Your role in the chain of command?" Clayton repeated the question twice. Duvenoix did not respond.

"Okay, seems like we have to call on our friends next door. Perhaps you would like to tell them what you do for a living."

Duvenoix had spent three years in an Israeli jail after intense interrogations. He had heard horror stories about Turkish interrogation techniques. When he refused to cooperate with Israeli intelligence officers, Duvenoix had a chance to experience a large dose of Turkish arm twisting. Duvenoix flinched every time he recalled his ordeal. He had been released along with several Hamas and Hezbollah leaders after one of the many false starts of an elusive peace process.

Duvenoix and his fellow travelers did not want peace in Palestine. As long as the hatred and the killing continued, their Islamic cause had a reason to exist. With peace there would be less incentive to recruit martyrs. Achieving peace would be like eliminating poverty.

Without poverty, there would be less incentive to recruit donors with an altruistic bend and reluctant terrorists willing to cross the rubicon of human decency. War in the Middle East was expedient. It kept peace at bay and helped TOVAIR reach its goal with less effort than otherwise possible.

Duvenoix hated Jews and he hated some fellow Muslims as much as he hated Americans. The mere thought of another encounter with Mossad made him sick to his stomach.

"Please," he said as if in pain, "I need to go to the restroom. I cannot wait much longer, please."

Will looked at Clayton and when his friend nodded, Will began to untie Duvenoix's ankles. Clayton held the gun and followed him into the bathroom. He towered over the short Algerian as he untied the wire around the clammy wrists. Clayton walked back into the bedroom after closing the bathroom door to give Duvenoix some privacy.

"Should one of us watch him in there?" Will seemed a bit uneasy. Clayton was more confident, and handing the gun back to Will, replied, "He's not going anywhere. You keep an eye on him when he comes out."

Will felt the sharp blade cut right through his ribcage as he struggled to free himself from Duvenoix's suffocating grip around his neck. His attacker was rabid, stabbing, kicking, biting, and scratching all at the same time. Will had lost the gun and his balance when Duvenoix suddenly spun around and delivered a disabling karate kick right above Will's navel.

Clayton had just pushed the "Send" button on his e-mail to Morton giving him a more detailed account of the Duvenoix interrogation, when he heard Will fall down with a thump and a groan.

"You son of a bitch." Clayton leaped from his chair and threw himself on top of Duvenoix, who was holding Will down and stabbing him one more time.

Clayton pushed the needle deep into the back of Duvenoix's neck while hitting him hard on the side of his temple. Duvenoix attempted to free himself from Clayton. He was unable to wiggle his way out from under the nimble American, who was pounding his head without mercy, and he faded into a stupor before he could think about his next move.

✲ ✲ ✲

Morton wasted no time after receiving Clayton's message. He called his contact in London and gave the order to move in. The FBI team had had "The Breakers" under surveillance since Clayton's arrival. British intelligence had received clearance from 10 Downing to cooperate fully in the American operation, and British agents moved swiftly to execute the job.

The capture of Francoise Duvenoix was an intelligence coup on both sides of the Atlantic. The Americans and the Brits had high stakes in uncovering TOVAIR's secrets because the organization used European capitals as operational headquarters to destabilize Western governments and economies. While, Morton received real time reports, a joint FBI and M16 team loaded Duvenoix into an unmarked sedan and paramedics evacuated Will to an undisclosed location to patch up his wounds. Morton's team of encryption experts were busy breaking the Ajnadayn codes and Clayton was en route to Washington. Morton was pleased with the positive turn of events on this long day. Another battle won in a nasty war that raged on across the globe. He picked up his briefcase, and satisfied with the day's work, he walked out of his office, looking forward to a quiet evening at home.

The phone on his desk rang, and when he picked it up, his heart sank. It was an old friend's voice.

"Morton, this is Calloway."

General Calloway did not make calls just to chat about the weather. He was a four-star army general, and he had just been appointed to the highest position in his distinguished military career, Chairman, of the Joint Chiefs of Staff.

"There has been an accident. We have people on the way to assess the situation. I'm afraid it does not look good."

Morton felt a tight knot in his chest but collected himself. "Thanks for letting me know, General."

Calloway replied, "It's the least I can do. I'll call you back as soon as I know more. Take care, Morton."

Morton hung up the phone and wondered how he was going to find the strength to break the news to Susan.

✲ ✲ ✲

"Did you really mean to kill him?" Will's voice was faint as the paramedics wheeled him out of Clayton's room. His friend held his hand and with a wide grin said, "You bet." Will smiled back. "Thanks. I still think you were bluffing. You always beat me in poker. You were bluffing."

Clayton put his hand on his friend's shoulder and replied, "Maybe yes and maybe no. We caught a big one. This guy is no rainbow; we'll never release him. We're going to lock him up and throw away the key."

Will was lifted into the ambulance. Clayton tapped his shoulder. “You’ll be fine. Take care. I’ll see you when you get back home.”

Mrs. Barton gave Clayton a big hug when he checked out. He had doubled the amount on her bill, apologizing for the afternoon ruckus.

“Thank you, dear. Think nothing of it. Indeed, I reckon we are all a little bit safer without the likes of that nasty-looking man in our neighborhood.” Clayton nodded and thanked Mrs. Barton for her hospitality.

“Always glad to have you, Mr. Harcourt. Do come back soon. You never know, perhaps you might even run into Ms. Chang again. Nice girl, Ms. Chang. Kind of mysterious, don’t you think?” Mrs. Barton paused as if to find a more appropriate description for the slim guest that looked as if she had stepped out of a high-fashion magazine. Then, pleased to have found the right words, she offered a more precise appraisal: “A bit exotic, I say.”

Clayton grinned as he walked out the door. “Indeed. So long, Mrs. Barton. Take good care.”

Chapter 9

Death at Dawn

"Only a few minutes ago, the blast rattled the buildings along this residential neighborhood." The reporter adjusted his earphone, and looking straight into the camera, continued his assessment.

"The Pentagon declines to confirm eye witness reports. Our sources tell us that the van carried a secret team assigned to carry out paramilitary operations throughout the Middle East. Their job is to wage covert, unconventional operations against our enemies." The TV camera zoomed in to get a closer shot at the crowd gathering around the announcer.

"The vehicle exploded instantly after a rocket-propelled grenade hit it. CNN camera crews are on their way to get live pictures to you from the scene of the accident." Beads of sweat made the young reporter's freckles sparkle against the early morning sun. Allegedly, the victims were to execute an operation in the early hours. There were no survivors. The reporter winced to keep a fly from landing in his forehead and then continued: "We will standby to report any further developments. This is Jon Collins reporting live for CNN from Riyadh. Over to you, Joe."

Susan shut the TV off and stepped out into her garden. A gigantic black and yellow butterfly landed on a bed of English thyme along the edge of the rock garden. The ethereal creature settled for an instant; it seemed an eternity. Then, it fluttered above the gardenias and disappeared behind the rose bushes. Susan closed her eyes and prayed. Holding hope against all odds that her son was one of the men in that van, Susan waited for the phone to ring. Somebody would call. Perhaps someone would drive up to the house, like in the movies. She refused to believe her son was gone, and yet she was prepared to hear the worst.

Susan did not hear Morton walk into the house. Morton saw her through the open window. She looked so brave, sitting alone in her garden waiting and hoping. He took a big breath and walked over to hold his wife.

"I just heard the news. What do you know about Jeff?"

"We don't know yet, honey. General Calloway will let us know as soon as he gets his men on the ground. We must be strong now for Jeff and the rest of the family." She nodded and held on tight to the father of her son. Soon thereafter, the call came in. Morton was relieved to hear General Galloway report that a chopper was transporting all the victims to the USS Eisenhower. The aircraft carrier and floating hospital was on standby in the Gulf. The General then spoke gently.

"Morton, some of the victims were in very bad shape. We lost two men and two are in critical condition." He paused to give his friend time to take the blow.

"No names available yet, but we know that it was Jeff's team."

Morton swallowed hard and wanted to thank Calloway for the call, when he heard the veteran soldier reassure him one more time.

"I'll keep you posted as soon as I hear more. You know they are getting the best medical attention in the world."

"I know. Thanks again."

Morton sat next to his wife and held her hand. They sat in silence watching a butterfly swirl in playful abandon among the daylilies. The last rays of light swept across the garden. Morton tried to convince himself that Jeff had survived. Susan knew otherwise.

"Everything will be alright."

✫ ✫ ✫

The chopper landed shortly after Dr. Patrick Gordon briefed his team of ten surgeons as to the condition of each of the victims now arriving at the emergency and trauma centers aboard the USS Eisenhower. The Navy assigned the best and the brightest among its medical personnel to serve in this state-of the art military hospital. Life on this floating city was demanding and rewarding. The crew served with pride to save lives. Dr. Gordon approached the gurney carrying the commander of the Delta team and was surprised to see Lt. Col. Jeffrey Rourke awake. The Navy SEAL's injuries did not look good.

The head surgeon put his hand on Jeff's shoulder and said, "We'll take good care of you and your men, Commander." The wounded sailor closed his eyes.

Minutes later, Dr. Gordon and his team battled to live up to the promise he had made to a dying man.

☆ ☆ ☆

Clayton landed in Washington's National airport and asked the cab driver to take him to Georgetown. His temporary home was a renovated studio in a narrow building overlooking a cobblestone alley near the canal. Georgetown reeked of old money and power. The permanence of this historic neighborhood made his temporary residence there that more obtrusive. As far as Clayton was concerned, Georgetown had a sense of place, an attitude steeped in quiet elegance. Clayton appreciated the quaint charm but he did not feel at home. After a shower and shave, Clayton grabbed a cup of coffee while listening to MSNBC. Clayton was eager to get to his office and find out about the results of Morton's analysis of the Ajnadayn files.

The anchor announced a special update "On the Riyadh accident." The news stunned Clayton. He dialed Morton's office and was not surprised when his assistant answered the private line.

"Yes, it is a terrible tragedy," she said, "we found out a few hours ago. We are all devastated."

Clayton asked if any of Jeff's men were alive. "Only one is still fighting for his life. I think his name is Anthony. That's all I know." Clayton hung up the phone and stepped out into the street.

The morning air was stale and a humid breeze blew across the alley. Clayton walked along the canal for several blocks and then headed toward Main

Street. Georgetown shoppers and commuters mingled in the heart of the town. Clayton needed to walk, sort out his anger, and prepare himself for the grief that was sure to follow. He had learned early on to compartmentalize his emotions. Today, he was going to put those lessons to the test.

Walking past the newsstand around the corner from his place, Clayton spotted the *Washington Post*. Out of the corner of his eye, he caught a glimpse of the front page headline: "Attack on Americans in Riyadh." Clayton shook his head. He knew them. They were ordinary men living extraordinary lives.

✲ ✲ ✲

Mack Cumberland set his reading glasses on his desk and rubbed his tired eyes. He had slept five hours. That was enough rest for one day, but the last two days had been anything but normal. When his chief of staff asked him how he was doing before the daily intelligence briefing, Cumberland joked:

"Okay, considering that last night I slept like a baby; woke up every half hour crying."

The president was increasingly worried about a resurgence of violent attacks against American forces in the Middle East, Africa, Asia, and in just about every hot spot around the globe. Attacks came in waves. After a pause, they came back again, and again. The attack against the Delta team was unsettling because it came on the heels of two similar attacks in Asia and Africa. More attacks could follow.

Cumberland felt responsible for every life he put in harm's way. He liked to either call or write a personal note of thanks to each family of a fallen American soldier. He attended each funeral and mourned each loss. The latest attack in Riyadh was personal. Mack Cumberland's voice cracked when he thanked Morton and Susan Rourke for their son's ultimate sacrifice.

Jeff's death was a stark reminder of the president's own loss of an infant son. Time had healed those scars, but the president knew the depth of a parent's grief. He wept when he hung up the phone. He had known Jeff since he and Morton returned from Vietnam. Their kids were in grade school together. The president had fond memories of simpler times when the two families had gone to Little League games together and shared the kids' victories and defeats during outings on the lake or summer BBQ's in the backyard.

"*Those were happy times, so long ago*," thought Mack Cumberland as he pulled himself together to call the grieving family of another Delta man.

The president's worries about foreign policy usually overshadowed his domestic concerns. In the last few days, his worst fears had become a reality. The latest Gallup poll showed his opponent Priscilla Parks within reach of becoming the next President of the United States. She waged unrelenting attacks against American foreign interventions and her call to "Bring our Boys Home" seemed to resonate with the American public. Against the advice of his senior campaign advisors, Cumberland refused to attack the junior senator on a personal level. His opposition research team had uncovered a big story about Ms. Parks. Leaked at the right time, the story could tarnish her reputation and drive a big nail into her political coffin.

The media had reported her husband's escapades when she announced her candidacy, but her dutiful wife image discouraged opponents from bringing up her husband's romantic dalliances. Priscilla had reminded voters during her senatorial campaign that she loved her husband but he was not perfect. With a confident smile, she had added:

"This campaign is not about Gregory. I'll be representing you in the United States Senate." Divorcing her personal life from her public persona worked for Priscilla's Senate run. Mack Cumberland's advisors underscored the need to reap the rewards of his opponent's poor judgment.

"This is too good for us to keep from the media, Mr. President. The American people would be disgusted with this woman. She should not even be serving in the Senate." Cumberland's campaign manager insisted in slowly leaking to the media details of the senator's torrid romance with a staffer half her age.

"Mr. President, the American people care about leadership. Moral leadership cannot be divorced from the virtues necessary to lead a nation in times of war and peace."

The president remained unmoved by his advisor's pitch. A young staff member piped in. As he spoke, his chubby face turned red like a beet from the excitement of persuading the president to bury his opponent and win reelection.

"Duty, prudence and good judgment, the virtues that you have shown in serving the American people, can be weaved into subtle testimonials to expose Ms. Parks' vices."

Mack Cumberland could not visualize the effective campaign ads floating in his advisors' heads. He was a man of principle. He had promised Americans that the politics of personal destruction would end with his administration.

"Stubborn," mumbled the red-faced assistant as he walked out of the Oval Office empty-handed. There would not be either subtle or unsubtle campaign ads about the Senator's debauchery. His boss, the campaign manager, was blunt.

"Stupid. Principles do not win elections."

✲ ✲ ✲

Tom Munroe woke up with a searing headache. Since the start of his administrative leave, he had taken two lie detector tests and had met with his lawyer on a daily basis. His friend at State did not return his calls. His daughter became hysterical when he confessed that the funds he had transferred into her account were now part of a federal investigation.

"What have you done? I do not care if you ruin your life. All you care about is yourself. You always have. You ruined mother's life. You have no right to ruin mine! I'm getting my own lawyer." She had stormed out of the house. She would not answer his phone calls anymore.

"So much for filial loyalty," Tom told his lawyer, while recounting his daughter's rage and pouring himself a gin on the rocks before lunchtime. The lawyer advised Tom to give investigators a full accounting of how he had become involved in selling information to build up his net worth.

"The next round of questions will come from the FBI," explained Tom's legal counsel, and then he added, "Don't lie to those guys, Tom. Tell them all that you know. We can always find a way to plea bargain. We can give them what they want in return for a lighter sentence."

Tom could not face up to the idea of spending time behind bars and after hearing his attorney's somber advice, he contemplated the idea of skipping town. After meeting with his attorney and realizing that deception was no longer an option, Tom drove back to his place in Bethesda. He dismissed the idea of an escape when he spotted a blue car following him and another just like it parked in front of his house.

"They want me to know that I'm under tight surveillance. There is no way out." He drank enough gin to pass out and forget about retiring in the Bahamas.

The next morning, Tom drafted a detailed memo telling his attorney some of the motives and circumstances for his fall from grace. "*This damn headache*," he told himself as he pecked away at the keyboard. Tom wrote that his estranged wife had acquired expensive tastes when they lived overseas, where he served most of his thirty-five year career. Four years ago, when they returned to Washington his salary was not enough to keep her satisfied and through a friend at the State department, he learned that there could be ways to supplement his income through some consulting. Tom put Alex Keynes III name in parenthesis wondering how many eyebrows this revelation would raise within the Beltway.

"The bastard won't even return my calls. Maybe this will get his attention. And I thought we were friends." Tom gulped down his drink and continued typing his confession. He admitted to exchanging information for cash and explained that he never passed along classified information to any enemy of the United States. He worked through Mr. Keynes and his associate, Mr. Sanford Gillman. Both assured him that the information was heading to friendly allies who wanted more details than those received through official channels. Tom signed the memo and hand delivered it to his attorney, a senior partner in a prestigious Washington law firm.

"Good job, Tom. We'll rehearse some of the questions you'll get tomorrow. We'll get you out of this mess."

Sam Smelter scanned the ten pages and complemented his client. The law firm of Smelter, Giddeon, and Harris had a reputation for handling high profile cases with one of the most effective PR teams in the nation. Sam Smelter could put a lid on a client's scandal before it reached the evening news and could cloak his clients in the mantle of innocence necessary to win cases. Legal prowess and media savvy earned Sam the dubious honor of being called Teflon Shark among his colleagues.

Sam leaned against the back of his swivel chair and grinned when he re-read the name of a prominent Washington lobbyist smack in the middle of Tom's confession.

"Well" he said out loud, "Well, well. What a nice surprise." The prospect of defending a high profile case had not occurred to Sam when he accepted Tom as a client for an initial fee of $250,000. Sanford Gillman would add some spice to the case. Alex Keynes III was another interesting addition. Sam wondered if this was the same Keynes who had been interviewed about the "Cumberland Purge," and had given an angry account of his reassignment to Washington. A frustrated bureaucrat was hardly newsworthy but this crabby snob had made a fool of himself on CNN last week. Yesterday, CNN reported that Mr. Keynes had been demoted again. He was now toiling in trivial affairs of state in some Foggy Bottom hallway.

"Very well, this will be fun." Sam Smelter smiled as he read the details of Tom's memo. Fun for Sam Smelter translated into collecting hefty fees.

What Sam Smelter did not read was the part of the story that worried Tom the most. Tom Munroe had resorted to literary license to explain his motives for complementing his government paycheck. More importantly, Tom omitted his unofficial relationship with a foreign national who was now an enemy of the United States. During a CIA tour of duty in Riyadh, a young Tom Munroe met a shy, newly wed American woman married to a Saudi prince. The couple gave lavish parties. During a reception at their home, Tom approached Ada Hassan. Her husband was busy with some business partners at a safe distance. Tom kissed her hand.

"One day, I'll peel away your veil, and make you the happiest woman in the kingdom."

She smiled and did not reply. Months later when her husband took a second wife, Ada became Tom Munroe's lover. Over the years, the relationship between Ada and Tom survived his long absences. Tom bonded with her son Khalid. While the youngster studied at MIT, Tom spent a weekend each month with his lover's son, and hoped that the boy would remain in the United States and follow his own career path. But Khalid returned to Riyadh to visit his mother and never returned. When Tom discovered that Khalid was working at the Ministry of Oil, he recruited his illegitimate son to work for him before he found out that a radical Islamic cleric had already approached the youngster.

On a visit to Riyadh, Khalid gave Tom a copy of a printout he had retrieved from the Minister's office. At that time, the shy young man confided that he had joined an Islamic movement to bring back glory to the culture of his ancestors. Khalid desperately wanted to live up to Prince Hassan's expectations.

"This movement means a lot to me. Maybe my father will accept me if I become a martyr."

Khalid informed Tom that he would no longer retrieve information to help the enemies of Islam. Tom knew that he could persuade Khalid to deliver information once again, but he was horrified by the troubled young man's confession. Tom pleaded with Ada to dissuade their son from becoming a terrorist. Horror turned to panic when Tom studied the documents Khalid retrieved from the Minister's office. Financial records suggested that the funds he was regularly receiving from Sanford Gillman were coming directly from TOVAIR's coffers.

Chapter 10

Blood and Tears

A busload of tourists was making its way along the Wall. Some stopped and touched the names of heroes. Some brought pictures or flowers. A girl dressed in a red, white, and blue shirt hugged a teddy bear. Her mother pointed to a name high up on the wall. Some wept in silence. All seemed in awe as they walked on hallow ground. A soft rain began to fall, and Clayton walked up to the place he knew well. He stood still, his head held high, proud of his father and the men whose names symbolized the determination of a free nation. His thoughts turned to Jeff and the men he had gotten to know. Their names would not be carved in stone. There would be no monument honoring these men. They would receive their medals in quiet ceremonies. Few would attend and fewer still would see these medals once they were stored in a glass case displayed along a hallway dedicated to fallen heroes. Like other quiet men before them, who had gone to Saigon in 1954 to join the SMM, Jeff and his team had worked to stabilize a volatile region. They had completed their work. They had paid with their own lives for the freedom others would forever enjoy.

The Delta team, like the Saigon Military Mission before it, had been engaged in a secret struggle to bring order out of chaos and turn tyranny into liberty. The Delta team's successes never made the prime time news. Any defeats remained shrouded in mystery. Clayton walked along the wall and noticed a young couple taking pictures. Behind the camera, the woman could have been Lyn Chang. He noticed that the photographer was considerably shorter than the intrepid journalist he had met in London. The Washington sky darkened and a steady downpour made the rain-washed sidewalk look like glass. Clayton headed to the Foggy Bottom subway station.

✲ ✲ ✲

The Ajnadayn files yielded valuable information about the multiple TOVAIR funds managed from London and were particularly useful when compared to the documents found in the Saudi Oil Minister's safe. Since returning to Washington, Clayton had spent many hours examining the large volume of data he had collected on his "fishing expedition," his whirlwind adventure from Cairo to London.

One missing piece of the puzzle still kept Clayton awake every night. Morton told him that the Swiss refused to divulge the identity of S.G. Clayton spent long evenings running a sophisticated content analysis tool across classified TOVAIR reports to unearth possible clues to the S.G. clandestine account. His search was of little use.

Morton assigned a special InterIntel team to assist Clayton in his quest to identify S.G. The team was working day and night. With each passing day, everyone grew tired and grumpy.

"I'm going home guys. Let's all get some rest and reconvene tomorrow morning." Clayton's announcement lifted tired spirits on that late Saturday afternoon.

As an incentive to return to work on a Sunday, he added, "After work tomorrow, Sunday brunch is on me. Let's meet at the Sound of the Whale." The invitation meant an early start at 4:30 am. The analysts joked that Clayton's clock was set on Idaho fly-fishing time.

The headline for the inconspicuous article on page eight of the Sunday *Washington Times* caught Clayton's attention. He and the team of analysts had combed through reams of data with little success. Back in his studio, Clayton stretched on the couch and read the story. He mulled over the headline: "Tom Munroe, hires Smelter, Giddeon, and Harris to defend his case." The article explained that since Carlton Harris, a scion of Harris Advertising on Madison Avenue, had recently joined the older partners, the firm had become a powerhouse for high profile cases across the nation. Clayton repeated aloud, "Smelter and Giddeon," and then he jotted down the initials S.G. on the newspaper margin.

✲ ✲ ✲

In the weeks following Jeff's funeral, Morton and Susan found solace within a small circle of family and friends. The twins and the Grands, as they liked to call the grandkids, had left for their respective homes on the West Coast. Morton thought it would be nice to invite Clayton over for dinner. Just as he was about to ask Susan if he could ask Clayton to join them for supper, his phone rang. It was Clayton with a question about the prestigious law form hired to defend Tom Munroe.

"Morton, I'm sorry to bother you on a Sunday afternoon. What do you know about Smelter, Giddeon and Harris? "

After telling Clayton how Harris had just joined the firm after his marriage to Smelter's daughter, Morton said: "Hang on, Clayton," and turning to Susan asked: "Honey, would it be alright with you if I ask Clayton to join us for supper tonight?"

After a light meal, Clayton complemented Susan. Then, he talked about her son. "In Cairo, Jeff made your oxtail stew for all of us one night. It was the best." Clayton paused, uncertain about his comment, worried that his candor would open the raw wound.

"I'm sorry."

Susan smiled and reached across the table. She patted his hand. "It's okay, Clayton. We love to hear about Jeff. He was looking forward to fly-fish with you."

Susan sensed that Clayton knew much about grief. His lips tightened and his pale green eyes became translucent as he spoke. "I wanted to show Jeff my favorite river. He would have liked my part of the world. He told me about your fishing outings on the lake, when he and his sisters were little. Jeff and I connected in the way that old friends do. I miss him."

Morton and Susan remembered those happy times and exchanged subtle looks as if to assure one another that they would never forget. They appreciated Clayton's words.

"Life is like a waterfall. You first see water flowing unencumbered. The river is lazy until it approaches the edge of a rock. There, the smooth ride ends abruptly and a torrent gushes down a steep incline. Water roars and knocks everything in its path, just like life. When you least expect it, calm turns into chaos."

Susan was certain that Clayton had experienced a huge loss in his life. "Jeff rode the rapids with dignity and honor. He taught me how to lead a team. I'll remember his lessons as long as I live."

Susan fought back tears. Morton felt pride swelling up in his chest. He smiled and motioned for Clayton to follow him out to patio.

"Come on Clayton, let's go out and check out Susan's garden."

They walked in silence and sat on the bench under the willow oak tree. Morton lit up a cigar, a Nicaraguan Flor de Jalapa Presidente. The smoke was thick and sweet.

"While you and Jeff were in Riyadh, the president told me that he served with your dad in Vietnam." Clayton turned to face him, and Morton noticed the few fine lines around his eyes. Clayton looked younger than his forty-eight years. Born exactly one year before the last American troops left Vietnam in March 1973, the very same year the last US prisoners returned from captivity, he had his dad's youthful looks.

"President Cumberland knows you want to learn more about your father. He'll make good on his promise to you." Morton took a deep breath. Smoke swirled above his head. "It's hard to talk about war when you've been in it. It's hard on fathers and sons."

Clayton looked at the daylilies. "I know."

Morton savored his cigar, and after a long pause asked,

"Do you suspect Tom's lawyers are linked to SG?"

Clayton stretched his arms above his head. He explained that he only had a hunch, no specific evidence at this time. "Suppose for a moment, that S.G. dates to the time when it was just the two old partners. It's a long shot but it's worth checking out, don't you think?"

Chapter 11
The Lion's Den

Sam Smelter was fond of his assistant in more than one way but was not amused when she came into his office. She bent over and whispered in his ear:

"Dr. Harcourt is here to see you. He is cute and young. But don't worry you are stuck with your Bunny." The woman annoyed Smelter with her silly games but she could make him feel young. He promised himself to get rid of her. Every time he made up his mind to let her go, she managed to come into his office and persuade him of her indispensable skills. Just like this morning before lunch when she walked in with that low cut, tight dress. He stood up and straightened his tie.

"Tell him to come in and hold all my calls." Smelter greeted his visitor with obvious disdain.

"Good afternoon, Dr. Harcourt. I hope you realize that I do not usually meet to discuss client's cases. Come on in."

Smelter sat behind his desk facing the window, his back to Clayton. The view from his corner office was expansive. Clayton got right to the point:

"Mr. Smelter, your client, Mr. Munroe may be innocent. I've worked for him for a number of years."

Clayton paused. Expecting the lawyer's reaction, he waited for a response. Smelter did not move. Clayton waited for Smelter to show some sign of civility. The lawyer did not turn around.

"Go, on I'm listening," he said.

"Tom made mistakes but he is not a criminal. Here is my theory."

Clayton went on to explain how Tom had broken the rules of the game. He became the case officer of a dangerous terrorist in Riyadh, while his recruit was in Washington. This was a most irregular way to manage intelligence assets. Case officers worked in the field and reported through well-established channels.

"I suspect that through this informal relationship, Tom learned sensitive information. In the wrong hands, this information could bring down our government and implicate him in a direct way." Clayton paused. Smelter shifted his weight and his swivel chair squeaked as he turned to face Clayton.

"I need your help. If we work together, maybe I can help you build a case for Tom's defense and you can help me uncover a deadly terrorist plot intent on destroying our nation." Clayton got up, walked around the coffee table, and with his hands in his pockets, stood in front of the patrician lawyer's desk. Smelter was taking notes and he did not look up.

"Sit down, young man. What do you know?"

Clayton ignored the invitation and said, "We have only a small clue, a pair of initials and a Swiss account. The initials are S.G." The old man straightened up his back and raised his left eyebrow. A sly grin crossed his lips.

"Very clever, Doctor." Then his face turned grey and his voice rose in anger. "Very clever, indeed."

Sam Smelter pounded his desk with a clenched fist and reminded Clayton of the ridiculous picture of Nikita Krushshev pounding his shoe on a table at the United Nations in the midst of the Cold War. The old lawyer erupted like a volcano. "You think those initials stand for Smelter and Giddeon, don't you? That is what brought you here."

Clayton nodded. Sam Smelter stood up and pointed angrily toward the door.

"Well, you are wrong. Wrong. Get out of my office. Right now, get out."

Clayton did not move. "I apologize, Mr. Smelter, you have a right to be upset. But I had to see you reaction first hand."

Smelter was still fuming mad. "How dare you?"

Clayton ignored the remark: "For an entire week, a team of seven analysts and I have tried every possible avenue to make a connection. The Swiss will not cooperate. We are working against the clock. You are our last resort. Please help us out."

The old man walked around his desk and sat down. He looked at Clayton and barked his order.

"Sit." Then he asked, "What do you propose we do next?" Sam Smelter listened as Clayton suggested that he ask Tom to think about any names with the initials S.G.

"And if Mr. Munroe cannot recollect any acquaintances with the initials S.G. what is it that you propose we do next?"

"Ask him to write down the events, dates, places and people he has been associated with in the last twenty five years."

"Why twenty five years, Dr. Harcourt?" The lawyer seemed genuinely curious.

"It was twenty five years ago when Tom Munroe was first assigned to Riyadh. I think you'll have to go back that far back to find any answers for his case.

"Twenty five years, interesting." Sam Smelter jotted down some notes with a gold Mont Blanc fountain pen, and then walked Clayton out of his office door. Without offering a handshake, the crusty old man gently pushed Clayton out the door.

"I'll call you, Doctor. Good day." Bunny blew a kiss behind Clayton's back, as Smelter slammed the door to his office.

"Twenty five years, very interesting." He reached for Tom's file. Reading over his client's notes, Smelter came across a name that made him smile broadly, just as he had done earlier that day before lunch.

"The initials match nicely," he said aloud and dialed Tom Munroe's number.

✡ ✡ ✡

Abdul Hakim, a.k.a., Ahmed Assoud paced his office angered by his inability to control events around him. The recent Riyadh hit against the Americans was a welcome relief to a string of obstacles and defeats. The disappearance of Khalid Hassan, a new recruit, and son of a close associate, coincided with the devastating news of the break-in at the Oil Ministry. Minister Sar-al Diab had assured Hakim that there would be a full investigation to uncover any accomplices.

"I promise you, those responsible for stealing documents from my safe will be killed." Sar-al Diab did not tell his friend Hakim which vital documents related to their joint TOVAIR operations were missing.

In turn, Hakim did not tell the Minister, that he had recently recruited the young engineer for planning a future suicide mission as reward for his loyalty. Even among friends, TOVAIR's secrets remained highly compartmentalized. Both Sar-al Diab and Hakim agreed that Americans had to be behind the break-in and launched an intense effort within the region to identify the responsible parties for their recent setbacks.

Khalid Hassan, was cooperating with Saudi authorities, who were drilling him for any information related to his abductors. He could not identify any of the men who had held him in the safe house. The engineer reported that during his captivity he had heard the name "Layton" or something like that. Hakim suspected that Clayton Harcourt could have been one of the perpetrators of Hassan's abduction and subsequent break-in.

"This American is sure persistent," thought Hakim, *"he evaded death once. He will not survive next time. I'll have to rely on a trusted ally to eliminate Harcourt."*

Hakim's frustration did not end with the Oil Ministry fiasco. Trusted affiliates in London reported the abduction and subsequent capture of Francois Duvenoix by British authorities. Hakim had a hunch that the charges were phony and Duvenoix was being held without bail to get him to talk. Hakim also had a hunch that under pressure, Duvenoix would falter.

TOVAIR's top leader trusted his instincts and was working around the clock to get someone in Duvenoix's cell block to persuade the Algerian to keep his mouth shut. Duvenoix knew too much. He was a loyal soldier, he was an accounting genius, he could hide transactions and create smoke and mirrors like a magician. He had other valuable skills; he had good rapport with key arms dealers around the globe. Like his father before him, Duvenoix had a knack for dealing with shady characters.

In London, free to operate far from where most of his work mattered most, Duvenoix was an asset for TOVAIR. In a British jail, Duvenoix was a liability. Duvenoix's capture had severe consequences for an operation of great interest to Hakim. The "US Domestic Politics" account was part of Duvenoix's portfolio. Now this responsibility had to be reassigned immediately. At stake was a valuable relationship TOVAIR maintained in America. This relationship was the single most delicate link to the highest levers of Washington power. Hakim decided to assume complete control over his most valuable asset, and invited his American power broker to meet him in Paris.

✲ ✲ ✲

Sanford Gillman loved French food, wine, and young men. He was delighted to accept Abdul Hakim's invitation to the French capital. He was disappointed that his stay at the exclusive Regency Hotel had only lasted one night but with the presidential election in full swing, Gillman's Washington calendar was full. His meetings with Hakim generally amounted to a review of the lobbying activities the Egyptian industrialist financed but this latest meeting was different. Hakim handed Gillman a blank check for "any amount you deem necessary to elect your next president."

Gillman had politely explained that such funds if discovered would be in violation of national election laws, and that he could face severe penalties for accepting such funds. Hakim had smiled and in the most reassuring tone had calmed Gillman's fears.

"My friend, why would anyone find out about this money? Consider this a personal gift from me to you." With a wink, he had added, "Surely, you can accept a generous gift from a trusted friend."

Hakim then suggested that Gillman put this money to work for the candidate that could bring the most professional rewards for a hard working lobbyist like himself. After a six-course dinner, they shook hands and Gillman put the blank check in his pocket. Hours later, his flight was about to land at Dulles International Airport and Sanford Gillman fastened his seat belt before a smooth landing.

Chapter 12
High Politics

President Cumberland and the First Lady hosted the lunch held in honor of the fallen members of the Delta team. The gathering was a private ceremony to thank the grieving families. The president introduced Anthony Marks, the sole survivor of the Riyadh attack. His wife, two daughters, and parents stood behind his wheelchair.

"I'm proud to serve my country. So were all the members of our team." Then Tony paused and looking at his Commander in Chief added:

"Mr. President, I look forward to get back to the field. I'll be ready in no time, as soon as this cast comes off, Sir." Tony was a fearless warrior but he was petrified of getting a desk job. President Cumberland smiled and Tony received a standing ovation.

Clayton and Morton drove back to Morton's office after the White House ceremony. Clayton pulled into the parking lot and told Mort how Tony had saved his life in Cairo.

"He's a tough fellow with a big heart," said Mort, "Jeff always could count on him when things got rough." Clayton followed Morton into his office. As soon as the two men sat down, Morton took a call and informed Clayton of the latest news from London.

"Duvenoix hung himself in his cell last night. The Brits are investigating." Clayton pointed to the stack of documents on the conference table.

"Guess he's not going to be of much more help than this." Morton nodded.

"He was beginning to break under pressure. We'll get the British report in a day or two." Clayton reached across the table and set two printouts side by side in front of Morton.

"The evidence is pretty clear. As you can see, TOVAIR is underwriting sovereign debt for developing countries, and they are buying these debt issues to collect interest, sometimes in the double digits. It's quite a scam."

Morton compared the numbers across both documents and took a second look at the chart Clayton had put together to graphically show the way TOVAIR was siphoning funds from strapped governments. He got up and began to pace. Morton always paced when he had to solve a complex puzzle just as Tony had to draw to think clearly.

"Well, looks like your hunch was right all along. Now, the question is how do we stop them?"

Clayton looked out Mortons's window as if to search for an answer. The Washington monument and a partial view of the Lincoln memorial reminded Clayton that since its founding, America faced adversity with determination and ingenuity. Across generations, enemies loomed large but Americans always prevailed against the enemies of freedom.

"Morton, I do not know the answer to your question, but I know that we will figure this out." The confidence in Clayton's voice reminded Morton of Jeff's eternal optimism.

Morton enjoyed spending time with Clayton. Knowing that he had never had a chance to meet his loving father, Morton wanted to tell him what he knew about Jack, but he did not. That was a promise Mack Cumberland had made, and Morton would honor the trust the president had placed in him.

✲ ✲ ✲

"We have to stop them from running these countries into the ground," said President Cumberland when Morton briefed him about the TOVAIR financing scheme.

A grim picture emerged from the documents and computer files snatched by Clayton and the Delta team. Clayton had given Morton a detailed report linking fiscal chaos to political chaos from Argentina to Zambia. The president had paid close attention to Clayton's conclusion.

"Countries with high foreign debt levels are burdened with high interest payments and are unable to pay for basic services. TOVAIR is filling this gap across Latin America, Africa, Asia, and the Middle East through social safety nets used to recruit and finance radical Islamic movements. This strategy replicates what the organization's predecessors did in Afghanistan, Saudi Arabia, Pakistan, and other countries. Operating in failed or weak nations was ideal to nurture hatred and violence against the West. The objective was to force the United States and its allies to engage in immediate hot spots around the world while TOVAIR pursued its destructive longer term aims."

The report concluded that based on its intricate connections to the financial stability of developing nations, TOVAIR was likely to have an interest in destabilizing the U.S. and other Western nations through domestic political channels. These were softer targets than American and European financial institutions, which had achieved a high degree of transparency and were very difficult to infiltrate.

"Mr. President, we think that TOVAIR has to be stopped right here at home. My hunch is that the ultimate targets are our economy and our political institutions." Clayton's report had stopped short of pointing out one of Clayton's concerns. It was premature to present inconclusive evidence, but Clayton convinced Mort to raise a sensitive issue with the president. Clayton had argued that the presidency and the very survival of the republic were at stake if Assoud found a way to influence American politicians. He stressed that TOVAIR could even manipulate the outcome of the presidential election. Mort chose his next words with great care.

"We have not connected all the dots yet, but there is some preliminary evidence suggesting that TOVAIR might have its sights fixed on our electoral process. Key players might be involved in the presidential campaign."

The president seemed calm but his voice shook a bit, as he spoke the first two words of a question Mort had anticipated.

"What exactly do you mean?"

Mort explained Clayton's findings and hunch, particularly in terms of a Swiss bank account for someone with the initials S.G. He also explained that the huge amounts of dollars swirling around American presidential campaigns provided a tempting target for manipulation.

"A few well-connected players could cause a great deal of damage, Mr. President." Cumberland did not hesitate and he gave Morton orders to act at once.

"We need to get to the bottom of this. Do whatever you need to do and find the answers. This is very serious business. I want you and the Attorney General to get together and start a full investigation."

After his meeting with Mort, the president placed a call to his campaign manager. The day was off to a bad start.

✡ ✡ ✡

After work, Clayton drove out to the Virginia countryside. Accotink Creek had a good number of riffles, runs, and pools. Although it was late in the day, Clayton did not notice much insect activity. He approached the stream with caution, stepping lightly over moist grasses. Squinting to avoid the last rays of sunlight, he saw three rises. He tied on an 18 Parachute Adams, made a single upstream cast, and caught a 14-inch rainbow. He found more satisfaction releasing the trout back into the creek than catching it. Wading into the stream reminded Clayton of why fly-fishing was his passion.

It was in places like this one, close to trout and wilderness that he was able to consider the way in which he chose to live. Holding a fly rod and attempting to imitate the natural landing of an insect on the surface of the water reminded Clayton of the essence of life. It was a humbling experience to imitate Mother Nature. During his younger days, futile attempts to repeat his infrequent successes had caused him anger and frustration. Anger had no place in a seasoned angler's journey, and the sheer joy of discovering the irrelevance of daily routines was now enough to erase any sign of aggravation. Fly-fishing was a healing enterprise for Clayton. The quiet sport taught him patience and pointed his way home. Clayton smiled as he recalled a favorite Norman Mclean quote: "In our family, there was no clear line between religion and fly-fishing." For the Harcourt family fly-fishing was a way of life.

Jack's premature death did not leave Clayton immune to the pain that came with each subsequent loss. Jeff's death was the latest episode in a string of relationships cut short by destiny. Standing there alone, in the middle of Accotink Creek, Clayton released all the anger of losing the chance to gain a true friend.

☆ ☆ ☆

Priscilla Parks had few friends in the Senate and within the Beltway. Women tended to distrust her political maneuvers while supporting her liberal agenda, proving that in politics the end often justifies the means. With the exception of her lover, most men including her husband tended to keep a safe distance from her. One man in Washington understood Senator Parks well and knew exactly how to make her happy. For her, politics was not a popularity contest. She did not seek public admiration, and did not care if her supporters liked her, or her foes hated her. She paid little attention to the media attacks, the rumor mill, and public opinion polls.

Senator Parks was interested in only two things, money and raw power. Sanford Gillman knew how to provide access to both. Priscilla seldom answered her private line but she always took Gillman's calls.

"Hi, sweetie," she purred after noticing the familiar number on her caller ID, "we missed you. Everyone asked about you, and I just said you had an important meeting. How was London?"

Gillman did not like to miss dinners at the Parks' residence but he could not ignore the London invitation from Hakim on the previous week.

"The trip exceeded all my expectations, Senator. I appreciate your understanding. Sorry I missed your dinner last Friday, and thank you for keeping my travel plans confidential." He paused, and then reported his accomplishment.

"I want you to know that this morning I made a contribution to AFF. Are you sitting down Senator?"

Priscilla Parks smiled broadly and took a deep breath. Her sweet Southern drawl slowed down, and her words rolled out of her pursed lips like molasses.

"Yes, Sandi, I am."

Gillman then told her that another forty five million would help get into 1600 Pennsylvania Avenue.

"What do you think, Foxy?"

Gillman liked addressing the senator by her nickname, because it gave him a sense of absolute power. Not even Gregory Parks got away with such infraction. She hated being called "Foxy," but Sanford Gillman could call her anything he wanted.

"Love you, honey," she told him and hung up.

The Americans For Fairness (AFF) was a coalition of trial lawyers, environmentalists, feminists, and labor organizations financed by a handful of wealthy contributors. AFF worked the loopholes in campaign finance laws to its advantage and operated in the shadow of campaign contribution limits. AFF provided no accountability, no transparency, and most important of all, no paper trail showing the source of contributions. Sanford Gillman and other large contributors liked it that way.

When the Clean Campaign Act banned soft money contributions to political parties, AFF became the avenue of choice to fund liberal candidates. On the other side of the political spectrum, the Coalition for a Free America (CFA) routed money to conservative candidates just the same way. At times, wealthy contributors would contribute to both organizations when faced with close races. Some of these fat-cat donors were hedging their bets during the final leg of the tight contest between Senator Parks and President Cumberland.

Chapter 13

The Chinese Connection

Lyn Chang unpacked her bags and called her contact at the Chinese Embassy. She followed instructions and requested an early morning meeting with Mr. Hu, the Commercial Officer. His official title had little to do with his actual Washington assignments. He had been expecting Ms. Chang's visit and had heard much about her accomplished career. She was in America for a sensitive assignment, the details of which Mr. Hu did not care to know. His responsibility was to provide any support she needed to help her get the job done. Mr. Hu did not take his responsibilities lightly. As soon as he hung up the phone, he logged on to his laptop to learn more about Ms. Chang's client.

✡ ✡ ✡

Sam Smelter knew a few Washington lobbyists, but he had only met Sanford Gillman once. Most of what Smelter knew about him came from the social pages of the *Washington Post*. In many ways, the Beltway was just like a small town filled with partisan cliques who seldom traveled in the same circles. Only a select group of political insiders moved back and forth across party lines, but neither Smelter nor Gillman belonged to this elite. Smelter had compiled a thick file of notes about the relationship between his client, Tom Munroe and Sanford Gillman.

Alex Keynes III had introduced the two men, when Tom had returned to Washington D.C. from his first assignment in Riyadh. According to Tom, Keynes claimed to have put Gillman in contact with "prominent people" outside the United States. Smelter deducted that Keynes's Foreign Service posts and his high profile stint at the United Nations were the chief sources for these foreign contacts. Smelter calculated that looking into Keynes's past would be less costly than digging for information about Gillman. Gillman had high-paid lawyers to keep his wealth and privacy safe from prying eyes.

"Besides," Smelter concluded, "why should I make it easier for Harcourt? Let him figure this out on his own."

Smelter was unforgiving and held his grudges for a long time. Clayton Harcourt had annoyed him with his false assumptions, and the old lawyer was not going to make Clayton's life easy. Besides, he did not need some government bureaucrat to help him defend one of his own clients. Sam Smelter gave Clayton only the information he had on Alex Keynes III but left out the name, claiming Tom's right to privacy.

"More detail would be helpful," pushed Clayton, "a name, at least the posts where this State Department FSO served."

Tom's lawyer paused. As if to look for a quick way out, he added, "Well, he did a stint at the UN. Sorry, Harcourt, that's the best I can do for you. I'm sure your outfit can pull the pieces of this puzzle together. Good day."

The old man hung up before Clayton could respond, and Clayton wondered how anyone could have such a nasty disposition. The morsel about the UN and the time line for the FSO's overseas assignments might yield some results. Smelter's information did not provide any further clues on S.G., and Clayton decided to pass on the details to his team for further analysis.

☆ ☆ ☆

The State personnel records office was the Inter-Intel team's first stop in search of an FSO who had served in the same posts as Tom Munroe and subsequently at the UN. Initially, seventeen names came up as a result of the initial data mining effort.

"Drill down further, let's just pick the highest ranking posts at the UN and compare that to the highest positions overseas," recommended Clayton. Three names came back in the next report. "That's more like it," announced Clayton to a relieved team leader. "Let's talk to the State Department folks."

Dealing with the State Department Personnel Office to get clearance and interview the three names that appeared on his short list, reminded Clayton as to why he had left Washington years ago. The Personnel Director was not about to take any shortcuts, and she unrolled the red tape at a snail pace. After three phone calls and several e-mails, Clayton was finally informed that one of the three individuals was now retired, one was serving in Paris, and only one was in D.C.

"Good, let's start with the fellow that's here."

Clayton's logical choice did not persuade the director, as she informed him that before anyone outside of State could get near the FSO to ask any questions, the personnel department would have to handle this as an internal matter. Rather than argue with her about procedural roadblocks, Clayton asked Morton to move the process further along. To no avail, moving the wheels of the bureaucracy forward was like turning an aircraft carrier 180 degrees. It took time.

"Like it or not, we have to wait for their internal investigation, Clayton. I checked with our legal counsel, and there is not one thing we can do about it." At that moment, Clayton knew he wanted to flee Washington and return to his beloved mountains. He did not share his frustration with Mort, but his mentor, a veteran of bureaucratic battles quickly figured out Clayton's feelings and placed a personal call to an old friend.

Later the same day, the president's personal call and his invitation to a private dinner at the White House surprised Clayton. He was certain that President Cumberland had questions about the preliminary assessment of TOVAIR's possible infiltration of the electoral process.

"Thank you, Mr. President, look forward to seeing you, sir."

Two days before the presidential dinner, Clayton struggled to get answers but was still unable to get his arms around the S.G. identity. His team showed the signs of stress and mental exhaustion. He realized that everyone was on edge when one of his best analysts called in sick and the team leader asked for some time off. The analysts had been working around the clock to unravel TOVAIR's secrets and their progress in the last few days had been minimal.

Late into the evening, Clayton approached a small group of his colleagues who were comparing notes.

"Is anyone ready for a brake?"

He knew that Mort would be still in his office waiting for them with a fresh pot of coffee and Susan's giant chocolate chip cookies.

"Let's go see the boss for a brainstorm and some home baked goodies."

Since his return to Washington, Clayton had become Acting Deputy Director of InterIntel, the position left vacant by Tom Munroe's forced leave of absence. A key priority of the Cumberland administration was to identify any links between TOVAIR and the presidential election. Clayton assigned three InterIntel teams to work exclusively on this problem. The late night strategy session in Mort's office helped his top team leaders prioritize their next moves.

The State Department roadblock would delay any interview with Alex Keynes III for at least a few weeks. If funds were moving from the Swiss account to the campaign coffers of either Senator Priscilla Parks or President Mack Cumberland, the InterIntel analysts had to move quickly. The election was only three months away. The Attorney General's investigation was underway, and Clayton suggested that the teams work closely with the Justice Department to widen the scope of their efforts. Pacing the floor, Clayton pointed to a large flow chart behind Mort's conference table.

"The folks at Justice are combing through donor lists and coordinating with bank regulators and Treasury to tease out any suspicious international funds transfers." He paused and gave everyone in the room time to digest the players and the process he had sketched graphically. Like an engineer presenting a complex drawing and explaining each component part, Clayton pointed to a cluster of acronyms listed under the subtitle "Other." He circled them with a red marker and noted their significance.

"Here, we have the toughest part of our puzzle. In addition to individual and corporate donors, we find that these few donors make substantial contributions. We do not know amounts nor do we know the individuals behind these campaign-financing schemes." He paused again to give everyone around the conference table time to think about each one of the names as he read them aloud.

"Friends of the Environment (FOE), Women in Power (WIP), The National Coalition for Security (NSC), Americans for Fairness (AFF) and all the others listed in your handout." Clayton took a sip of coffee.

"We need to zero-in on these outfits. These groups often fund candidates along party lines but some hedge their bets and contribute across partisan lines. Electronic surveillance is now underway but we will need a little time to collect more data and establish communication and fund transfer patterns."

After answering some tactical questions, Clayton thanked everyone for their hard work, and reminded his analytical team of possible ways to solve the puzzle.

"Let's keep thinking in terms of what if scenarios. He then added, "Don't rule anything out. Rule everything in. Get creative. Question everything. Put yourself in the enemy's shoes. Don't just figure out how they think but figure out how they will act. Get some rest."

It was shortly past midnight when the three analysts who accompanied Clayton to Mort's office left to catch a few hours of sleep.

* * *

"You ran a good meeting last night." Mort's compliment pleased Clayton, as he was becoming closer to his mentor. The two men respected one another's judgment and Mort was increasingly fond of sharing quiet moments, smoking a cigar, or taking a walk with someone who lessened the pain of losing a son.

"Thanks, Mort. I just followed your lead. Appreciate your suggestion of coming over to get everyone focused and change the pace. Sometimes, it's good to get outside of the confines of the office. I do my best thinking away from it all."

Mort smiled and said: "You've got to keep them motivated. You are working with the most talented people in town. They'll work around the clock until the job is done." He paused and then asked:

"Anything on this morning's report I need to know about?" Clayton glanced at the report he had been reading before Mort's call.

"Looks like Assoud is working around the clock. We have picked up lots of TOVAIR chatter around a large Indian arms smuggling ring previously affiliated with Duvenoix. With Duvenoix's recent demise, Assoud is trying to reconnect with the ring leaders, the Tansari brothers operating out of Punjab."

Mort recalled reading about the Kanhpor arms dealers. They had been in the arms smuggling business for five generations and were instrumental to the rise of terrorist activities from Afghanistan to Indonesia. TOVAIR was one of their major clients. Mort looked at his watch. He did not want to run late for a meeting with the Attorney General.

"Clayton, I've got to leave the office in about five minutes but I want to hear more about the Kanhpor connection. Let's have lunch at our usual place, say noon?"

Washington was sticky in late summer, and Clayton walked briskly from his office to the Sign of the Whale, where he was to meet Morton for lunch. K Street was crowded and traffic crawled to a halt as two black limousines with their respective police escorts roared past a red light. No one paid much attention to this common capital sight. Often, VIPs traveled across town disrupting the normal flow of pedestrians and cars.

"Important people within the Beltway always seem in a hurry," thought Clayton, *"Much movement but very little movement forward."*

He did not notice the slim woman approaching him as he was waiting for the light to change. Before he could step out into the curbside, she touched his arm.

"Do you always leave without saying good bye?"

Clayton recognized the voice.

"Small world. Last time I saw you, we were across the pond. You are a long way from Hong Kong!"

She pulled her sunglasses over her head, and ignored the question. Lyn Chang looked stunning in her low-cut silk tunic. Clayton tried to ignore her inviting looks. She had pulled her black hair up, which made her long neck seem longer. Her eyes danced in the sunlight.

"*Exotic is how Mrs. Barton put it*," he thought.

She brushed a wayward strand of hair off her forehead. "Any chance we can pick up where we left off?"

Her directness did not surprise him but something about this chance encounter made him feel cautious. "Give me your number. Maybe I'll call you," he replied and then added another note of uncertainty: "It's a busy time for me. I may have to leave town later today."

Lyn Chang tried another tack. "It's about lunch time. Can I join you?"

"Afraid not, I'm already late for a meeting."

Sensing his impatience, she pulled her sunglasses down, reached into her bag, and took out her business card. She scribbled a hotel name, pulled her sunglasses back on and handed him the card.

"Here is where you can find me." Before hailing a cab, Lyn Chang called Mr. Hue and left a short message: "Difficult customer. Will advise of any change in our plans."

Clayton spotted Mort and made his way to their usual table towards the back of the restaurant. "Sorry, I'm late. I ran into someone I did not expect to see again." He pulled Lyn's card out of his pocket and showed it to Morton.

"Does the name ring familiar? She is a Chinese journalist I met in London. She was staying at the Breakers. Now she is here. Somehow, I have a hunch she did not just run into me by accident on my way here."

Morton glanced at the menu, and peering over his reading glasses. "You are right. Lyn Chang does not run into people by chance." Clayton was stunned.

"You know her? Who is she?"

The waiter approached their table and took their order. Morton took a sip of water and looking Clayton straight in the eye, said, "In our business there is little we do not know. Lyn Chang was on your Nile river cruise. She is a close associate of Assoud, his Chinese connection you might say. She followed you to London."

"I probably should not have…" Morton interrupted him.

"Don't worry about it. You had no way of knowing about her. We have been tracking her for a while. We have had a couple of people working on Lyn Chang for some time. She is the daughter of a prominent Chinese trader from Xinjiang, who converted to Islam while growing up in Indonesia. Her family owns an oil, shipping, mining, and agribusiness conglomerate operating from Jakarta to Bombay. She serves as her father's envoy throughout the Middle East, and moves in official circles around the region. In her spare time, she works on special projects for the Chinese government. One of her close confidants is Assoud's daughter. I believe you met her on the Salinah?"

Clayton began to feel like he was in a fishbowl. He was thinking, "*What doesn't Mort know?*" Instead, he asked, "Why is Lyn Chang here now?"

Lunch arrived. The waiter poured vinaigrette dressing over a mound of succulent shrimp atop a bed of baby spinach garnished with fresh asparagus and cherry tomatoes. Mort reached into a basket filled with warm rolls, and while generously buttering one, responded: "We are not sure why she is here. She contacted the Commercial Officer at the Chinese embassy shortly after arriving day before yesterday."

He paused and reached for the butter again. Clayton pulled the butter dish away from Mort with a grin.

"Hold it, go easy on that cholesterol."

"Thanks, Clayton. My arteries do not need any additional clogging." Morton's triple bypass two years ago had saved his life. His old eating habits were hard to break.

"Our source at the embassy thinks that she is on an undercover mission. Her contact is not only the commercial guy; he is also a high ranking intelligence operative."

Clayton scanned the room as if to look for any suspicious individual and said, "She wants to get together. I told her I might have to be out of town. Did not want to commit to anything."

"You might want to reconsider," Morton suggested and then added, "Just be very careful."

Over a cup of coffee after lunch, Clayton briefed Morton on the latest reports linking TOVAIR and their major arms supplier: "In the last twenty four hours we have discovered increased communications between Assoud's Paris associate, a French arms dealer we think is taking over Duvenoix's arms smuggling operations and the Tansari brothers from Khanpur."

Clayton explained that a more alarming report came just before he left his office: "A large French shipment of air-to-surface missiles failed to arrive at its destination. We traced the cargo ship ownership. The Tansari brothers control the holdings of various multinational shipping companies. The missing cargo was aboard one of their vessels." Morton shook his head.

"It does not smell good."

Clayton agreed and then added more details of the plot. "It gets worse. DIA reports a sharp rise in Chinese military activities along the eastern Russian border. Our Russian friends are getting nervous and lining up defense positions from Vladivostok to Khabarovsk. A Sino-Russian border skirmish could distract attention from more substantive TOVAIR operations."

"Why do you think the Chinese are behind this move?"

"Deception can turn their weaknesses into strengths. This is right in line with what I call the *iceberg* strategy. The idea is to keep the opponent focused on surface activities, while the more important work takes place out of sight."

Morton lowered his voice, as the waiter cleared a table nearby. "Creating havoc along the Chinese-Russian border is not just any kind of distraction. If you are right, the greater the distraction we see, the more dangerous the work we do not see. Let's go. Maybe by the time we get back to the office, we'll have some answers."

Clayton and Mort walked in silence and neither one of them noticed the grey sedan following their every step.

Chapter 14
The Kitchen Cabinet

The White House dining room on the second floor was President's Cumberland favorite place to entertain his closest advisors and friends. The First Lady had redecorated the room in the Federal-style period, with replicas of furniture produced in America during the Revolutionary War. The effect was stately yet restrained. The mahogany accent pieces gave the room a warm glow. Satinwood inlays and patriotic emblems complemented the symmetrical lines. Simple curves gave each piece of furniture unusual distinction. Pale yellow walls, matching flower arrangements, and casual family pictures displayed on the blue-green marble fireplace mantle softened the formal setting. Above the mantle, an eagle, a most patriotic motif, seemed to keep a watchful eye over the entire room. The eagle surmounted a mirror framed in gilded wood, with delicate latticework and gilded rope with pendant balls draped around each corner of its frame.

The Irish linen and the amber candlelight reminded Clayton of his grandmother's traditional dinner table, set with heirloom silver and china brought out on holidays and special occasions. For Clayton, this was a special event. Like his grandfather before him, he was having dinner at the White House.

The small group of dinner guests included Jay Jones, the Attorney General, Al Grant, the National

Security Advisor, the President's Chief of Staff, Troy Hatfield, Roger Miles, the Secretary of Defense, and the Senior Domestic Policy Advisor, Cory Black. Mack Cumberland seemed at ease with this special group of loyal appointees, his kitchen cabinet members. Clayton realized that he had been included in this select White House working dinner not as another member of the president's team, but the expert outsider. He was certain that eventually, small talk about the searing Washington summer would turn to the most pressing issue of the day, TOVAIR.

Looking around the table, Clayton observed the guests as they turned their attention to Mack Cumberland, who presided over his flock of advisors with magnanimous charm.

"I like to propose a toast," Mack Cumberland held his wine glass steady and high, "To all of you. For your service and love of country, thank you." He paused as everyone mumbled almost in unison, "Thank you, Mr. President."

"You must be wondering why I asked you to join me for dinner this evening on such short notice."

Cory Black, the only woman in the group, cleared her throat, and sat upright, as if to rise above Al Grant to her right and Troy Hatfiled to her left. She was a petite woman. Her piercing eyes matched her designer royal blue outfit. She wore no jewelry and no makeup. The short crop of thin hair made her head loom large in relation to her frame.

"Friends, we live in dangerous times. As all of you well know, our enemies aim to derail our domestic and international agenda and destroy our political and economic freedoms. This war defines us as a nation. It tells the world who we are and why we fight. Our enemy changes strategies from time to time but our destruction remains his mission. Defeat, my friends, is not an option. I have asked Dr. Clayton Harcourt to join us because he is in a unique position to help us uncover the motives and plans of our enemies."

"Officially, Clayton serves as Deputy Director at InterIntel."

Al Grant shifted in his seat and raised his eyebrows as the president announced that he was pleased to have Dr. Clayton Harcourt aboard his team. Cory Black nodded in agreement and tilted her head to the right, as if to hear every word the president spoke. She scribbled a comment about Clayton on her note pad and placed a question mark next to "official position." She made a mental note to get to know Dr. Harcourt and learn more about his unofficial duties.

The president looked straight at Clayton across the table and added, "I appreciate your service, and want you to join this fine group of friends. We get together from time to time to talk about important things in an informal setting." Clayton was not sure if he had heard a formal invitation to join Mack Cumberland's kitchen cabinet, but the President erased any doubts.

"Welcome to my kitchen cabinet."

"Thank you Mr. President, I am honored."

Jay Jones, was sitting next to Clayton, turned to him with a big smile, and said: "I hear you fly-fish.

At these dinners, we try to read the water the best we can, if you know what I mean. We try to find the best spots to reel in a trophy. We try to anticipate problems before they happen. We brainstorm. Welcome!"

The Attorney General was a childhood friend of the President and former Governor of Montana. He was loyal to Mack Cumberland because he owed the President much of his political capital. Clayton gathered that for Mack Cumberland, the biggest domestic trophy would be to gain reelection and the biggest foreign policy trophy would be to defeat TOVAIR.

There was another reason Clayton was having dinner at the White House with such an exclusive group of advisors. Clayton was making progress in cleaning house at InterIntel and a short week after taking over Tom's position, fired three of Tom's collaborators, analysts who had manipulated intelligence reports. These men were appealing Clayton's personnel action but the evidence against them was great, and the IG's office had a solid case.

With the exception of Jay Jones, the president trusted Clayton more than he trusted some of the advisors around the dinner table. All other members of the kitchen cabinet were Washington insiders. The president appreciated their advice but questioned their motives. Many would remain in Washington long after Mack Cumberland retired to his Montana ranch.

Mack Cumberland did not trust Washington insiders. Cory Black, a former campaign speech-writer, was entrenched in Beltway politics. She was not a bold thinker but she could read the partisan tea leaves. More importantly, she had access to powerful players on Capitol Hill. She seldom spoke at meetings but always took copious notes. The president trusted Cory Black because she had sound political instincts and like no other in his inner circle, she understood congressional politics.

Mack Cumberland was a millionaire entrepreneur and cattleman who appreciated risk takers, bold thinkers, and Washington outsiders. Clayton not only was a bold thinker, he was entrepreneurial in the field as shown through his actions in Cairo and London. Mack Cumberland admired courageous men. He also felt that he owed Jack's son a long explanation about his father's death. The president felt guilt about Jack's death and in a way having Clayton close felt like some sort of redemption.

After dinner, the president invited his guests to join him for a chat in his private study. This was his way of taking his guests into his own turf, a far more relaxed setting than Mrs. Cumberland's renovated dining room one floor below. Mrs. Cumberland never attended the kitchen cabinet meetings. When her husband met with the "Eagle Scouts," as she called his close advisors, she preferred to schedule time to visit her relatives in Colorado.

Mack Cumberland's study combined a cozy library and family room, decorated with leather couches, Western paintings, and mounted hunting trophies. It was a man's room and it reminded guests of their host's humble beginnings growing up in the family ranch in Montana. Clayton felt instantly at home.

"Well, this is as close as we get to the ranch, out here," said the president, "I had my way with this room. Only place, where you can put your feet up on the furniture. So go right ahead, folks, settle in."

It was an invitation to get to work. The dinner conversation had been informal, with the exception of the official announcement of Clayton's membership in the president's kitchen cabinet. It was always after dinner when Cumberland would start with a question and then let the conversation flow from there.

"Clayton, tell us your assessment of TOVAIR's campaign involvement. How real is this threat?"

Right to the point, thought Troy Hatfield. Roger Miles smiled to himself admiring the precision of this vintage Cumberland question to kick off the evening discussion.

"Mr. President the threat is real," said Clayton and then proceeded to give a brief summation of the key reasons underpinning the AG's investigation.

"Good point," interjected Jay Jones, after Clayton told the group that the most critical problem was to identify sources of funds for coalition groups like the AFF and others with no accountability. "Clayton is right, we need to get to the heart of these groups because they can hide contributions right under our noses."

President Cumberland smoked his pipe with deliberate calm. He puffed once and a small curl of smoke twirled above his head. He looked at his most trusted advisor.

"You are saying that these groups could be funneling terrorist money into my campaign?" Jay Jones did not flinch, and gave the president the straight answer he expected.

"Yes, Mr. President. That is exactly what I am saying."

✡ ✡ ✡

Will Rogerson had just returned from London when Clayton called to check how he was doing. Will was recovering from his injuries and had read about Duvenoix's demise. Clayton asked his friend to remember any possible conversations about other contacts his former business associate might have had in the United States.

"Do you recall anything that might indicate that Duvenoix was doing business with others here at home?"

Will could not remember any specific names but recalled Duvenoix's interest in knowing more about lobbyists in America.

"At the time, it just seemed like a casual dinner question. We were in London about three years ago. He wanted to know names of prominent lobbyists," Will paused and then added, "I did not know any names, but I told him that usually lobbyists are registered with the government and that he could look up those lists online." Clayton wanted to know if Will and Duveniox had any follow-up conversation.

"Nope, he never brought it up again, and quite frankly I never thought about until now." Will told Clayton that he wanted to help in any way he could. The FBI was conducting a separate investigation and Will was collaborating fully. Clayton suggested that he begin to think about all the details of his relationship with Duvenoix.

"Would you mind spending some time with a couple of our analysts? I'll clear it with the folks at FBI." Clayton called Morton who worked out the clearances for a team of two InterIntel analysts who would be visiting Will soon.

After talking to Will, Clayton assigned one of his best junior analysts to comb through the list of registered lobbyists and suggested he cross-reference this list with their client lists and political contributors to both parties. Late in the day, a beaming analyst came into Clayton's office holding a short list of ten names.

"These match our profile, sir. I've circled the top three. We may want to run these names through the Wringer."

The Wringer was the latest data-mining package capable of literally connecting dots across massive amounts of data in mere seconds. Clayton reviewed the three reports and focused his attention on Sanford Gillman, the name he had seen just hours before. After his first White House kitchen cabinet meeting, Clayton had had an opportunity to ask President Cumberland for a list of special guests and top donors to all campaign fundraising events in the last twelve months. The campaign staff had faxed the list to Clayton and he had noted that Sanford Gillman and two other lobbyists with the initials S.G. had made the maximum contribution. Only Sanford Gillman had attended three of five major fundraising events for Priscilla Parks. Clayton wondered if Mr. Gillman had made additional contributions to Cumberland's campaign perhaps through any of the coalition groups under investigation. Clayton also discovered that unlike his colleagues, Mr. Gillman was a big contributor to Senator Parks' campaign.

The Wringer was an effective tool to search through various databases, make connections, and identify patterns not visible to the naked eye. Clayton's team was able to solve problems by jumping into a multi dimensional pool of data. The analysts traveled through data to discover causal relationships not evident through traditional quantitative methods of analysis. The Wringer provided a 360-degree view of a problem and enabled analysts to ask "What if" questions, envision unimaginable scenarios, and plot strategies. Artificial intelligence could take analysts to the roots of a problem, but it could not yet replace their judgment. A group of scientists in a lab not far from Clayton's office was testing the prototype of a second generation Wringer capable of closing the gap between technological capabilities and human decision-making skills.

Chapter 15

At Close Range

Lyn Chang's team was in place. Mr. Hu had arranged the service of one of his most trusted and lethal operatives to wait in the dark alley behind the home of Ms. Chang's client. She had not heard from her client in a couple of days and time was running out for her to act. Ms. Chang liked to take care of high profile clients personally but Mr. Hu had advised against it.

"Too much risk when you deal with a client that does not want to dance. We are better off taking care of this with one of our regular client representatives. Let him get the job done."

Ms. Chang insisted in having a chance to observe the operation nearby to make sure that all details worked according to plan. Mr. Hu thought she was stubborn. She insisted. "I have to report back, Comrade, and I want to see first hand that we completed our mission. Figure it out."

Mr. Hu gave in and against his own judgment, arranged for Ms. Chang to wait in a cab around the corner from the accident. The accident was planned to look like a random mugging. A passerby would walk by the scene two minutes after the perpetrator had vanished to make sure the job was completed and to call 911 on his cell phone. At about this time, Ms. Chang would arrive near the scene of the accident and she would walk a few blocks to confirm the execution.

☆ ☆ ☆

Clayton decided to walk home as usual. It was late in the evening and he planned to work a few more hours after dinner. He liked taking the shortcut to Georgetown across the bridge and along the banks of the Potomac. The smell of water, any water, even this polluted river was a pleasant distraction from the city confinements. By the time Clayton reached the alley behind his townhouse, it was dark. The street lamps were throwing the first faint rays of light, yet the alley was darker than the rest of the neighborhood. Georgetown was quiet.

A stray grey cat scavenging for mice darted off knocking a metal garbage can that rolled across the alley clanking and bumping against the cobblestones. Clayton could barely see the street corner where he would turn right and walk a few steps to his front door. He did not see the figure lurching from the shadows. The first blow to his head made him stumble but he spun around to face his attacker, and he noticed that the man was wearing a torn coat and a cap. A second blow hit him just above his right eye. He lost his balance and fell back. The stranger kicked Clayton hard and pulled a knife right up to his throat.

Clayton felt the sharp blade rip his skin and felt dizzy from the blows to his head. He struggled to grab the knife and turn it against his assailant. Bleeding from a cut on his right temple, Clayton seized the knife and freed himself from the attacker. He punched the man as hard as he could. His anger overcame the pain and he warned his attacker, as he grabbed him by the coat collar.

"The police will be here any second. I'm going to take care of you until they get here." Clayton reached into his pocket to get his phone, and as he began to dial 911, the man in ragged clothes pulled himself free and ran away.

Just as he was giving the police the details of the attack, Clayton spotted a man walking briskly along the alley. When the passerby saw Clayton on the cell phone, he ran and disappeared into the night. Minutes later, the police and ambulance arrived. A small group of curious neighbors gathered, but no one could give a description of the attacker. Clayton noticed a familiar face in the crowd out of the corner of his eye, as the paramedics lifted him into a stretcher.

"It was her again. I'm certain of it."

Clayton was home after a night in the hospital and Morton had come to see him with some home made cookies from Susan. He wanted to convince Clayton to rest for a day. Morton had read the police report.

"How can you be sure it was Lyn Chang? Assume it was; what does that prove? How would she be connected to a mugger?" Clayton sat upright and became somber.

"Look this was the second time someone tried to get rid of me since I took this job. Lyn Chang seems to be close to the scene of my accidents every time. I do not think this is a coincidence."

Morton made a fresh pot of coffee and handed Clayton a cup and a chocolate chip cookie with paternal care.

"It's your favorite kind. Susan said this will help you get well fast." Then in a more serious tone, Morton added, "We traced calls to the Chinese embassy. As expected, Ms. Chang has been in constant communication with Mr. Hu. We checked her hotel and she has vanished. She left no trace. The airlines have been on red alert since yesterday. Lyn Chang is on the no-fly list."

Clayton knew that the no-fly list, an intelligence black box targeting individuals posing a high risk to national security was not fail proof. Many of these individuals traveled with multiple identities and could often trick the airport eye scanner cameras used to identify travelers as they boarded airplanes. As scanning technology became more accurate, counterfeiters began to develop contact lenses with irrefragable imprints to avoid detection. Clayton doubted that Lyn Chang would risk the red alert scrutiny at any airport. The media treated the national security alert system like the weather, giving the public daily updates on the rating changes. Red alerts received instant attention because this highest level of security measures imposed huge air travel delays. Clayton was certain that Lyn Chang would find another way out of the United States.

"What if she drives to Canada or sails a leisure boat up the coast? If there was a plot to kill me and it failed, she will try to get away at any cost." Morton picked up his cell phone.

"Good idea. I'll contact the Coast Guard and the Border Patrol just in case our Mata Hari tries to get creative with her exit strategy."

☆ ☆ ☆

Assoud, a.k.a. Hakim paced up and down his presidential suite in Cairo. The father of the First Lady of Egypt stayed at the Royal Renaissance during his unofficial visits. He had just received a fax from his daughter's trusted friend.

"Dinner cancelled. Our guest of honor is ill." Assoud pounded his fist on the marble countertop.

"How could she possibly fail? I should not trust a woman to do a man's job." Aisha sat across from her father and did not respond. In times of stress, he found solace in her advice and she waited for her father to vent his anger before speaking.

"Father, maybe this worked out to your advantage. Lyn Chang values your support. She owes you now. We don't know why her mission failed but we know that she is a loyal warrior. You need her but now she needs you more." Assoud took a sip of coffee and smiled.

"You always walk on the sunny side of the road we travel." He paused and added, "We are on a perilous path and cannot afford too many mistakes."

Aisha walked toward her father with a bright smile.

"Focus on your success this week, father. The Kanhpor operation turned out better than you expected," and then pointing to the sunset unfolding across the horizon, she added, "Just like the sun sets in the West each day, with each passing day, the West yields a little of its power to us. Let's be patient and concentrate on the big picture."

Aisha had a calming effect on her father, and he was glad that he had groomed her to be his successor. She opened the sliding door to the balcony and motioned to her father to join her.

"Come father, let's watch the sunset and figure out how wc can get Senator Parks to win the presidency and become our friend."

✲ ✲ ✲

The duty officer at the Northern Command center did not have time to enjoy the stunning views. The Colorado peaks seemed to rise like sleepy giants across the horizon in the early morning hours. Not far from the Northern Command, the very mountain streams Clayton and his grandfather had once explored now flowed behind a locked fence with a prominent sign, advising intruders: "Danger. Trespassers will be prosecuted." The national forest surrounding the Northern Command was off limits to anglers and anyone else without the proper security clearance.

On the second floor of a sleek building shaped like a mini-pentagon, military and intelligence personnel worked around the clock analyzing intelligence flowing in from Alaska to Chiapas and Yucatan, states bordering Mexico and Guatemala. The mission of the Northern Command was to identify and stop any terrorist activity threatening national security. Such threats were not limited to the Canadian and Mexican borders. The Northern Command had established close relations with the governments of both countries to create a regional security zone. All three governments deployed joint cross-border immigration and law enforcement personnel in a seamless security web stretching across North America.

On this day, the duty officer was busy scanning the data crossing his laptop screen. His shift was about to end and he felt energized, confident that in doing his job with surgical precision, he saved lives, at least most of the time. Reports from Newfoundland pointed to a suspicious vessel unloading cargo in St. John. Canadian authorities were moving quickly to identify the cargo, which they suspected included weapons. Concurrently, the Canadian Coast Guard reported that this same vessel sailed on to Halifax an hour ago.

"For a Monday morning, this does not look good," said the duty officer, as he picked up the secure emergency line to the Halifax FBI liaison officer. The duty officer did not waste any time in sharing his conclusion: "I am e-mailing you the details as we speak. The vessel named "Entourage" sails under a French flag." He paused, and read the bold letters in the alert box on the right hand corner of his screen.

"This fits the operational pattern of arms smuggling rings connected to TOVAIR." With great relief, the duty officer read the "Real Time Response" update on his screen and reported the reply to his FBI counterpart.

"The Coast Guard is on top of this situation for now. When Entourage docks, you guys can spring into action."

The FBI field team would place the vessel under close surveillance and monitor all activity around the ship. Northern Command would track all reports and distribute intelligence on a "need to know" basis across the entire intelligence community involving over two dozen agencies around the country. The duty officer hung up the phone and leaned back on his chair. For the first time since he had entered his office eight hours earlier, he looked out his window. The sun was coming up behind frosted peaks and the aspen were just beginning to glow in their dazzling fall colors. A first and light dusting of snow had fallen overnight marking the early start of a cold winter.

✲ ✲ ✲

Lyn Chang had traveled all night, her Canadian passport under the name of Lee Ann Culver securely tucked in her zipped leather tote bag. Her briefcase contained papers supporting her identity as a freelance writer from Vancouver. The train ride from Washington to Boston had been uneventful. The car rental clerk had offered a special discount and had not asked many questions.

Lyn drove straight from the airport to Augusta, where she spent the night and then continued her journey north. She was approaching the border town of St. Stephen, when she noticed the flashing light, dutifully slowed down, and pulled off the side of the road. The young officer approached her car and asked for her identification. Lyn Chang smiled and handed him her Canadian passport.

"I hope I did not break any rules," and then with an impish grin added, "I hope you'll be kind to this Canadian neighbor."

He entered the faked passport number into his notebook, and read the instant reply. He handed Lyn the passport back with a small smile.

"You are along way from home, Ms. Culver. We like to treat our Canadian guests well around here, so I am just going to give you a warning. You were going ten miles over the speed limit. Please watch the signs and drive carefully. Have a good trip, Ms. Culver." Lyn Chang smiled.

"Thank you, officer. I appreciate your kindness. Have a nice day." She rolled up the window and for the first time since she pulled over, she felt a drop of cold sweat running down her spine. Halifax was only thirty miles away, and Lyn was eager to board the Entourage for a safe passage home.

Chapter 16

The Summit

The city of Khotan in Xinjiang province was the gateway to the southern stretch of the ancient Silk Road. Here, the cultures of India and China had clashed in times of war and melded customs in times of peace. Buddhist art from India and Sanskrit literature found a home in Khotan until the Islamic conquest swept across the desert. In this remote region of Central Asia, the Uighur represented the largest Chinese ethnic minority. Originally, the Uighur were Buddhists but converted to Islam during the third Caliphate in the tenth century. They now represented over thirty percent of the Chinese population inhabiting a vast oil rich territory bordering Russia, Afghanistan, Pakistan, Kazakhstan, Kyrgyzstan, and Tajikistan. Liao Chang was proud of his Uighur heritage. He controlled the oil fields in the Tarin Basin and at Turpan, the largest sources of power, fueling the Chinese economy.

Although the Chinese government retained majority ownership of oil production, Chang was the largest private stockholder with a twenty-five percent stake in these largely untapped oil fields. The land of his mother's Uighur ancestors and the oil empire he now controlled were only part of the legacy he wished to pass on to his children and to Chang generations to come. He had left Khotan when his father accepted an appointment as Chinese Ambassador to Indonesia.

Young Liao grew up torn between his father's Buddhist teachings and his mother's Muslim traditions. His father traced his lineage all the way back to the expansionist Han dynasty, a peasant group of leaders ruling China for about four centuries between 206 B.C.– A.D. 220.

While attending the university in Jakarta, he became increasingly interested in learning more about his mother's religion, joined a radical orthodox community, and converted to Islam. It was expedient for Liao to retain his father's family name, and he refused to adopt a Muslim name. His father's diplomatic and business connections opened many doors and yielded much influence across the capitals of Asia.

Liao Chang was a radical with a pragmatic streak and he taught his children the virtues of strategic thinking. Tsu and Lyn Chang grew up learning about their father's obsession with Uighur separatism and radical fundamentalism. They also learned to hide their deep resentment against Han Chinese settlements in Xinjiang. They committed their lives to a single cause, the reestablishment of an Islamic Caliphate.

Liao Chang had convened the secret meeting of TOVAIR principals in his ancestral estate. The Saudi delegation arrived clad in white robes and black-checkered *kaffiyeh.* Oil Minister Abduhl Sar-al Diab, Prince Mohamed Hassan, and Ahmed Assoud sat around the large mahogany table resting on a thick East Turkestan carpet. Young servants hidden behind light blue *burkas* served tea and sweet candy. Liao's son Tsu, arrived shortly after the Saudi guests were seated. He ushered the Deputy Chinese Minister Li Chui, member of the largest Chinese minority, the Zhuang, into the lavish room decorated with bronze vases from the Zhou dynasty and a collection of horse sculptures from the Han dynasty.

Chui, named after a famous river bordering Russia, was born in Kunming, known as the "city of eternal spring" along the shores of the Dianchi Lake in the Yunnan province. The Zhuang were poor, open, and ready to receive foreign ideas that could lift them from their dire existence. They lagged behind the rest of the Chinese population. Their poverty and lack of education provided fertile ground to sow the seeds of discontent. Islamic fundamentalism resonated in the streets of Kunming. In the city where the Flying Tigers had set up their headquarters in World War II, Islamic militants were now catering to large numbers of uneducated and resentful young men filled with hatred against the West.

Two brothers, Mansour and Jalees Tansari from Khanpor, India were sitting next to Tsu Chang. Just before Liao Chang called the meeting to order, the last guest on the list rushed into the room. He was a tall man with thick, black eyebrows and a bushy beard with a few sprinkles of grey. He approached the men seated around the table, and a servant bowed ceremoniously as he made his way to the only empty chair. Before sitting down to the right of his host, he dabbed a drop of sweat off his turbaned forehead.

"My security detail took extra travel precautions on our way from New Delhi. I'm sure you understand."

Mansour and Jalees rose in unison as the Indian Prime Minister joined the secret summit, and both men smiled and welcomed their distant cousin. Prime Minister Jahan was a militant Sikh, who rose to power convinced that holy war was a family affair. Some years back, an uncle and cousin had served as bodyguards to Prime Minister Indira Ghandi, gained her trust, and assassinated her. Since that time, militant Sikhs escalated their attacks beyond Punjab. They carried their banner of hatred across rural India, spreading their teachings of Hinduism and Islamic Sufism. Their anti-modern, anti-western rhetoric found a receptive audience among poor, uneducated peasants. Their charismatic leader, Jahan, stayed far away from the politics of violence, delegating operational details to trusted lieutenants, mostly members of his immediate family.

Jahan stayed above the fray of street demonstrations, assassinations, and bombings. He joined the ruling Congress Party and climbed to its presidency. From his powerful legislative perch, he launched a moderate national campaign and became Prime Minister. Once he reached his goal to lead a nuclear power, Jahan set his sites on even higher ground. TOVAIR was the key to unlock India's destiny. The Tansari brothers like the militant Punjab brotherhood before them were useful pawns in Jahan's highest stakes game to control the affairs of the world.

Liao Chang disliked interruptions. He did not appreciate late arrivals, prime minister of India or not. Seated at the head of the table, he straightened his back and began his scheduled meeting in a low, monotone voice, while a sweaty Jahan settled into the large velvet chair. Chang enjoyed making his listeners strain to hear his words, and watched with delight, as they leaned forward to hear each sound.

"Gentlemen, you must be wondering why I called you for this emergency meeting." He paused, and continued to talk with his eyes closed.

"We need to reassess our strategic agenda. We need to make sure that all of us remain on target to avoid mistakes." He paused briefly, and added:

"I am most grateful to Ahmed for his efforts in the matter of my daughter's failed mission in America. I also want to thank Mansour and Jalees for arranging the getaway vessel." He paused and the named guests shifted uneasily in their chairs as if recoiling from a slap in the face. Liao Chang barely moved his lips, as he continued. His tone was grave.

"Lyn Chang's recent capture should be a wake up call to us and our cause." Chang paused again, as if to emphasize his next point spoken in an even graver tone.

"We are at a crossroads. We must reassess our strategy because the future of TOVAIR is in peril."

Liao Chang opened his eyes and looked around the room to capture the mood of his guests. No one said a word, as he expected. He cleared his throat, and continued:

"My daughter will sacrifice her precious life before she betrays us. Of that, I give you my word of honor. We must avoid the events that led her to this preposterous operation at all cost. We cannot afford another fiasco."

All nodded around the table, with the exception of Ahmed Assoud. It had been his idea to deploy Lyn Chang in a mission to eliminate Clayton Harcourt. Liao Chang fixed his eyes on Ahmed Assoud and continued without raising his voice.

"We cannot afford to risk one of our principals in a low priority mission. Help me understand, Ahmed, why is Harcourt's elimination on the top of our agenda?" Assoud did not hesitate to respond.

"He is a key target who could obstruct in a major way our long range plan to gain access to the White House. This man came out of retirement, and he just knows too much."

Liao Chang looked puzzled. Assoud did not waste time explaining that Clayton Harcourt had once worked for the CIA, was responsible for the capture of Duvenoix, and was now a high-ranking official in the U.S. government.

"We do not exactly know what he is up to. Years ago, he was working on one of the most secret projects in the U.S. intelligence community. He is a major threat to our mission." Assoud looked around the table for confirmation that his assessment was on target. Jahan was the first to speak.

"I agree with brother Ahmed. This is not a matter we should delegate to lower level operatives."

Oil Minister Abduhl Sar-al Diab and Prince Mohammed Hassan spoke next, both agreeing with the Prime Minister. The Tansari brothers concurred.

Deputy Minister, Li Chui and Tsu Chang remained silent. Liao Chang closed his eyes and said in a lower voice than usual.

"My friends, I disagree. Your perceptions about this Mr. Harcourt are misplaced. You underestimate the power of our own commitment and that of our followers. No single man can stand in our way."

Li Chui nodded in agreement but remained silent. Like Liao Chang, he distrusted all the men around the table. They were convenient allies in a war against the West. Like his Han ancestors, Liao Chang dreamed of expanding the power of China beyond its borders. Li Chui was a useful partner when it came to Chinese domestic politics because he was the next in line to become Prime Minister. Li Chui was not a strategic thinker and his vision for China was strictly nationalistic. He did not envision the grand expansion Chang planned for his homeland.

Chinese nationalism could act as a counter force against Uighur separatism and radical fundamentalism but ultimately it had to be suppressed. For now, Chui served as a catalyst for change. Moreover, Chang would not let anyone stand in the way of his vision. Chang was certain that he could control Li Chui.

Confronting Assoud about their significant ideological differences would have to wait. Chang was certain that Assoud had lured Lyn Chang into a deadly game to entrap Harcourt in order to get rid of her. Lyn Chang would have been a formidable rival for the leadership of TOVAIR, but Assoud was grooming his own daughter for that position. Chang's distrust ran deep when it came to Prime Minister Jahan, a man driven by blind ambition and ruthlessness.

Chang felt contempt for the Tansari brothers; they were Jahan's pawns, who rubber-stamped their master's whims without resistance. To their credit, they were nimble when it came to the arms trade. For that reason only, it was wise to keep them in the circle of power. Besides, their presence gave Jahan a false sense of security, and that suited Liao Chang just fine. Chang's maneuvers kept TOVAIR's mission intact. He did not believe that alliances should be permanent; alliances were temporary, made to be broken when they no longer served their purpose. He would not let emotions get in the way of success. The summit host looked around the table fixing his eyes on each individual as if to read their minds.

"I realize that I hold the minority view on this issue. So, for the sake of moving forward and achieving the goals of the Transnational Organization of Victorious Asian/Arab Islamic Republics, let us put this issue to rest. You win. Go ahead and pursue Mr. Harcourt."

Chang smiled, paused, and added, "But let us concentrate on the larger picture. Let us minimize risk in our operations and sharpen our strategic focus. If our American mission is our first and foremost priority let us put more resources to work there." All around the table nodded. Once the summit guests had left the meeting, Liao Chang and his son took a long walk. The estate's manicured garden was a place for reflection. Tsu listened attentively to his father's advice, because he knew that he was destined to take the helm of TOVAIR.

"Always remember never to trust friends who have hidden agendas. Remember the words of Sun Tzu: *All warfare is based on deception. When you are far away pretend to be near, when you are near, pretend to be far away.*" Liao Chang then placed a call to his daughter's friend in Washington D.C. She received Chang's orders and set in motion the first steps of a delicate mission with the code name, Autumn.

Chapter 17
Hidden Agendas

Assoud and Prince Hassan had forged an alliance of convenience. An ancient family feud over the control of *halawas*, informal money transfer networks across Muslim communities from Asia to Africa, pitted their grandfathers in a deadly dispute spanning many generations. Assoud and Prince Hassan had arrived at a truce in their youth when they both had attended a *madrassa*. Upon graduation, both joined a secret society, the Al-Muhtadi Brotherhood. This militant organization was the brainchild of Prince Hassan and served as the training ground for suicide missions against the West. After several Al-Muhtadi leaders were killed or captured, Hassan convinced Assoud to step into the void. Assoud envisioned a global network, and realized that to accomplish his goal he had to form cross-cultural alliances outside the region.

Gradually, Al-Muhtadi expanded its operations beyond the Arabian Peninsula. After an informal meeting in Jakarta attended by Assoud, Chang, and Jahan, TOVAIR was born. Since the inception of this improbable alliance, Chang assumed strategic leadership of the organization persuading its members to shift violent tactics against the West to systematic dismantling of Western economic and political institutions. He was aware that his culture and that of his allies could not compete and advance within the framework of Western democracies and free markets. More importantly, Western democracies and free markets were the antithesis of his belief in centralized power and control. His mantra was simple and he repeated it often.

"Give the enemy incentives for self-destruction. Use their weakness to our advantage. Be patient."

✲ ✲ ✲

Oil Minister Abduhl Sar-al Diab, Prince Mohammed Hassan, and Ahmed Assoud had arrived together at the secret summit in Khotan. Prior to their departure from Liao Chang's estate, Assoud convened a meeting of his Saudi counterparts in his suite.

"Well, my friends, it looks like we agree with Liao on the basic strategy but disagree on how to achieve our goals." Assoud paused but before he could continue Abdhul Sar-al Diab, a rotund man who wheezed as he spoke, interrupted him.

"We have a majority, so what is there to worry about? Jahan and the Tansari brothers are in our camp. We proceed with our operational plans, and let Liao continue to think about the big picture. After all..." Prince Hassan, interjected as Sar al-Diab began to cough and gasp for air.

"I agree we proceed, but I think we need to become more aggressive against our enemies, not just around the world, but against high profile American targets on their own turf. Patience is not working. The business of letting the West fall apart from within is not viable."

He paused and with a wide grin showed off his gold front tooth. He seldom smiled but the thought of inflicting fear and pain on his enemies gave him a sense of savage satisfaction, like an adrenalin boost for a marathon runner about to reach the finishing line.

"We must return to our original operational tactics. We must strike again. We must deploy the most unexpected means to crush the West." Assoud expected Hassan's recommendation, and taking advantage of Sar al-Diab's lasting coughing spell, added, "This is a good idea, given that the most recent Vancouver arms shipment arrived undetected. We need to step up the violence as we pursue our electoral objectives."

The Saudi Oil Minister waved his chubby hand in the air as if to stop the conversation and once his cough subsided, he offered his view.

"My friends, I think you are heading in the wrong direction. We need to continue to create trouble for the enemy around the world, but violence on American soil has diverted many of our resources. Why not stay with our low-violence approach for now, and devote all of our attention to the financial side of the American campaign?" Hassan was about to respond but Assoud cut him short.

"My dear Abdhul, your moderate views no longer work. The Americans are getting too close to our most valuable financial and political asset. The Canadians confiscated our latest arms shipment in St. John, and Lyn Chang is in American custody, compliments of the FBI. Our entire American mission is in jeopardy."

Abdhul Sar al-Diab began to object once again gasping for air.

"But we need to..." Hassan interrupted him pointing to Assoud.

"Decision is made, two to one. We have a majority."

✡ ✡ ✡

The Tansari brothers boarded Jahan's helicopter for the flight back to Kahnpur. Mansour was the eldest of the two brothers and always spoke on their behalf. He managed their businesses with an iron hand and was often rude to his subordinates and business partners. He took swift action against his enemies, and those who crossed him paid with their lives. His arrogance irked his brother Jalees, but the younger sibling respected Mansour's stature in the illicit world of arms trading.

"Congratulations, cousin," said Jahan to Mansour as they flew over Liao Chang's vast estate. "It looks like the next few months will be very profitable for you, as business picks up across the Atlantic."

Mansour replied while looking out at the vast territory below. "Business is good. I just hope, that Assoud's insurance company pays for the St. John shipment." He paused and looked his cousin in the eye: "After all, that loss amounts to over $50 million. It was his fault that we lost the shipment."

The confiscated cache of weapons included several hundred shoulder-fired missiles intended for secret locations near North American airports. It was the first shipment of its kind in support of operation Harun, named after caliph of the Abbasid dynasty, who ruled for twenty-three years at the pinnacle of Islamic power. Mansour's voice revealed deep frustration.

"I told him the St. John port was vulnerable. I know my business. But he insisted and had to have it his way."

Jahan was soothing. "Calm, calm brother. Assoud will pay, and besides he's given you additional business now that you are a full partner."

"He better pay," replied Mansour. "He better pay soon." Jalees did not wonder what would happen to Ahmed Assoud if he failed to meet his obligation.

☆ ☆ ☆

Li Chui's limousine pulled up to his private residence at the edge of Kunming. He felt renewed each time he returned to his modest home along the shores of Dianchi Lake. The seasons blended into each other in this mild region, where spring temperatures remained almost constant throughout the year. Chui liked the predictability of his country home. He was a methodical man, as meticulous with his personal appearance as he was with his thoughts.

The trip back from the Khotan summit had left him exhausted, mostly from worry about the direction TOVAIR was taking under pressure from the Saudis and Indian partners. He had not spoken during the meeting, not so much to appease Liao Chang, but because he believed that he could learn more from listening than from talking. Li Chui had survived the factionalism of the Chinese Communist Party since Mao's death. As a young CCP member, Chui rose through the *nomenklatura*, the party leadership, all the way to the Central Committee. From there, the quiet Li Chui established strong ties with key members of the Politburo.

His cunning political maneuvers landed Li Chui key committee assignments and more importantly assured him the ultimate prize of becoming a first-line leader. Now in his mid-sixties, Li Chui had plans to rise to the very top of China's hierarchy. Liao Chang was an important ally, mostly because of his position as TOVAIR's strategist. On his journey home, Chui concluded that one day Chang would become a liability.

"When that day comes," Chui wrote in his personal journal, "apply Sun Tzu's lesson. *In war, as in art, the rules change according to circumstances*." He paused, recalling the ancient master's advice, and then jotted down other ancient words of wisdom: "*Order or disorder depends on organization; courage or cowardice on circumstances; strength or weakness on dispositions.*" Li Chui closed his journal and his eyes. He was confident that soon he would displace Chang as the top leader of TOVAIR and revamp the organization to advance Chinese nationalism.

Chapter 18

Red Tape

The State Department completed its internal review of the Alex Keynes III file and concluded that there was no evidence to support InterIntel's allegations of misconduct. The lead State investigator contacted Clayton's office and reported that his findings did not warrant the next step, an interview of Mr. Keynes by a team of InterIntel agents.

"So much for interagency cooperation," retorted Clayton to which the State Department official replied, "The best I can do for you is to fax you the report. There is nothing there but at least you cannot accuse us of stonewalling."

Clayton hung up and picked up the fax arriving just as Morton walked into his office.

"State is behaving at its collegial best," Clayton said sarcastically, as he showed Morton the fax. "The dinosaurs in Foggy Bottom claim Keynes is clean and oppose any further investigation. Our friends at State don't lead, they don't follow, and they just get in the way. Congress should just shut down the entire place."

Morton smiled as his friend and colleague vented his frustration. He knew that Clayton had left his government position once before because of his contempt for the bureaucratic hurdles and malfunctions that often pushed entrepreneurial types over the edge.

"Hey, relax. Don't let State get under your skin, we can always run circles around them," said Morton, with the confidence only a veteran of many bureaucratic battles could muster. He handed the State report back to Clayton and added, "Forget the State department. Good news. We are closing in on Sanford Gillman. His lawyers agreed to a meeting tomorrow at ten in the morning, my office. That ought to make you happy."

Clayton gave Morton the thumbs up. "Good. I'll have a list of questions ready before the end of the day. I'm still having trouble connecting Gillman to the Swiss account."

Clayton walked over to his desk and picked up a stack of printouts he had been reviewing before the State department call ruined his morning.

"Your Swiss contacts finally came through, Mort. They would not confirm that the S.G. account belongs to Gillman but at least they sent us the transaction history since the opening date four years ago."

Morton put on his bifocals and his eyes narrowed as he strained to see the fine print.

"Take a look at the last month. Zero activity. It's like the account shut down." Clayton had circled the last three transactions in red and pointed them out.

"Now take a look at the last three transfers. We deciphered the account numbers. The sequence of numbers and letters coincides with off-shore accounts at the Transcontinental Bank of the Bahamas. Our friends at the Treasury Department are working on that trail. So far, it's pretty cold." Morton pushed his spectacles up with his index finger, and drew a question mark next to each of Clayton's red circles.

"Clayton, what are our chances of connecting these accounts to any of the most recent large transfers into The Americans For Fairness (AFF) coffers?"

Clayton grimaced as the scar on his neck pulled tight, sending a sharp pain right down his shoulder and making the end of the fingers in his right hand tingle.

"Are you alright?" asked Morton showing genuine concern for his protégée.

"I'm fine. Just fine," replied Clayton brushing the pain off his mind.

"You just put your finger on the most delicate point here. Connecting these transactions to AFF or any other organization will be tricky. I suspect there are additional financing layers between this Swiss account, the Bahamas bank, and the final destination of any TOVAIR money. These funds are not flowing in a straight line."

Morton was about to tell Clayton to go home early and get some rest before the next day's meeting, when his cell phone rang. After he hung up, he walked up to Clayton. The good news had just turned sour.

"It was the Attorney General's Office. Will Rogerson refused to plea bargain, his case is going to trial. I'm afraid you'll be testifying for the prosecuting team." Morton slumped into the brown leather chair at the head of Clayton's conference table. After the death of his son, Morton had become close to

Clayton. He was protective of the quiet professional who reminded him so much of Jeff. Morton's dismay was sincere.

"I'm sorry about this raw deal, Clayton. I wish we could have avoided going to trial." Clayton was disappointed but knew that Morton had pushed hard for a plea agreement and thanked him for his efforts.

"Look, Morton, since I came back to Washington life has been anything but normal. This war does not distinguish between friends, family, or foes. We all have to pay our dues. In London, I forgave Will for his personal lies and deception but the trial has nothing to do with my personal feelings. I can separate the two. Don't worry, I'll be okay. I'll testify for the prosecution. We do what we have to do."

For the first time since he had returned to Washington, Clayton considered just packing his bags and heading back to his mountain home. The prospect of testifying against Will Rogerson did not disturb him as much as the frustration with the red tape and bureaucratic wrangling which slowed down progress in a war that seemed to have no end.

✲ ✲ ✲

In his short tenure as Deputy Director at InterIntel, Clayton Harcourt had tightened internal controls, and the results were a higher quality and reliability of the intelligence reports prepared by the agency. The culture of this hybrid organization was another matter. InterIntel housed analysts and field officers from various intelligence agencies, private sector contractors, and academics who did not speak the same language nor shared the same values under the same roof. This diverse group had an important mission: to protect Americans from deadly terrorist attacks. Petty squabbles often blurred the task fostering gridlock just like the ones caused by traffic jams clogging the main arteries of the capital during rush hour.

Clayton decided that after the Gillman interview, he would take some time and fly back to Idaho. After all, he was still recovering from the Georgetown attack and it had been too long since he had waded into a cold mountain stream. Just a few days away from Washington would be sufficient to recover from life in the city. He was about to leave his office and thinking about netting a brown in a mountain stream, when his cell phone rang.

On the other end of the line, a junior analyst at Treasury reported that she had just uncovered some strong evidence linking transfers from Transcontinental Bank of the Bahamas to a Union Bank in Virginia. Almost simultaneous transfers from Union Bank to AFF and other organizations followed each transfer from the Bahamas bank. Her report was encouraging.

"We've got a perfect match. We ran the data through several filters and the results are consistent across the board. All our models show positive correlations ranging from .992 to .998. I'm faxing you the report as we speak."

Clayton was pleased. "Great work. This is terrific news. We are preparing a key witness for an interview and your call could not come at a better time. Thanks again."

"Glad we could help, Dr. Harcourt."

Clayton picked up the fax on his way out of the office and made a note to thank the young analyst's boss at Treasury for a job well done. The Treasury breakthrough gave Clayton renewed hope that cracking the S.G. investigation wide-open was within the realm of possibility. Sanford Gillman was a powerful K Street lobbyist who had retained the law firm of Smelter, Giddeon, and Harris to respond to InterIntel's inquiries.

After weeks of negotiation, Giddeon had finally agreed to meet with Morton and Clayton was glad that Smelter was not involved in this case. The crusty old lawyer had been an effective gatekeeper protecting Tom Munroe's secrets and Clayton was certain that if involved in Gillman's case, Smelter would obstruct the investigation while maintaining the illusion of legal decorum. As he jotted down some questions for Giddeon, Clayton remembered his grandfather's advice: "Always hire an old lawyer and a young doctor."

Before midnight, Clayton stopped working and stretched out to read *American Angler*, one of his favorite magazines about his beloved sport. When far from a river or stream, Clayton enjoyed reading about the art of discovering wild trout in remote places. Thumbing through the pages of an article about the joy of fly-fishing, he came across a quote by Russell Chatham, and smiled as he read it.

"It's simply a matter of learning to find those places where the river will allow you to fish. Each river tells you in its own way. All you have to do is listen." Clayton closed his eyes. The quote was a great metaphor for life itself. He then fell into a light sleep, punctuated by the constant pain of his recent wounds.

Chapter 19
Fathers and Sons

Breathless and resting on a cane, Oil Minister Abdhul Sar-al Diab welcomed young Khalid Hassan into his home. Sar-al Diab, had served as a loyal advisor of the late Saudi King and had known Khalid since Prince Hassan brought the toddler to a gathering of royal family members. The Oil Minister knew that his health was quickly deteriorating. Khalid Hassan was his last hope to shape TOVAIR's future. A veiled servant brought a tray of tea and dates, placed it on a heavily engraved brass table, and left the room as quietly as she had entered.

The men settled into two big chairs facing an atrium filled with plants and exotic birds in fancy iron cages. The captive creatures reminded the young engineer of the brief interrogation he endured the previous week. Before his father bailed him out of jail, Khalid wondered how he would survive behind bars. He was angry for his own failure to meet his father's high expectations. Khalid was not ready to sacrifice his life and convinced his father that he could become a key planner for TOVAIR rather than a martyr. After masterminding a failed plot to blow up the Canadian embassy in Riyadh, Khalid had become even more withdrawn than his usual self.

Sar-al Diab sensed the time was ripe for breaking Khalid away from the man Khalid believed to be his father. The Oil Minister spoke in a raspy voice but his tone was gentle.

"Khalid, I know how difficult the last few weeks have been for you." Khalid avoided Sar-al Diab's intense stare and nodded.

"You are a true hero. Never forget that only you can lead the fight against our enemies in ways that no one else can accomplish. Because of who you are, you can destroy the West …" a brief coughing spell followed. When it subsided, Sar-al Diab continued: "You are one of them." Khalid looked confused and fixed his eyes on Sar-al Diab.

"You are saying that because my mother was born in the West, I can accomplish what others cannot? I don't understand."

"Khalid, listen very carefully to what I am about to tell you. The future of your country and the destiny of your own people are in your hands. While you were growing up, your mother hid the truth to protect you. You are a man now. You should know that there is a reason for your difficulties with your father."

Sar-al Diab paused to give Khalid a chance to digest every single word. Knowing the truth would make the young man angry, hopefully angry enough to eliminate Sar-al Diab's nemesis within TOVAIR. Khalid was malleable. Once Prince Hassan was out of the way, Sar-al Diab hoped to manipulate Khalid and put him at the helm of TOVAIR. The move was risky but time was running out for the Oil Minister. He no longer wondered what would happen if

Khalid turned against him instead of eliminating the intended target.

"Go on," said the young engineer eager to hear more. The Oil Minister coughed and then continued.

"Prince Hassan does not know it, and perhaps should never know it. Your father is Tom Munroe, who is now serving a life sentence for spying for us against his own country."

Khalid felt like he was going to faint. The words he had just heard floated around his head like fog hanging low above the ground. They seemed easy to grasp but remained elusive. Somehow, his connection to Tom since an early age was now clear. The bond connecting him to his American "uncle" had faded in the last few years. In its place, a troubled relationship with Prince Hassan filled his life with anger. The shock uncoiled emotions bottled up since early childhood: the sense of security he felt as a toddler whenever Tom visited and held him in his arms; the despair he felt when his mother announced Tom's departure.

"Tom will be moving back to the U.S., but he'll come to visit as soon as possible." Khalid remembered the joy he felt when as a teenager he visited Tom and together they took the train to Boston to watch his first baseball game. He recalled the shame he felt as Prince Hassan pressured him severe his ties to Tom. He had struggled with mixed emotions as the presumed son of a militant Saudi prince and an American woman, who converted to Islam and kept her secret to survive. The young engineer now understood who he was.

Tom Munroe's son had always been indecisive. Knowing that the words he had just heard were true, he had no trouble now deciding what he would do next. Sar-al Diab's heavy breathing broke the silence, and Khalid took a sip of cold tea. He then spoke measuring each one of his words.

"Mohammed Hassan is my father. I think he would be very upset to know that a loyal friend is attempting to plant lies in his son's head. Why should I believe you?"

Sar-al Diab was a calculating man and knew that to win Khalid's trust he would have to rely on the truth. He would also rely on his close relationship to the woman who played a key role in Khalid's life. He had become Ada Hassan's best friend and she had confided in him her son's identity.

"Your mother felt very isolated and she trusted me, is that not enough for you to trust me?" al-Diab then gave Khalid a detailed account of his involvement with TOVAIR, Hassan's role in the organization, and the feud among TOVAIR's leaders.

✲ ✲ ✲

Clayton had received the news about Sanford Gillman shortly after waking up.

"You won't believe what just came over the wire!" Mort still used the term 'wire' to refer to real-time electronic communications between field offices around the globe and Washington InterIntel headquarters. The prominent Washington lobbyist had died in his Georgetown home of an apparent heart attack. Autopsy results were not yet available, and Gillman's lawyers cancelled the scheduled meeting in Mort's office.

After a call to FBI investigators, Clayton became convinced that Gillman's death was not accidental. Now it seemed that Mort had an additional surprise for the day. Clayton did not hesitate to show his sarcasm.

"After Gillman's accidental death, I'll believe anything. What's up?"

Mort still held the copy of the urgent electronic message in his hands as he briefed Clayton. "This just came in from Riyadh. Oil Minister Sar-al Diab has been killed in a helicopter crash. The Saudis are investigating and our own team is on its way to scene of the crash." Mort paused recalling that if alive, his son Jeff would probably be leading that team in the Saudi desert.

Clayton replied as if thinking aloud. "Interesting. Very interesting. I wonder if these deaths are related. I wonder who is behind these accidents and who will be next." Mort did not comment but suggested a trip out of town.

"Let's just take the day off tomorrow and go for a drive. Maybe we'll brainstorm and maybe we'll just enjoy the fall colors. It's time to regroup. What do you say?"

Clayton welcomed the opportunity to spend time with Morton away from the office. He recalled that the next day marked one month since Jeff's death, and knew that Mort was still grieving the loss of his son. It seemed like an eternity and yet it seemed like yesterday. Mort offered an action plan.

"I'll pick you up. Let's get an early start so we can have breakfast in Colonial Beach with plenty of time to swing by our cabin in Mt. Holly and get back before dinner time."

Clayton and Mort drove into the Virginia countryside just as the first rays of sun turned the landscape into a rich palette of red, yellow, and orange hues. The further they got away from the city and the closer they seemed to their destination, the more comfortable Mort seemed to let Jeff's memory enter the conversation. Without mentioning his son's name, as if knowing that Clayton would understand, Mort shared his recollection of his last trip to Mt. Holly.

"We always liked to get an early start and stop for breakfast before getting to the cabin. Just the two of us came this way in early spring only a few days before the last deployment." Mort smiled as he talked.

"We encountered a flock of geese and a sea otter basking in the sun. Once we got to the cabin, we replaced a couple of screen doors, repainted the deck, and worked out plans to build a gazebo, a sort of wildlife lookout spot." Mort sighted and Clayton did not interrupt his train of thought.

"That last weekend was special. We walked in silence along the beach, cooked steaks on the grill, and laughed recalling how we survived a summer storm in the cabin while playing poker when the kids were young."

Mort paused and drove in silence. Then, as they approached the turn into Colonial Beach, his heart ached. "I miss Jeff. I miss him very much." Clayton understood the void, the empty space left behind for those who mourn.

"I know. I miss him too."

After a hearty breakfast, it was Clayton's turn to drive and on the way to Mort's cabin, Clayton shared memories of his own.

"The closer we get to your place, the more I can smell the ocean. It's amazing how far inland you can detect its presence. The first thing I learned about the Atlantic is that it does not roar like the Pacific. Growing up in Colorado, I was excited to make my first trip to Oregon to visit my cousins. I discovered the roar of the Pacific and attributed that sound to all oceans. Years later, I was surprised to hear the mellow sounds of the Atlantic, more like a whisper than a roar."

Clayton paused and at the next turn of the road, he spotted the widening Potomac preparing itself to flow into the Chesapeake Bay.

"I miss my rivers and mountain streams, Mort. I miss their sound and their smell. I want to go home soon."

"I know."

The drive to Mt. Holly was like a reprieve from the daily pressures of life in the arena. On the way back to Washington, Clayton and Mort discussed the latest presidential polls and agreed that Mack Cumberland and Priscilla Parks were in a very tight race. In the next few weeks, anything could happen to catapult either one of the candidates into the Oval Office. With the election looming larger and the intelligence chatter from Middle Eastern, African, and Asian field offices growing more ominous, the top brass at Inter-Intel was on a heightened state of alert.

During the week before the deaths of Sar al-Diab and Gillman, it appeared that TOVAIR was reshuffling resources across the globe to disguise its strategic objectives and its drastic leadership changes. Just as Clayton and his team were getting closer to connecting the dots between TOVAIR's subversive financial and political operations, the terrorist network seemed to be refocusing its mission.

Mort offered some advice before dropping Clayton back in the office. "Think some more about those questions you raised when I gave you the news about Sar-al Diab. You are on to something. Let's try to figure out who is behind these moves and what the possible consequences are for our domestic risk assessments. I know this is a Gordian knot. Do the best you can."

"Yeah, all we can do is guess and work overtime to identify small crumbs of data leading to some big answers."

✲ ✲ ✲

The drive to Mt. Holly gave Clayton a glimpse of a father's pain and pride. The drive also gave Clayton a chance to spend some time near water, which for him was reinvigorating. That evening, as he was about to settle in for the evening, his phone rang. He recognized the baritone voice beaming through the secure line.

"We are close to seeing the light at the end of the tunnel! Someone I know wants to meet you. He can help you find answers."

Tom Munroe's financial and personal indiscretions provided a timely cover to serve the national interest. Under the guise of serving a life sentence for spying, he was able to gather intelligence unavailable to Washington officials. InterIntel's public affairs office made sure that news of Munroe's conviction reached across the enemy network. Munroe informed Clayton that working through a tight group of Saudi detainees, he had just made contact with a Chicago cleric, who delivered an urgent personal message from a valuable asset in the Middle East.

"Clayton, my son wants to talk to you. You met him in Riyadh not long ago. His name is Khalid Hassan." Munroe paused and added: "He'll be in Puerto Vallarta day after tomorrow. Be there."

Tom Munroe still liked to give orders, and Clayton relished the irony of getting an assignment from his former boss, while holding his position.

"Yes, sir. Anything else I should do? Anything I should know?"

"Tell Mort to widen the net of informers across prisons in NFL cities. TOVAIR is recruiting big time in these swamps." He paused and then added,

"Khalid is a bright kid but he has a lot of anger bottled up inside. I think he is ready to channel that anger toward Hassan." He paused again. Then, before hanging up, he shared something he had kept secret for a long time.

"Handle him with care. I never told him that I love him."

Chapter 20

The Root of Deceit

Clayton was not surprised to hear that Khalid Hassan was Munroe's son. The internal memo outlining his plea bargain spelled out the details about the personal and financial choices that landed Tom Munroe in jail. In exchange for a light sentence and his full pension, Tom agreed to work undercover to tap into the vast TOVAIR recruitment efforts in U.S. prisons. Two days later, Clayton was surprised when he entered the private waterfront villa just outside Puerto Vallarta, where Khalid Hassan was waiting for him. The slightly hunched man he had questioned in a safe house half way around the world now seemed to stand straighter and taller, more in control. There was a confidence about him that made Clayton approach him with great caution.

"I trust you came alone, Dr. Harcourt?"

"Of course. I promised your dad that I would. My word is my bond." Khalid invited Clayton to join him and Clayton stepped out into the sun-drenched Tuscan balcony overlooking the Pacific. The villa had breathtaking views of Mismaloya Bay and seemed to be precariously perched on a cliff. The tropical jungle drew its vibrant energy from the ocean mist now enveloping the estate. Khalid squinted and put on a pair of sunglasses. Clayton followed suit.

"My father thinks highly of you. I do not know if I can trust you, but I know that you will hear what I have to say."

He paused and turned to face Clayton, who wished that he could see the young engineer's eyes. Khalid's hands trembled as he reached to pour himself a glass of iced tea.

"Please help yourself, make yourself at home," he said to Clayton, and then added as if picking up the thread of his previous remark, "I also know that you will act on any information I give you to defend your country."

Khalid then told Clayton, that he had recently learned about his father's identity and that the man who told him was now dead.

"Sar-al Diab was killed by the man who claimed to be my father all these years. I think I know the reason. Hassan and a close associate, Abdul Hakim, had a fundamental disagreement with Sar-al Diab over a major operation to be carried out against your country."

Khalid's mouth felt dry and he sipped his tea slowly, as if to let his last words hang in the damp air. Across the Western horizon, the sun began to set in motion a symphony of color.

"Operation Zamzam was the brainchild of Sar-al Diab. Before his helicopter crash, he told me of the power struggle at the top of TOVAIR. He told me that I should lead the organization some day."

Clayton was eager to ask questions but knew that the time was not now. He waited in silence as Khalid sat motionless. The sunset was spilling an orange hue across the horizon and the line between water and sky melted into the distance. Khalid looked at Clayton and a small smile crossed his thin lips.

"When we last met, you asked many questions. Is there anything you would like to know now?"

Clayton's eyes narrowed as he calculated his answer. He wanted to know the targets for Operation Zamzam, he wanted to know names, he wanted to know places, and he wanted to know more about the tensions among TOVAIR's leaders. He spoke softly, as if measuring the potential impact of each word.

"Why did you want to talk? Why now?"

Khalid took a deep breath and began to recount his anger the day he was hauled off for questioning after a failed bombing attempt and then again after the break-in at the Saudi Oil Ministry. Hassan had bailed him out of jail both times and had given him a lecture about bravery.

"You are a weak man that is why the Americans picked you off the street and made you give up secrets. You'll never amount to anything."

Hassan's words were still ringing in Khalid's ears, when he learned that Tom Munroe was his father. At that point, he came to realize that the only man he had trusted was Tom. His anger grew stronger against the man who always made him feel inferior and he decided to reach out to Tom.

"I knew that my real father was in the intelligence business and I knew he could help me bring down Hassan. When I found out that Tom was in jail, I contacted him and he told me to talk to you."

Clayton figured revenge was a double edge sword, and he probed to uncover Khalid's true motives.

"I understand your anger and frustration against Hassan. Let us assume for a moment that you succeed in bringing him down. What will that accomplish? Will it help you rise to TOVAIR's top leadership? Will you then use your position to destroy Tom and all that he and your mother worked so hard to protect?"

Khalid had been listening, while gazing out into the Pacific. At the mention of his mother, he leaped from his chair and turned to Clayton looking puzzled.

"Take a seat, Khalid. What I am about to tell you can either save or end your life," Clayton sounded extremely calm.

"Your mother was a deep cover agent for the CIA; she worked closely with Tom to infiltrate the Al-Muhtadi Brotherhood. Almost three decades ago, her charm and good looks served to smitten Hassan. Soon after their marriage, Hassan took a second wife, and moved your mother into one of his Riyadh penthouses. Shortly thereafter, you were born and your parents, Tom and Ada, continued to work together."

The sun was now setting low in the horizon and a salty ocean breeze filled the balcony. Clayton paused and Khalid remained motionless, holding his breath to make sure he heard every word.

"Your mother collected important bits and pieces of intelligence for us. She did so at great personal risk during her brief visits with Hassan's family and staff. Your father put a network of informants in place to keep critical information flowing into our hands. Three years ago, your mother earned the highest distinction after a quarter of a century of service to her country. In a secret ceremony she was awarded a Patriot Medal of Honor for risking her life in the defense of liberty."

Clayton paused again, and in the dim evening light, he could see Khalid's eyes glistening bright with tears of anger and pride. After a light dinner, Khalid and Clayton walked along the garden path surrounding Villa Nueva. The discovery of his mother's role in the long war against terror triggered a rush of unanticipated anger against both of his parents.

"My whole life has been a big lie. Why did they keep these secrets from me? Why?"

"Ada and Tom love you very much. They wanted to protect you. The less you knew, the safer you were. Now you know and you will never be safe. You have two choices and each carries great danger. If you choose to help us destroy Hassan and his network, keep in mind that TOVAIR does not forgive its enemies. On the other hand, if you choose to side with our enemy, your parents can no longer protect you."

The two men walked in silence for nearly an hour, and returned to the balcony, where they had started their conversation earlier in the day. Neither one broke the silence. The damp air had thickened and seemed to breed reflection. The Pacific Ocean roared below, while bright stars sparkled like diamonds in the dark sky. Clayton walked back into the dining room. Khalid followed him. For now, he had made up his mind.

"I am ready to do whatever necessary to bring down TOVAIR and Hassan's evil designs on the West. What do you need to know? What do I need to do?"

Khalid briefed Clayton on Hassan's upcoming video-conference with other top TOVAIR leaders. The meeting was intended to be Khalid's introduction to the group and his first official briefing on Operation Zamzam. Clayton suggested that Khalid volunteer to help carry out U.S. operations.

"Be sure to follow every order they give you, no matter how insignificant. You need to establish a track-record of success before they trust you with bigger and more sensitive missions."

"Hassan has indicated that perhaps I could be useful in recruiting. I think he wants to keep me busy in this longer-term effort to keep me out of immediate operations."

"You are probably right. Play along. Suggest that you can be useful in more than one way. From our end, we'll help you. We'll plant some of your successes in recruiting operatives on U.S. soil."

"All of this will take time, years perhaps."

"Khalid, we don't have years. TOVAIR plans to inflict much damage in the near future. We are running out of time."

Clayton explained that with the U.S. election only weeks away, it was imperative to tap reliable sources to identify any plots to execute deadly attacks or manipulate the electoral process. Khalid reiterated that he was not aware of any details regarding near term missions but promised to do his best to find out. Late that night, the two men went over the rough outlines of a short and long- term plan to put Khalid at the center of TOVAIR's operations in America. Clayton went over the intricate logistics and communications strategies twice to make sure Khalid committed all details to memory.

Early the next morning, as Clayton was on his way to the Puerto Vallarta airport, he heard a loud explosion. His cab pulled up to the Southwest terminal just as sirens wailed in the distance. The driver seemed apologetic as he tried to explain the blast.

"It was probably another attempt by angry *ejidarios*. You know, the Campesinos are demanding more land and they are getting more violent all the time, *Señor*." Clayton nodded and handed the driver his fare and a generous tip.

Before boarding, Clayton overheard the rumor that there had been an accident at Villa Nueva. He was certain angry peasants demanding land reforms were not the culprit. Had he been the target? What about Khalid? Either way, if the rumors were true, his carefully laid plans would be far more difficult to implement.

Chapter 21
War Memories

The rustic splendor of Camp David seemed more pronounced in autumn, when heaps of leaves blanketed the grounds of the secluded presidential retreat. FDR had come here to find refuge from the pressures of WWII and named the place, Shangri-La. After the Navy completed a major remodel project following Mamie's first visit to the spartan quarters, president Eisenhower and his family enjoyed the solitude of this remote estate high up in the Catoctin Mountains. President Eisenhower renamed the retreat after his grandson, David.

In the seclusion of Camp David, presidents had time to rest, reflect, and recover from the unrelenting pressures of public service. Eisenhower had come here to spend time, as he would tell the press, "quietly, doing nothing." Carter chose this place to sign the Camp David accords, a fragile peace among Middle Eastern enemies waging war against each other across the centuries. Now, President Cumberland came here often to reconnect with nature. He reckoned a Westerner needed to escape the city from time to time to focus on the important things in life. Growing up the country song line "*Don't fence me in*," pretty much defined his outlook on life.

Clayton had come to Camp David to brief the president about his meeting with Khalid. The Saudi Press, reported that Prince Hassan's son had survived a random attack by angry peasants against wealthy landowners in Puerto Vallarta, while vacationing in Mexico. The latest intelligence from Riyadh suggested that Khalid had managed to identify three U.S. sleeper cells positioned to disrupt the upcoming election but the details of the plot were still sketchy.

Walking along the same path where another president had walked to ponder the challenges of a collapsed Soviet Union, Cumberland stopped and shared with Clayton his recollection of that time.

"Here we are in the very same spot, where in November of 1986 Reagan and Thatcher worked together to preserve the free world. Those were uncertain times but we knew our enemy well and the enemy was predictable. We are still fighting to defend our freedom, the very freedom for which your father gave his life. This is a different war, but the fight is about the same issue, our freedom and survival. The fight is far from over."

President Cumberland paused. The two men walked in silence for a few minutes and then the president stopped to take in the views of blue and purple mountains etched against the grey sky.

"Vietnam was a sideshow on a larger stage. It pitted the West against the evil force of totalitarianism and Marxist ideology. After Ho Chi Ming negotiated with the French to eliminate Chinese Nationalist troops in 1946 and Chinese Communists established the PRC in October of 1949, Secretary Acheson tied America's interests to French colonialism in the region. The bottom line was stability at a time when

Soviet imperialism threatened the free world. Once again, freedom is in peril. This time it's another "*ism*." This time the stakes are higher; the enemy is over here, rather than somewhere in a remote jungle."

They resumed their walk in silence, until the president spoke again. His train of thought was bare, unencumbered by place or time. Cumberland free at last from the demons of Vietnam spoke in choppy sentences, as if digging deep to retrieve memories buried long ago. Clayton Harcourt was the first and only person to hear his story.

"Jack was a quiet guy. I liked him the minute we met in boot camp. After we arrived in Vietnam, we would often go on night patrols together and watch one another's backs."

Clayton could hear dry leaves crumbling under his feet. He wondered what his father and Mack Cumberland could hear on those night patrols in the jungle so long ago. The president's voice was steady.

"We were young kids, fresh out of high school; we were like brothers. We were family. Shortly after you were born, Jack got your picture tucked in a letter from your mom. He carried that picture everywhere and pulled it out often. *I want to make sure I remember my son's face*, he would say. The night of the ambush was like a movie in slow motion." Cumberland stopped and lit up his pipe. The sweet smell of Cavendish filled the air.

"Jack and eight other guys from our unit were coming back to the base, after a tough rescue mission. When they emerged from the edge of the jungle and into a road near the base, Viet Cong trail watchers, who had been monitoring their movements signaled to a regiment of hidden comrades. A hellish firefight broke out. Outnumbered, our men ended up in hand-to-hand combat for hours into the night. Shortly before dawn, two fellows barely alive themselves brought the bodies of our fallen brothers. One of the wounded was Ken Baines."

Mack Cumberland's voice broke up as he recounted the vivid picture of that morning in hell. "Ken stumbled into the base on that rainy morning, and I can still see the tears flowing down his bloodied face. He carried Jack over his shoulder."

Mack Cumberland felt a tight knot in his chest as if the pain he had hidden for so long was finally breaking loose. He took a deep breath and looked at Clayton straight in the eye.

"I should have been fighting alongside Jack that night. Maybe he could have survived and lived to raise you. I'll always blame myself for your father's death and all others who never came back that bloody night. I was supposed to be out in the bush that night."

The damp air seemed to run straight down Clayton's spine as he walked in silence. Mack Cumberland kept walking. At his side, Clayton could only hear autumn leaves rustle under their feet. They climbed the rugged path to a clearing with grand views of the estate. Mack Cumberland stopped and pulled his collar tighter around his neck. His eyes moistened as he recounted the events that kept him alive the night Jack died.

"A new commander, who had just arrived the week prior to the attack knew my father and arranged for me to swap assignments. Jack volunteered to take my place on the rescue mission. He should never have been on that trail. It was wrong. Damn wrong. I have lived with this shame for the better part of my life. I do not expect your forgiveness but you need to know the truth."

"There is nothing to forgive, sir. A commander made a decision and one man took another man's place in the battleground. The men who fought in that jungle were warriors without leaders. America lacked political leadership in those days. My father and some 58,000 Americans gave up their lives to keep us free. They paid the highest price. You paid a price too, sir; the shame and pain you buried all these years. The memories you hold and cannot tell because they are still too raw."

Clayton sensed that the president needed to hear more after opening up the floodgates of his Vietnam nightmare. Clayton had learned early in his life not to probe. Men, who had seen war close up, did not like to talk. He understood the healing power of silence. Now, it was different. The president had spoken, he had shared memories too painful to describe. He had traveled back in time to show a son the love of his father.

"Sir, my dad would have said that the night of the ambush, he was just doing his job. You did your job. Just let go of the rest. Let it go."

Clayton and President Cumberland walked in silence. They approached the guest cabin, where Clayton was staying, and the president put his hand on Clayton's shoulder. Their eyes met. Both men knew that their lives had touched to heal their pain.

"Thanks, son. Jack would be very proud of you."

Chapter 22

State of Siege

Back in his office, Clayton read the latest report from Khalid. TOVAIR was activating sleeper cells throughout the United States. These cells were to conduct simultaneous attacks on key officials during the eve of the presidential election to weaken the incumbent administration. Clayton wanted to know places and names, but the intricate underground communications network established to access Khalid's latest intelligence posed an increasing threat of exposure. Clayton wanted to know if anyone was coordinating the attack plans in America. The footprints of previous attacks led to a command and control center – directed by a high-ranking TOVAIR operative – each time, strategically placed far from to the scene of the action. Khalid could only provide a sketch; it was up to InterIntel to draw the final blueprint to counter the wave of terror in the making.

Just as Clayton picked up the phone to call Morton, his secure line rang. The operator's voice sounded faint, the result of a bad connection.

"Dr. Harcourt, please hold for President Cumberland."

"Clayton, I'm on my way to San Francisco and wanted to thank you again for your support. I'm glad we had a chance to chat about your dad." The president's voice came through as clear as the California sky, and then his tone became somber. He wanted to know if Clayton had heard any more from his Riyadh contact. After hearing the latest report, the president asked for Clayton's advice.

"What would you do?"

"Mr. President, we cannot assume the attackers will wait until the day before the election, we need to take preventive measures right now. We do not know the place, the time, or the means but we know the targets. Anyone in your administration, venturing out of Washington for official or personal business is at risk. For all we know, they are at risk even right here in D.C. I recommend you go directly to the American people, announce a national alert, and mobilize our domestic security forces."

The president did not respond, and Clayton wondered if Mack Cumberland was still on the line.

"Hello. Sir, can you hear me?"

"I hear you just fine."

"Sir, there is one more thing. Is there anyway we can have a list of everyone with access to the campaign schedule? We'll need a list of anyone at the White House, election headquarters, the media, anyone with access to travel schedules for any member of your cabinet?"

"Call up my Chief of Staff, Troy Hatfield. He will give you anything you need." Cumberland hung up the phone and placed a call to his Chief of Staff.

Clayton scanned the list of names coming through the fax and recognized that of the president's Domestic Policy Advisor at the bottom of the page. Cory Black seemed aloof and cunning. She was a woman in a man's world, a skilled political operator with an icy disposition under the guise of her professionalism. Clayton did not remember her voice but he remembered the way she raised her left eyebrow when she first met him at the president's dinner. Cory Black's handshake made Clayton uneasy. He was not able to pinpoint what bothered him about this woman, but he knew not to trust her.

Clayton finished scanning the list of names and was again ready to call Mort when a CNN news alert flashed at the bottom of one of his desktop monitors.

"Attorney General Jay Jones killed this afternoon." Clayton dialed Mort's number as the scrolling text moved across the screen: "Mr. Jones was hit by two sniper bullets as he spoke at a gathering of law enforcement officials in Atlanta. Minutes later, another sniper gunned down Al Grant, the president's National Security Advisor, as he left a foreign policy forum at UCLA in Los Angeles. Almost simultaneously, ten explosions ripped trough major city freeways clogged up with rush hour traffic killing thousands of commuters from coast to coast."

"Mort, I just heard the news about Jones, Grant and the rest. Do we know anything more than what CNN is reporting?"

"I'm afraid not. Any ideas where we need to look for clues?"

"TOVAIR. In fact I was about to call you after reading Khalid's report a few minutes ago. This is definitely TOVAIR's signature and there is more to come along these same lines."

Clayton sketched the outlines of TOVAIR's pre-election offensive and told Mort that he wanted to conduct a preliminary investigation of those individuals listed on the sheet Hatfield had just faxed from the White House.

"Just as a precaution," he explained to a reluctant Mort. "I have a hunch that TOVAIR cannot be targeting their prey without help from the inside."

"These are folks with top security clearance, Clayton. I think we would be wasting our time. There must be some other explanation. Besides, we would be stepping into a political minefield if word got out to the press right before an election. Just think of the headlines: "President investigates his own staff; suspects someone in his administration works directly with the enemy." Mort paused and then added, "I think this could just energize the Parks camp and give credence to the conspiracy theories swirling around town."

"I'll take care of this myself, Mort. Trust me on this one. TOVAIR lost a key player when Gillman expired. I doubt that they did not have another high-level player in place. The sleeper cells are only executing the plan. The snipers, the truckers and their deadly cargo are ready to execute their orders at a moment's notice. There is a key operative pulling the strings. I believe that person has access to actionable intelligence inside the administration. We need to choke off the sleeper cells' main controller before his next move. We need to catch the key U.S. player in this deadly game. TOVAIR cannot achieve this type of precision against high value targets without an insider pulling the strings."

Clayton's concern was not for the political survival of president Cumberland but for the survival of the presidency and the republic. His political instincts were sharp but his love of country was stronger than the respect he had for the man who admitted responsibility for Jack's death. Since returning from Camp David, Clayton had little time to reflect on the discovery of his father's death. His focus on the short timetable he had to stop the enemy was a higher priority than dwelling on mistakes of the past.

☆ ☆ ☆

Mack Cumberland approved Operation Troutfly giving Clayton sole responsibility to avert further attacks. With only two weeks before Election Day, the murder of Jay Jones began to erode public support for the Cumberland Administration.

Priscilla Parks intensified her attacks on the incumbent. She claimed that Cumberland's hawkish stance towards terrorists had backfired, unleashing TOVAIR's ire once again on American soil. The argument began to resonate with much help from the mainstream media. All major newspaper editorials called for the president to negotiate with terrorists and reach a cease-fire. Anti-war demonstrations erupted in major cities calling for an end to violence. A massive mobilization of the National Guard around the country and particularly in major NFL cities gave the public a queasy feeling. America was under siege. Urban life looked more like the unsettling pictures of the Gaza strip than the familiar pictures of American urban life. Military patrols, checkpoints, and curfews became the order of the day. Priscilla Parks began to lead in the polls by double digits.

Clayton received the message from agent Chu Teh, the main conduit for Khalid's reports, late in the evening. He reread the secret message warning him of a high-ranking mole, code-named Autumn, who seemed to be in direct contact with Liao Chang about an ultra secret operation against the West. Clayton deduced that the operation was underway and he had a hunch that Autumn was a high-ranking official he had suspected for some time. Before leaving his office for the emergency meeting at the White House, Clayton checked the progress of the president's staff background investigations. Before leaving for the White House, Clayton placed a call to Mort.

"Any surprises yet?"

"We are moving right along and have retrieved the FBI files on each individual. We have a preliminary report. During the transition, a senator requested that the vetting process be speeded up, leaving some big holes in the files of at least three of the president's appointees. We are now checking to find the source up on the Hill so we can isolate the individuals and step up our search."

"Great. I'm on my way to the emergency meeting and will keep my eyes and ears open. Maybe our elusive prey will be there."

✡ ✡ ✡

President Cumberland welcomed his Cabinet to the emergency meeting, and the faces around the conference table were somber. Clayton watched as members of the president's inner-circle took their seats around the room.

"Ladies and gentleman, while our nation grieves we must act. I've called you here today to ask for your advice and your continuing support in fighting the enemy at home and abroad."

Clayton sat right behind the president along a row of chairs reserved for non-cabinet members and other senior members of the president's team. One by one, cabinet members seated around the table submitted their recommendations, most reaffirming Cumberland's stance against terrorist attacks. Secretary of Defense Roger Miles cleared his throat and looked around the table before presenting his views.

"Mr. President, as I hear my colleagues support our current actions, I concur on all points made regarding our tactical response at home and abroad. I respectfully differ, however, as to the strategic steps we must to take to win this war. Sir, we must launch a secret offensive to reach TOVAIR leaders before it is too late."

Miles paused and looked across the table toward Secretary of State, Vivian Lacey, who put on her reading glasses and opened her leather folder. Clayton noted the Defense Secretary's tight jaw. Cory Black raised her left eyebrow once again. She was sitting across the room from Clayton right behind the Defense Secretary and was not taking any notes. Miles continued, looking straight into his notes.

"Secretary Lacey and I have developed a plan for your approval, sir. We propose to send an envoy to meet with top TOVAIR leaders. We should negotiate a cease-fire. We believe negotiation will defuse criticism of our policy at home and can ensure your reelection, sir."

Mack Cumberland did not show any emotion. He sat impassive like an expert poker player, taking notes and looking at each one of his Cabinet members. Secretary Lacey presented the details of the negotiation plan. When she concluded, Mack Cumberland thanked everyone around the room and announced that he would get back to them later in the day. Secretary Miles approached Mack Cumberland and whispered something in his ear. The president shook his head, and said:

"Sorry. We cannot meet today, Roger. I need to get back to the office. I'll call you soon."

Right after the Cabinet meeting, Troy Hatfield led Clayton into the Oval Office, where Mack Cumberland sat behind Thomas Jefferson's desk. The president's Chief of Staff picked up a stack of papers and looked at his watch.

"These letters will be ready for your signature in an hour, sir."

"Thanks Troy. Please tell Amy to hold all calls."

"Yes, sir."

Cumberland walked across the room and motioned for Clayton to join him. The president looked tired, as he slumped into a chair across the fireplace. He stared at the dancing flames and lit his pipe. Clayton sensed the letters requesting the resignation of close advisors caused the president much grief.

"I hope I won't have to use any of these resignation letters. What do you make of the Miles-Lacey proposal?"

Clayton had read a copy of the proposal on his way to the Oval Office and noted that the envoy was to deliver a message to TOVAIR leaders along the same appeasement lines as the policy proposed by Senator Parks.

"Mr. President. You need to be very careful with this." Clayton conveyed Mort's latest findings and shared his concerns with the president.

"Mr. President, if Priscilla Parks was the senator who sped up the vetting process, and Miles and Lacey were the targets of the rushed investigation, the enemy is much closer than we ever imagined."

"This is impossible. I've known Miles for over twenty years. He cannot be part of this mess. There must be some other explanation."

"Sir, you need to be ready for the possibility of a mole at the highest levels of your administration. If not Miles, it could be anyone else in that Cabinet room today."

"When will we know?"

Mack Cumberland stared at the fireplace. His outer expression was calm. His stomach felt like a tight knot. He worried more about the presidency than about his own re-election. His personal ambition to leave a legacy during a second term was now relegated to a lower priority. Saving the country from its enemies within was now his primary mission. If indeed high-level officials were aiding the enemy, he no longer recognized his own country. He was determined to uncover the culprits of treason and let justice prevail. He was committed to defend his nation at all costs and trusted Jack's son to find answers.

"We are working around the clock, sir. I assure you we'll get to the bottom of this. In the meantime, keep playing your cards right just like you did during the cabinet meeting. Keep them guessing, sir.

A small smile crossed Cumberland's face for the first time in several days.

"Growing up, we played poker every Thursday night. It was tough. We had some fast thinkers around, who sharpened my body language. It's been a long time since those days."

Cumberland's thoughts drifted to growing up at the ranch, nearly 120 miles away from the nearest town. He could still remember the smell of sagebrush and the sound of the creek behind the stables. It was a simple life; rich in values that made a man steady in the midst of any storm. The lessons of daily survival had served him well. Those lessons would help him now. Then, as if snapping back to the moment, he added:

"Would you be ready to meet with TOVAIR leaders?" The question surprised Clayton but he did not hesitate to respond.

"Sir, I'll do whatever you ask. You know that."

"I do. But maybe it is best you stick around until we know more."

Troy Hatfield did not hesitate to interrupt the president's meeting. The president stood up and looked alarmed as his chief of staff entered the room unannounced, knowing that it signaled another emergency.

"Sir, they hit again. Secretary Miles is on his way to the hospital but it does not look good. Two of the men in his detail were killed instantly."

"Get the Deputy Secretary on my secure line."

While Troy placed the call to the Pentagon, Cumberland turned to Clayton and told Clayton that Miles had asked to see him right after the Cabinet meeting. The Secretary had insisted that it was important. The president had declined.

"I want you to visit Mike Perry, Roger's Deputy. I think…."

Hatfield interrupted, "Mr. President, I've got Mr. Perry on the line."

"Mr. President," Mike Perry sounded shocked, "we are still waiting for word from the hospital. Secretary Miles is fighting for his life, Sir."

"Mike, I know this is a tough moment for you but I need your help. I'm sending Clayton Harcourt over to your office right now. He'll have some questions. We need to find those responsible for this attack. I know you understand."

"I certainly do. We will find them, Sir. I can assure you that we are already working with DHS, FBI and others to find the culprits.

✲ ✲ ✲

Mike Perry was a retired Marine and a perfectionist. He seldom forgot a face or a name and his resume was as long as his memory. Before joining the Cumberland administration as Deputy Secretary of Defense, he had sold his oil exploration company for a tidy sum. His relationship to Secretary Miles was strictly professional, grounded on trust and respect. They met daily for two hours to set priorities and manage the mammoth organization. Miles likened the Pentagon to an aircraft carrier – it could not change direction at a moment's notice. The Defense Secretary relied on Mike Perry to get things done.

Mike Perry delivered what he promised. He had promised Miles a swift counter-attack against a Pentagon initiative to slow down the President's agenda and implemented the "Deadwood Offensive," a program to force generals into early retirement and promote young officers up the chain of command. Diplomacy was not Mike Perry's forte but his strong will served him well. He liked to joke that stubbornness was a gene invented by his ancestors. One of his relatives, Commodore Matthew Perry, sailed to Japan and demanded negotiations with the emperor to open Japanese ports in the 19th century. A picture of the family idol blazing his way into Edo Bay hung in Mike Perry's office.

"Well, it's good to finally meet you, Clayton. I've heard a lot about you from Mort Rourke. We go all the way back to Camp Pendelton." Mike Perry extended his hand. The solid grip concealed a missing finger.

"I am pleased to meet you as well. Morton thinks the world of you." Clayton had heard Morton praise Mike Perry's feats. After exchanging pleasantries, Clayton got right down to business.

"A few minutes before the attack, Secretary Miles presented a bold proposal on how to approach TOVAIR. Are you familiar with any of the details and how this plan came about?"

"Miles held a number of meetings with Vivian Lacey in the past couple of weeks. Last week, he seemed unusually tense after one of these meetings. He told me that she had proposed a plan that he could not support. He sketched the outline of what I believe he presented earlier today at the cabinet meeting. Yesterday, he informed me that he was going to go ahead and support her plan. We argued, and I advised him against it. Before he left for the White

House, he stopped by my office and told me not to worry. The Lacey plan is going nowhere. He was going to make sure of that."

Mike Perry sat back in his chair and studied Clayton's face. The angular jaw drew attention away from the clear eyes. Clayton did not blink under the intense gaze of the Deputy Secretary of Defense. Mike Perry decided the man sitting across from his desk could be trusted. He walked across the room to a safe, unlocked it, and handed Clayton a computer disk.

"Take a look at this. As soon as I received the news of the attack, I walked into Miles' office and found his computer locked on to a personal file. He must have been working on this before the Cabinet meeting."

Clayton began to read the document in which Miles acknowledged receiving a call from Senator Parks pressuring him to "keep his word" before the election, while Secretary of State, Vivian Lacey, pressured him to accept her proposal to negotiate with TOVAIR leaders. The Defense Secretary's conundrum became clearer as Clayton reached the last page: *"Vivian's proposal requires that we scale back on our military options. If I refuse to accept this shift in our defense policy, Senator Parks threatens to leak the story she helped cover up during my nomination hearings."*

The Secretary of Defense had decided to go to the president and tell him "everything as soon as possible." He had concluded: "I am prepared to resign before jeopardizing the president's re-election." Clayton closed the document and turned to Mike Perry.

"If you don't mind, I would like to hold on to this a little longer. Any idea what it was that Senator Parks covered up?"

"I have the same question. I wish I knew. If Miles makes it, I will ask him personally." Perry paused and then added, "I thought I knew him pretty well but sometimes people are not what they seem." Clayton detected anger in Perry's voice. Mike Perry did not like surprises, particularly from people he trusted.

✲ ✲ ✲

Mort Rourke sat behind his desk in disbelief. After reading Miles memo, he put down his reading glasses and handed Clayton the disk back.

"It's pretty amazing. Roger Miles one of Parks' protégées and potentially a TOVAIR mole?"

"Maybe and maybe not," Clayton rubbed his eyes and looked at his watch. It was shortly after midnight, and the latest reports from Morton's investigative team were still inconclusive. "What we know is that Miles was one of the three appointees that Senator Parks streamlined through the nomination process. Vivian Lacey could well be another."

"Let's hope that Miles pulls through in time to get to the bottom of this," Mort shook his head, "I still cannot believe he could be our guy."

"He is still in intensive care, and the next twenty four hours will be critical. Let's hope he makes it. After Mike Perry gets a hold of him, he may wish he hadn't." Mort grinned. He appreciated Clayton's accurate reading of his old friend.

"Miles is lucky that Mike Perry is no longer a young man. Back when we were in boot camp, we used to call him Mean Mike." Mort paused, and then added, "Don't let his appearance fool you. Mike has a big heart. You can trust him with your life."

✡ ✡ ✡

President Cumberland made the brief announcement during a press conference scheduled during prime time. The president spoke without reading any notes.

"The recent attack on Secretary of Defense Miles was an act of cowardice. While we pray for his family and his recovery, we are emboldened to fight our enemies to the end. I am happy to report that Secretary of Defense Miles is now out of intensive care. Shortly before his attack, I had approved an extensive internal investigation. Regretfully, we now have preliminary evidence implicating government officials and elected representatives in these acts of violence. I want to assure all Americans that the rule of law will prevail and order will be restored."

The president cleared his throat and looked across an audience of stunned reporters. One reporter turned a page of his note-pad and disrupted the eerie silence. Everyone waited for the president to give further details. Some reporters in the back of the room shifted in their chairs, eager to break the story. Only the first row of reporters heard the president sigh. Then, after what seemed to be an eternity to some members of the press, the president resumed his press conference.

"I also want to assure Americans that we will provide information on our investigation as further evidence becomes available. We will not jeopardize justice in the name of freedom of information. We are at war and we will not back down. We will hold anyone accountable who is responsible for attacks on innocent citizens and government officials. Thank you. I will now take a few questions.

"Mr. President, are any members of your administration implicated at this time?"

"It is possible."

"Who are they?" The president ignored the follow-up question and pointed to another reporter struggling to elbow his way to the front row, past a camera crew.

"Sir, are any members of Congress involved in the conduct of the investigation?"

"Last night, I informed Congress about our preliminary findings. Members of the Senate and House Ethics Committees are in the process of launching their own investigations."

The matronly reporter with the smoke-stained fingers asked the question, many in the room wanted to ask. The frame of her thick glasses was slightly crooked, and when the camera zoomed in on her profile, the paper clip holding her spectacles together came into full view under the bright lights.

"Given your sharp decline in the polls and the fact that continuing criticism from your opponent seems to resonate with the American people, are you launching this investigation to get reelected?"

The president had anticipated a question along these lines. Although he had sketched the rough outline of a reply before the press conference, his answer seemed spontaneous.

"You suggest that this investigation is politically motivated." He emphasized the word "politically" as if underlining it and paused for added emphasis. Then he continued looking straight at the camera. The collar of his starched white shirt looked impeccable – a sharp contrast against his tanned skin.

"After serving in Vietnam, I spent most of my life building a business. Four years ago, the American people elected me to this office, because professional politicians have been unable to end this war." He paused as if searching for the right words, and then added, "This war has turned our lives upside down. I came to this town to push politics aside and help us get back to normal. I never have, and I'm not about to put politics above my country. This is not about my re-election. This is about defending our way of life, our values and freedom. This is about giving our children hope for a peaceful and prosperous future, without fear of walking into exploding buildings, trains, or schools."

Another brief pause followed. The president turned to the reporter with the crooked eyeglasses. She recoiled when he called her by her first name. Cumberland addressed her in a fatherly tone.

"Ann, I want to live in an America free of fear where all of us can pursue our goals and achieve our dreams. We can't do this while living in a state of siege. The enemy wins every time a military convoy rolls through your neighborhood, every time your city is under an extreme alert and curfew sirens ring."

The president faced the camera once again, shifted his tone, and continued without pausing. "I want to end this war and the only way to do so is to defeat the enemy. If in fact, our very own people are helping terrorists destroy our institutions we must redouble our efforts to stop anyone involved in these acts of sedition. The enemy is testing our will to prevail. We will never let our enemies get their way. We will never surrender. Regardless of the outcome of this election, I will fight against extremists until I take my last breath."

There were no more questions. The president walked back into the Oval Office. For the first time since taking the oath of office, he felt the weight of a decision pressing hard against his chest. Before speaking to reporters, he had made the call to Mike Perry and now he wondered if his order to carry on with Clayton's recommendation had been wise. Mack Cumberland was about to talk himself into calming down, when his chief of staff walked in. Troy Hatfield informed him that Mike Perry and Clayton were on their way to Hong Kong. There was no sense in second-guessing a decision to move Operation Troutfly forward – it was now up to Clayton to accomplish the mission.

Chapter 23
Secret Encounters

Shortly after receiving Morton's report, the president had reluctantly approved Clayton's secret meeting with one of TOVAIR's leaders. The report included excerpts of agent Chu The's message to Clayton indicating that Chinese Deputy Prime Minister Li Chui was willing to attend a secret meeting to discuss "mutual" concerns about TOVAIR's latest attacks on U.S. soil. The president insisted on having Mike Perry lead the mission as diplomatic cover for Clayton's operation. Alone on such a mission, Clayton would be far more vulnerable than accompanied by a high-ranking government official.

Mike Perry and Clayton boarded the military cargo plane shortly before dawn and tightened their seat belts for the long flight to Hong Kong. Engine clatter and hard seats provided little comfort but kept both men focused on the thick TOVAIR files. It was imperative to zero in on Li Chui's main priorities. Clayton and Mike Perry knew that they needed to play their cards right to hand the Deputy Prime Minister of China a reason to defect from TOVAIR. The most difficult task would be to implement the domino effect of their plan, namely to knock off the rest of TOVAIR's leadership, one by one like a falling house of cards.

Mike Perry walked across the tarmac and immediately recalled the smells of Asia. It had been a long time since he had set foot in Hong Kong or for that matter any Asian nation. His once fluent Chinese was now rusty, but he recognized the characters "Welcome to Hong Kong" painted in deep red above the entrance to the customs building. Past the baggage claim area, Mike Perry spotted the familiar face. The hardships of war had carved deep lines across the old man's forehead, and the sunken eyes looked as defiant as the ones of the young prison guard Mike Perry remembered.

Chu The's crooked smile had not changed. He approached the secret envoys, and his eyes became moist as he shook Mike Perry's hand.

"Sir, I never thought I see you again. You kept your promise and saved my family. We never forget." The old man paused, embarrassed by his own display of emotion. He bowed his head and felt the firm grip of Perry's handshake. The same handshake had sealed his family's fate long ago.

"It's been a long time, Chu. Good to see you, my friend.

Chu ushered Mike Perry and Clayton through the crowded airport and drove them to a safe house across town in Repulse Bay.

"Bet you were surprised."

Mike Perry eased himself into a plush leader chair. Out of the corner of his eye, he caught a sailboat pulling into the Yacht Club marina just below the hill. If he had gotten up from his chair he would have seen an expansive view of the bay, but he was too tired now to take in the local scenery. The meeting with Deputy Prime Minister Li Chui was scheduled for the following morning, after just a few hours of rest.

"Yeah. Quite. I gathered you two met in Vietnam."

"Right."

Clayton did not probe. He knew that Mike Perry would tell him what he needed to know.

"You can trust Chu The. He is a decent man, the only decent human being I encountered at the Hanoi Hilton. His family fled Vietnam. He stayed behind and began to work for us."

For Clayton, the picture of how Chu The ended up being his main link to TOVAIR now began to come into focus. Mort Rourke, had recommended Chu The. Morton trusted him because he had been kind to his close friend Mike Perry, a former POW in Hanoi. In the last few weeks, Chu gained Clayton's confidence with thorough reports gathered through a network of TOVAIR infiltrators in China and India. Clayton had confirmed these reports through other channels established to communicate directly to Khalid in Saudi Arabia.

TOVAIR's leadership was breaking up at the very top. This created a unique opportunity to peel away key players starting with Li Chui, the most likely TOVAIR defector. Li Chui's relationship with Liao Chang had soured recently over their quest to gain absolute power. Liao Chang was willing to delegate operational plans in the U.S. by giving sole discretion to Assoud and the Tansari brothers, who determined targets and methods. Li Chui felt that violent attacks in the U.S. did not advance his nationalist agenda and could jeopardize his political ambitions to rise to the top of China's leadership. His nationalist vision was narrower than Chang's goal of Chinese global supremacy. Li Chui was an isolationist and he was willing to severe his ties to TOVAIR in order to reach his own pinnacle of power.

Clayton woke Mike Perry up shortly before daybreak. Together they waited for the signal to start the last leg of their journey to meet Li Chui. As they drove from Repulse Bay to Aberdeen Harbor, they noticed the shadows of wealth and poverty right next to one another but far apart like strangers in a crowded subway. As they approached the floating community of junks and sampans, they spotted the old woman clad in a black tunic and trousers loading vegetables and buckets of fresh water into her sampan. They boarded the vessel and squatted almost blending into the cargo. The old woman adjusted her mushroom shaped straw hat and pushed her sampan away from the dock. She paddled deftly. They glided in slow motion through the labyrinth of moored junks, container vessels, and sampans.

The water dwellers of Causeway Bay's Typhon Shelter had not yet started their daily routines. In this floating city, women were not yet squatting over stoves. Children were not yet sweeping, carrying buckets of salt water, or crawling on decks without worry of falling overboard. Old men were not yet playing Mah-Jong under faded tarpaulins. Pigs and poultry roamed the decks. Dogs slept and cats chased one another. Clotheslines hung heavy with wet clothes from the previous day. Before long, the boat people of Aberdeen Harbor, many of whom had arrived here from Vietnamese villages many years ago, would begin to rise unaware of the important meeting underway in the midst of their meager existence.

The first thing Clayton noticed when he boarded the junk was the smell of burning incense floating from aft. A Buddhist shrine and a motley assortment of paper flowers provided the only apparent color on the rotting wooded deck. The room below deck seemed out of place. The understated elegance was unexpected as was the casual demeanor of the short man extending his hand.

"Welcome to my home. The Deputy Prime Minister will be with you shortly." Li Chui entered the room almost instantly followed by two bodyguards. Clayton and Mike Perry rose from their seats and Li Chui greeted them in flawless English.

"I am glad you came. Please sit down." Li Chui turned to his bodyguards and instructed them to leave the room. He knew the two Americans were the intended high-ranking envoys. He had studied their files carefully before the meeting and was now satisfied that both had arrived alone. Li Chui offered his guests a cup of tea and settled into a rattan chair that seemed too big for him.

"I believe we share a concern over the direction of TOVAIR's activities in your country," he began looking straight at Mike Perry. Then turning to Clayton, he continued, "Your concern has to do with American national security; my concern has to do with China's national interest. You find the recent attacks on individual members of your administration abhorrent; I find them inconvenient. Although our motives differ, we share a common interest in stopping these activities."

Clayton glanced at Mike Perry and then interjected. "Why are these attacks inconvenient for you? Why should we care?"

Li Chui ignored the questions. In his view, Westerners had a way of being too direct. They had no regard for saving face, no regard for subtleties, no ability to leave things unsaid.

"As a single member of TOVAIR's leadership, I cannot impose my will nor do I have discretionary authority to change the course of operations in your country or any where else around the world." Li Chui paused, sipped his tea, and was relieved that no interruptions followed.

Mike Perry sat motionless, his eyes fixed on the Deputy Prime Minister. Li Chui recognized the look of defiance and superiority. It was the look of a free man willing to fight to the death. Mike Perry annoyed Li Chui more so than the younger American. Clayton Harcourt seemed brash and complex. The American Deputy Secretary of Defense seemed calm and single-minded. Li Chui decided to hide his disgust and moved right ahead with his agenda.

"I am able, however, to supply you with information that can help you stop these activities for your benefit and mine."

Clayton fixed his eyes on Li Chui reading each facial line and remaining silent. Mike Perry spoke first.

"We are most grateful for your offer. I am afraid, it comes a bit late." Mike Perry paused and detected a hint of disgust in Li Chui's slight frown.

"We have enough information to stop these activities. Stopping the perpetrators only provides a short-term solution. We are interested in long-term solutions."

Li Chui seldom smiled, but now a wide grin displayed an imperfect row of yellow teeth. He bowed his head as if to apologize for his indiscretion.

"Well, that makes two of us. Is that how you say it?" Li Chui raised his eyebrows and without waiting for a reply continued: "I am in search of long- term solutions for my country. At one time, I thought that TOVAIR could provide the answers. Now, I believe my country must find another path."

Li Chui unveiled his motive of becoming Prime Minister without the baggage of TOVAIR and painted himself as a pragmatic nationalist. He explained that gaining a place of prominence in TOVAIR's inner sanctum had enabled him to learn first-hand about the motives of China's internal enemies. He suggested that he was willing to share this knowledge in return for American acceptance of a One China policy, meaning Taiwan joining the mainland as a sole sovereign nation.

What Li Chui did not disclose was his intent of implementing a full-blown nationalist agenda, including the removal of China from the World Trade Organization, the nationalization of all foreign investments, and a rollback of local and state elections. He knew that such a China would be a threat to American interests.

Suspecting that Li Chui was not showing his entire hand, Mike Perry's reply was brief and to the point.

"We welcome an opportunity to work with you to destroy our common enemies. I am not in a position to negotiate any conditions on future policy."

"Would you reconsider your position, if I told you that I agree to work with Khalid Hassan to undermine TOVAIR's immediate plans to derail your election?"

The U.S. presidential election was only a week and one half away. Li Chui committed to provide Khalid with actionable and real-time intelligence regarding immediate TOVAIR targets. The plan was for Khalid to travel to the U.S. and pass on TOVAIR's plans to U.S. authorities under the guise of recruiting potential sleeper cells. A visit to Khalid's father, Tom Munroe in federal prison would provide additional cover.

On their flight back to Washington D.C., Clayton asked Mike Perry if he thought Li Chui would follow-up on his promise to cooperate.

"He'll follow through. He wants power and this a way to get it."

"So, you trust him to deliver the goods and not play both sides of the fence?"

"Yes and no. He'll deliver the goods because he believes we'll retaliate if he doesn't. He'll look out for himself and back-stab anyone in his path. He will not hesitate to kill Khalid or anyone else to save his skin."

"Nice work. You even convinced me that our China policy was in your hands."

Mike Perry smiled, leaned back, and fell asleep thinking about the battles to come, as they flew over the Pacific Ocean. After landing at Andrews Air Force base, Mike Perry shook Clayton's hand. Their firm handshake signaled both men's determination to win no matter the cost.

"In the days ahead, your job won't be easy. But from what I have seen, you're up to the challenge. Always remember that not all men understand freedom. Some are threatened by it, some don't want to know it, and some resent it. We will always have to fight to protect ourselves. Every generation needs to teach the next that freedom does not come with guarantees. Vietnam was your father's mission. Now you have your own mission. I trust you will prevail."

Clayton remained silent and wondered if Mike Perry had known Jack Harcourt.

"I did not know your dad, but I knew of him. He was a patriot who saved many lives and gave his own to defend our way of life. Your work honors his memory. Carry on."

Another voice from his father's generation brought Clayton closer to the man who inspired his life's work. The man Clayton wanted to emulate, the man who gave him life and lived on in his imagination. The man he talked to in a quiet way and to whom he asked the hard questions, those with no answers. The man, who never held his hand tight, led him up a steep mountain trail, or placed him on his shoulders to spot elk at a distance. The childhood dreams were a memory now but his father's absence was as real now as on the day when Clayton learned that Jack Harcourt would never come home.

Chapter 24
Revenge

Tom Munroe had settled into a routine of reading, writing, and tending a prison garden, where he pulled weeds and collected intelligence while he worked with fellow inmates. The federal facility in the outskirts of the small town of Trout, West Virginia housed high profile, white-collar crime felons with vast connections in the major capitals of the world. In his journal, Tom described the place as a "small pond with big fish." Here he had made the initial contact that led him to contact Khalid Hassan, and now he was waiting for his son's visit. It had been more than five years since Tom had last seen Khalid. The father waited for the son with cautious anticipation.

Tom Munroe did not spend more than three decades in the intelligence business without acquiring a good nose for spotting trouble. He trusted his instincts and his reaction to first impressions. He remembered Khalid's reticent nature, and his son's smug demeanor surprised him. The change was subtle. It had to do with the way Khalid looked down at the prison guard who escorted him to the garden, where Tom was raking leaves. When Tom approached his son, expecting to hug him, Khalid took a step back and extended his hand. A thin smirk crossed his lips as he pronounced his father's name. Tom sensed disdain in his son's greeting.

"Well, Tom. We finally meet again. It's been a long time."

Tom did not reply and shook his head, motioning Khalid to join him on a wood bench under an old oak tree. Father and son sat in silence, for what seemed a long time. Tom saw anger in the young man's eyes, but somehow he felt the anger was greater than that of a son holding a big grudge. He wondered if the lies and deceit he had learned to spin in his professional life were the source of his son's hatred. He wondered about what could have happened if only he and Khalid's mother would have had normal lives. Tom had asked himself the same questions many times. His answers were always unsatisfactory. He often wondered how to regain his son's trust. Khalid broke the silence and gave Tom a clue. Looking at his father, he spoke without trepidation.

"Since finding out who you are, I have managed to control my anger against you and mother. I spent many hours trying to sort it all out. I understand your motives against your enemies. I know you are loyal to your country. What I do not understand is why you thought I could be your pawn. In those early years, you could have accomplished more with the truth rather than with lies. Now I understand what I couldn't figure out then." Khalid did not look at his father as he spoke.

"When I was growing up, you came in and out of my life, as you played the great game."

Khalid's voice did not grow louder but his tone grew bitter. He was tempted to tell Tom, "*Now, I'm a big boy and you will play by my rules,*" but he refrained. He noticed how much Tom had aged. He also noticed deep sorrow in his father's eyes. Tom spoke softly.

"I'm sorry for letting you down so often and for so long. I will always regret the pain I caused you and your mother. I hope you will forgive me but I understand if you cannot."

Khalid was determined to play into his father's guilt to accomplish his own mission. His voice softened, as he probed further and risked exposing his own motives for this visit.

"Tom, there is much to forgive and we may not have enough time to do it. In the meantime, we have a job to finish. Our personal relationship cannot be fixed today, let's focus on what can be fixed. I trust you know why I came to see you."

Tom nodded, and Khalid handed him an envelope with names, places, and dates. Li Chui had kept his promise to forward TOVAIR's operational plans to Khalid. Tom tucked the envelope in his shirt pocket, and was ready to ask Khalid about specifics on TOVAIR's American operations, when Khalid surprised him with a question of his own.

"This place must be difficult for you, after all those years of making decisions about life and death, do you find yourself wanting to get back into the arena?"

Tom measured his response. The question raised a red flag and he proceeded with great caution.

"At times, of course I would like to be back at the center of counter-terror operations. This is no longer possible for me. I'll pass the information you gave me to the right people and get back to my daily routine."

"Would you be interested in getting back in the arena, if the opportunity presented itself?"

"Sure." Tom did not look up. He did not want to betray his son's newfound trust.

"Would you be willing to work for me?"

"Sure."

"Even if it means that you may betray your own country?"

"An old man in jail has nothing to lose. I just hope to regain your trust, son."

Khalid was blunt.

"I cannot promise you trust, I can only promise you revenge."

"Revenge?"

"Right. That is the price for all the lies, for all the years, I thought of you as someone I could trust."

Tom played his last card. He realized the game had deadly undertones.

"What if I decide not to work for you?"

"Same price. I have contacts right here in this prison. They will eliminate you." Khalid did not hesitate to add, "Traitors are beheaded in my part of the world."

"I see. Guess my choice is easy. What can I do for you?" Tom's training kicked in. He kept his composure, while his son closed the deal.

"I'll send you instructions soon. You will have a chance to practice your skills once again. This time you will deceive those for whom you worked. The lies will now run in the opposite direction. You will help America turn its guns against itself."

A cold chill ran through Tom's back as his son walked away without turning back. His own blood was a man without a moral compass, a killer bound and determined to extract a high price for the sins of his father. His life now seemed like a motion picture. He recalled the opening scene, when he first held Khalid in his arms. He was such a fragile creature. He wiggled his legs and his tiny fingers held Tom's thumb tight. He looked like his mother but as he grew older, Khalid resembled more and more the man he believed to be his father.

When Khalid was at MIT, Tom almost told him the truth, but twice he decided against it. As grown men, father and son seemed closer than ever before. Why screw up a good thing? Now the past seemed irrelevant. The truth had done more harm than good. The lies kept the lid on Khalid's anger. The lies had caught up with Tom's life. Tom walked back to his cell and tried to keep his thoughts from becoming visible to those around him. In this place, he had learned not to trust anyone, but then again distrust came easy; it was part of his life's work. He had to warn Clayton. Maybe it was already too late.

✲ ✲ ✲

Clayton had come to his office before dawn. He still felt jetlagged but liked getting to work before anyone else. It was a quiet time, a time to think and plan strategy for the days before the election. The nation was on a state of high alert and Washington was awash in rumors about the findings of the Senate Ethics Committee's investigation. Clayton's contacts on the Hill kept him apprised of the mounting evidence against Senator Parks, but no official reports were yet available.

A high stack of faxes spilled over Clayton's desk, but the one he was most interested in was on the very top of the pile. It was the list Chu The had just sent to provide evidence of Khalid's deception. The call from Tom late the previous evening over an unsecured line came as a surprise, but Clayton wasted no time to contact Chu The and requested a copy of the list Li Chui had provided to Khalid. Before his staff came in, Clayton compared the lists and quickly figured out that Khalid's list was a fake. It included some of the original information, but most of the names did not match Chui's list.

Clayton checked the time and decided that it was not too early to brief Morton. He was probably in his office by now. Just as he was about to dial Morton's extension, the phone rang. It was the secure line.

"Hey Clayton, have you checked your red inbox yet?"

"Good morning Mort, I was just about to call you to brief you on the latest caper. Khalid tried to recruit Tom. The list he brought over is tainted. He can't be trusted. Tom will play him along, keep him on the line for a while. We'll feed him bits and pieces of real and bogus facts to keep him interested and confused."

"That explains the latest news from Riyadh. Khalid's mother was found dead in her apartment. Beheaded."

"Mort, there are no boundaries for these fanatics. Khalid in now part of TOVAIR's inner circle. His main motive is revenge, personal mind you, but revenge nevertheless. Hatred and rivalry are also part of the equation. Khalid wants to lead in order to get even with those who manipulated his life. His quest is not ideological, so he will be a weaker leader. If he rises to power he will destroy TOVAIR. Eventually his targets will be Prince Hasan, Assoud, Chang, Li Chui, and to a lesser extent Jahan. We must exploit the divisions in their leadership."

"Are you telling me that we want Khalid to rise to the top?"

"Yeah. That's the goal. I met both Khalid and Chui. Khalid is full of hatred, Chui is full of ambition. We cannot trust either, but we can probably work with Chui to destabilize TOVAIR."

"Hope you are right. In the meantime, take a look at this morning's *Washington Post*. Roger Miles' story is front-page news. His resignation will probably come next. Hey, I just realize it's only 6:00 am, what are you doing in the office already?"

"Same thing you are, Mort. I'm trying to keep up with massive amounts of data coming in. There seems to be much movement, but little movement forward. Progress is slow when you try to anticipate trouble before it hits."

"Know what you mean. Technology is not the silver bullet the eggheads in the lab keep promising." Mort was skeptical of the power of the Wringer and other state-of-the-art technologies.

"If you cannot make any sense of data, I'm afraid nobody can. We are sunk if we do not avert the next attack. The closer we get to Election Day, the grimmer the scenarios." Morton was convinced TOVAIR planned major attacks to disrupt in the electoral process throughout the country. It was imperative to disrupt these terrorist plots before they could strike their targets.

Chapter 25
October Surprise

After hanging up, Clayton got himself a cup of coffee and glanced at the paper. Roger Miles had some shady business dealings prior to joining the Cumberland administration. During his nomination hearings, Senator Parks covered up his indiscretions in exchange for his loyalty to her foreign policy priorities. He planned to announce his resignation shortly. The news did not seem to affect Parks' standing in the polls. Her approval numbers continued to climb, and most political pundits were already writing Cumberland's political obituary.

Just a week before Election Day, only an act of Congress could derail Senator Parks' impending victory. The Senate Ethics Committee staff was working day and night. Their investigation progressed at a snail's pace. They dug for information, but they did not dig deep. Congress was not designed to operate fast; the founders intended this institution to be a deliberative body. The Senate was particularly deft in preserving its constitutional design.

"We need a breakthrough, soon." Clayton was going over a mountain of data that did not seem to shed any new light on TOVAIR's campaign to derail the presidential election. The latest attempt on one of the president's Cabinet members had come on the day Clayton and Perry arrived from their secret mission to Hong Kong.

Two snipers were caught with detailed maps of locations planned for Cumberland's schedule during the last week of the campaign. The suspects were not cooperative, and their false identities hid a long string of petty crimes, jail time, and travel to terrorist training camps in Latin America and Africa.

Three simultaneous attacks on members of Cumberland's security detail in the last four weeks added to Clayton's suspicion that TOVAIR's mole within the administration was ready to attempt a direct attack on the President. Clayton did not share his suspicion with his staff, but before they arrived at their desks, he had already sent them an e-mail requesting answers.

"TOVAIR is cherry-picking," he told his staff as he requested another round of data evaluations. "Keep looking for patterns. Drill further down. Who has access to the President's schedule? Go back to the same people you interviewed yesterday and ask the same questions again. Ask new questions. Go back to all Cabinet members, to all White House staff. Go all the way to the Chief of Staff. Don't take no for an answer; if you cannot see someone today, ask that they change their schedule. This investigation is top priority."

At the end of a long day of searching for answers without much success, a coded message from Li Chui arrived just as Clayton was getting ready to leave his office. A call to his boss followed without delay.

"Autumn plans to strike soon and will carry out final orders. Does this mean Autumn will try to kill the President?"

"Yeah. I think it's possible, Mort. We cannot rule it out. I'm on my way to the White House right now."

✲ ✲ ✲

Troy Hatfield was meticulous about his appearance. He favored white, starched, buttoned down shirts and wore ties with the colors of Yale, his alma mater. A strand of thin blond hair covered his prematurely balding head. With surgical precision, Hatfield placed his hair on the very same spot each morning. This ritual gave him a sense of self-confidence, just as the ritual of placing all papers on his desk inside a neat folder at the end of the day. He ate lunch at his desk and left the office late each night. He enjoyed having control over VIPs and important events. He was the best gatekeeper a president could have, because Hatfield knew how to anticipate problems and run a seamless operation.

"Hello Troy, mind if I come in?" Clayton's surprise visit distressed Troy Hatfield, particularly because it interrupted his review of papers destined for the overnight folder. The stack of memos for the president's signature was short this evening, and that lessened his annoyance over the unscheduled call.

"Well, good to see you Clayton. Come on in. I don't suppose you are coming for dinner? Didn't see your name on the guest list for tonight. I was getting ready to leave, but my plans for this evening can wait. What can I do for you?" Troy Hatfield knew that Clayton was not paying him a casual visit. The president had instructed his Chief of Staff to schedule Dr. Harcourt whenever he requested to see him. The president's schedule was full for the next two days, and Hatfield was trying to decide which appointment he would cancel to fit Clayton into the Oval Office calendar. "Need your help. I need to take another look at the personnel files for all White House personnel, particularly those individuals dealing with the president's schedule."

The request was unusual, but Dr. Clayton Harcourt seemed to operate outside of the normal flow of White House procedures. His relationship to the president was not a puzzle Hatfield wanted to solve. It was none of his business; he had plenty of daily pressures with his own job.

"Your staff was here this morning, and we provided all the information they requested. Anything in particular you are looking for?"

"Yeah. I want to see backgrounds of specific individuals, suppose that is in their vetting files and their background checks."

"I'll order the files first thing in the morning for you."

"I'm afraid that will not do, Troy. I need to see the files right now." Clayton's voice was firm, a negative answer did not seem like a viable option.

"The staff is gone, but let me call the security duty officer and get him up here with the files you need. Any names in particular?"

"All the members of the president's security detail and his kitchen cabinet." Clayton paused and looked Hatfield straight in the eye. "I'll need to see your file too."

Troy Hatfiled did not expect special treatment just because he had attended the same school as Clayton Harcourt. He understood official rules and knew that Clayton's request was far beyond his need to know. The tension around the White House had escalated in direct proportion to the polls and to the impending election. Although Hatfield relished his position, his secret wish was that Senator Parks would win, so that he could retire. After nearly thirty years of service, Hatfield was ready to get back to his little farm in the Virginia countryside. He placed the call to retrieve the files, and he offered Clayton a drink.

"Coffee would be great. This is going to be a long night. Mind if I work right here in your office?"

"Not at all, not at all." Troy Hatfiled did not like to share his office with anyone, even on a temporary basis. He abhorred the idea of anyone sitting behind his desk, messing up his sense of order.

"I think you'll be more comfortable working in the conference room. There is more room there to spread out the files. Be glad to stay with you and help out in any way."

"Not necessary, Troy. Thanks anyway." The two men walked down the hall. Clayton hoped that whatever he would discover in the files piled high on the large mahogany table would not shatter his first impression of Troy Hatfield, a decent man.

✲ ✲ ✲

Three hours into his review of the White House files, Clayton finished the pot of coffee and began to read a thin file. It was Cory Black's FBI background check. She grew up in San Francisco. Her parents were missionaries and her father moved the family to Hong Kong when Cory was ten years old. She attended UC Berkeley and majored in communications with minors in Mandarin and music.

A few years after working for the *San Francisco Chronicle*, she returned to Hong Kong as an independent correspondent, where she resided for three years. There was a blank in her file for this period, but an incomplete address was listed at the bottom of the page. Clayton jotted it down to check it against other data. Ms. Black was divorced and lived alone in Foggy Bottom. She did not belong to any service clubs or professional organizations. She seldom traveled outside the United States and had not returned to China for over twenty years. Clayton checked his watch. Maybe it was not too late to pay her a visit. Her phone rang twice and she delivered a familiar voice message.

"We are unable to take your call. Please leave your name and number. We will get back to you as soon as possible."

Clayton placed a call to his office and left a secure message on Mort's cell phone. He then handed the stack of files back to the duty officer and headed to the Executive Building.

Cory Black had a corner office on the third floor of the new Executive Building. Her office door was ajar. She was reading a thick report her back to the door and her bare feet on her desk. Without knocking, Clayton walked in casually and quietly approached her desk.

"Good to see dedicated public servants at work late at night."

Cory Black jumped out of her chair and spun around. Karate training kept her trim and fit.

"You scared me to death! What are you doing here?"

"Never sit with your back to the door." He was grinning broadly. "You never know who might walk in and scare you to death."

She straightened her skirt, put her shoes back on, and walked around her desk. "Still don't know what brings you here at this late hour."

Clayton looked relaxed as he sat down on the leather couch and put his feet on a red ottoman. The burgundy shade in the Oriental carpet matched the color of Cory Black's tailored suit. She poured herself some water without offering him any.

"It's been a long day, and I just finished a meeting next door. Saw the light in your office and thought I should stop by to say hello and put my feet up."

Cory Black sat across from him, took her glasses off, and shook her head. "Dr. Harcourt, I don't believe you. You do not seem to be the type that just wonders around and pops in just to put his feet up."

He grinned again. The grin bothered her. Clayton Harcourt never smiled during meetings. Now he was beaming. She did not trust him. This late night visit gave her a creepy feeling, but she decided to play along. She smiled and scratched her forehead, then pointed her finger at him. Her smile got a bit wider. Her teeth were even but a shade too light for her pale skin.

"Oh, I think you are here for a reason and I just figured out what this visit is all about," she paused. "I think you are here to find out if I have any secret sources up on the Hill. You are on fishing expedition. You are interested in digging up details on the Senate investigation." Cory Black straightened her back, but still looked diminutive against the wings of the Queen Anne chair.

"By the way, I hear you are quite an angler."

Clayton ignored the personal remark, and smiled. He looked around the room and fixed his eyes on a picture of Cory Back with two Senators and Sanford Gillman. He made a mental note to pass on the information to a contact close to the Senate Ethics Committee investigation. The pictures covering the walls of her office displayed her wide circle of influential contacts around town. She moved across party lines with professional ease and was highly skilled in the art of horse-trading.

"Tell me about your secret sources."

"C'mon. You know better than ask. First, I don't have secret sources on the Hill. Second, if I did, why would I want to share them with you?"

"Because, we are on the same team. Are we not?" He was deadly serious.

"Of course we are." Her mischievous smile seemed to invite Clayton to join her in game of cat and mouse. "But you have your turf and I have mine."

She paused, put her glasses back on, and proceeded to lecture Clayton about politics inside the Beltway. She had contacts in the media and on Capitol Hill and kept her rolodex up to date.

"You and I know that in this town turf matters. My portfolio is domestic policy, and I work very hard to stay on top of everything I need to know. I also keep my nose out of foreign and defense policy. That would be your bailiwick, if I'm not mistaken. The division of labor in our executive branch is replicated up on the Hill. I am sure you know that your contacts on the Hill are not the same as mine. You also must know that some of the Senate staff I know well has access to classified information coming out of the Ethics Committee. Now, that could be of interest to you." She emphasized "that," paused, and waited to see his facial reaction, but there was none. She decided to put one more chip on the table.

"Now, suppose there is some information I want to know about matters of foreign intelligence. I might have something from the Ethics Committee for you and you might have something I could use. We could swap information for our mutual benefit. That would make us even."

Clayton grinned. He got up to stretch his legs and as he sat back down, a CD on top of a stack of books on a side table caught his eye.

"Antonio Vivalvi, The Four Seasons." He paused and scanned the next couple of lines: *Concerto No.1, "Spring"; "Concerto No. 2, "Summer"; Concerto No.3, Autumn; Concerto No. 4, Winter.*" He fixed his eyes on Cory Black. She smiled and was about to say something, but Clayton interrupted. He was no longer grinning. He held the CD in his left hand, while tapping it lightly with his right forefinger.

"Vivalvi, my favorite, you enjoy classical music?"

"Very much so. I studied a little music in school. Long time ago." She blushed.

"Really? Who is your favorite composer?"

Cory Black did not trust Clayton but her defenses were down. Classical music was her passion, and she blurted out:

"Actually, Vivaldi. Were you serious when you said he is also your favorite?"

"Absolutely." He grinned again and made her queasy. "See, you and I have more in common than you think." He still held the CD in his right hand and was now tapping it against his knee. She wanted to get up and grab it from him. It was so distracting. As if he was reading her mind, he set the CD back on top of the books. When he addressed her by her first name, he unsettled her even more than when he fidgeted with the CD.

"Cory, you and I will have to take some time to know each other a little better one of these days, but first, where were we?" Then, answering his own question he continued, "Oh yeah. We were talking about swapping stories, or rather information I should say. A win-win situation. OK, I'll start. What I want to know is when the Senate Ethics Committee will release its report?"

"You must be kidding! Nobody inside the Beltway knows that. The best estimates I hear put the date right after the election; others think it will be a year or two at best. My turn?"

"Not so fast, Ms. Black, you have not told me anything new. The timetable favors the Parks campaign. What do you plan to do when she wins?"

The question caught her by surprise, but she recovered quickly.

"I know a lot of people in town. For now, I want to keep my options open. Maybe write a book; maybe get into the lobbying business, maybe consulting. Who knows?"

Clayton looked at his watch and got off the couch. "Well, I best get on my way. It's getting late."

"Not so fast, Clayton." She seemed to put special emphasis on his first name. "I still get to ask my question."

He grinned. Right then she knew he would not tell her much, but she asked anyway, just in case.

"How was your recent trip to Hong Kong?"

"Splendid. Got to do a little sightseeing. Ever been there?"

She wondered why he ended up asking all the questions. He wondered if she would tell him the truth. He wanted to know how she had found out about his secret mission with Perry. He also wanted to know whether she was working alone or with someone else at the White House. Those questions would have to wait. Maybe he should have stayed and worked his way through the entire stack of files.

Cory Black was not about to tell the truth. She wondered why he asked her about living in Hong Kong. He had no way of knowing about her past. Maybe he was digging up missing information from her files. Maybe during his recent trip to Hong Kong he found a link to her past. She was certain that there was no trail leading her to her best friend. Perhaps he knew something. She brushed the thought aside. This was not the time to let paranoia sneak into her world.

"*Don't be silly. Just stay focused*," she told herself, and then said, "No, I do not travel much, my work is right here."

"You'd like Hong Kong. Great town. You should visit some time."

"Well, I must get going. Good night, Ms. Black. Don't work too hard. Get some rest."

When she heard her last name, she became uneasy once again about Clayton's demeanor. Cory Black did not sleep much that night. She worked until midnight and went home still thinking about Clayton's last comments and his grin. She did not notice the blue sedan parked across from her apartment. Clayton's visit meant that she had to move fast to execute her mission. She decided to revise her plans. The logistics did not have to change much, but she needed approval for changing the timetable. She sat at her home computer and sent a coded request. The reply was quick and brief: "Proceed as you see fit."

On his way home, Clayton checked his inbox. Morton had called back to let him know that a team was on its way to Virginia Avenue to pay Ms. Black's apartment a short visit. A second message, just said: "Mission accomplished. We got some evidence. Will examine right away. You should have a report by early morning."

✲ ✲ ✲

The election was less than one week away when Secretary Miles held a press conference to announce his resignation. The announcement was drowned by a news flash from the Oval Office. Clayton and Morton sat in Troy Hatfield's office as President Cumberland's Communications Director announced to the nation that a first round of executive branch investigations had just uncovered evidence of close links between a high-ranking member of the administration and TOVAIR. The official was taken into custody early that morning, after coded files in her home computer revealed a plot to kill the President two days before the election and coordinate various attacks against key U.S. officials to disrupt the presidential election.

All networks cancelled their scheduled programming to report the story. The White House pool of reporters crowded the executive briefing room, and peppered the media director with questions about the person's name and position, the findings of the investigation, and the consequences for a normal election.

"Investigators are now questioning the President's Advisor for Domestic Policy, Ms. Cory Black, about her relationship to Lyn Chang, her former roommate in Hong Kong. Ms. Chang is the daughter of one of TOVAIR's leaders and she is also in U.S. custody."

The evidence linking Cory Black to the suspected "Autumn" mole was growing by the minute. Clayton's elite investigative team was interrogating the presidential advisor while continuing to peel thick layers of secrets from her files.

"What did Ms. Black's computer files reveal about her involvement with the alleged attack on the President?"

"No comment. Next."

"Does Ms. Black have access to legal counsel?" The CNN reporter wanted to know if Ms. Black's rights were protected while in custody. The media and academic elites were obsessed with the rights of suspected terrorists. After the attacks in previous weeks, public safety was a priority for most voters.

"She will." The White House Communications Director pointed to another reporter in the back of the room.

"Could you comment on any potential attacks? If the objective is to disrupt our electoral process, could we expect to see Senator Parks in the list of targets? If so, is the Senator at risk?"

"We have sent updated risk assessment reports to all cabinet members and elected representatives on Capitol Hill. At this point, we cannot rule anyone in or out. Last question, please."

The Communications Director pointed to an eager reporter who had managed to elbow his way from the back to the front of the room.

"Is this your October surprise? Do you expect that this announcement will help President Cumberland narrow the gap in the polls? Do you expect the election to tighten in the coming days?"

The White House Office of Communications director was a veteran reporter and former prosecutor. At 6'4", he was a towering presence during the daily media briefings. He was not camera shy and knew the secret of looking sharp for a national TV audience. He spoke with aplomb to rest the case and calm a nervous public.

"Those were three questions. First, this is not a White House October surprise; it is a terrorist plot. Our administration has been working day and night to protect our nation and keep all Americans and their elected officials safe. For months, we have been following leads pointing in the direction someone at the highest level of our government who was collaborating with TOVAIR to disrupt our electoral process. The capture of Ms. Black and the evidence connecting her to our enemies will prevent attacks on our citizens."

"The timing of this announcement has nothing to do with Americans going to the polls in a week, which leads me to the second and third parts of your question. It is up to the American people to decide who will be our next President. Americans know President Cumberland's record of service to our country. He is a dedicated patriot determined to secure our homeland and preserve the values that keep us free. His record speaks for itself. Thank you ladies and gentleman."

"Well done. The boss will approve. He usually does not care to watch the daily news conference down the hall, but I am sure that he tuned in for this one." Troy Hatfield looked at his watch, checked the presidential schedule, and led Clayton and Mort to the Oval Office. "The president is ready to see you now."

Chapter 26

A Delicate Lure

Mack Cumberland congratulated Clayton for exposing Cory Black as the "Autumn" mole. When the President first heard about the threat of a mole inside his own administration, he did not have a shred of suspicion. The FBI had vetted his inner circle with meticulous care. He trusted the integrity of his team without question. At times, he was leery of their advice; always, he respected their views. He figured the culprit was a man, probably one dealing in matters of foreign policy. More than likely it was a political appointee at the assistant secretary level; all Cabinet members and senior advisors had endured extensive background checks. Not a single presidential advisor had failed the FBI's thorough check before stepping into the White House. Not once did President Cumberland suspect his Domestic Policy Advisor, known around town for her deft moves on the Hill. Now her contacts might suggest something more sinister than anything the Senate Ethics Committee was willing to uncover.

"Hear anything new about the Senate investigation?"

The president's question did not surprise Clayton, who had asked his staff for a briefing on the matter just before coming to see him. The Senate, as intended by the Founders, was moving at a snail's pace. The Ethics Committee Chair, Senator Thomas, was a close friend of Senator Parks and was not about to divulge any information that could hurt her impending election. Staff leaks were a common practice in congressional investigations, but not this time around. Senator Thomas had buttoned up his staff members like a concerned parent pushing a stroller in a cold winter night. Not a word was leaking out, zip, nothing. The committee findings, wrapped tight, saw no light between the Senate chamber and the beehive of reporters toiling in vain to be the first in line to break the story. Bloggers speculated day and night filling cyber space with conspiracies and innuendo. Evidence and facts were hard to find.

"Cory has many contacts on the Hill. Do you think anyone there might be working with her? Is it possible that even Senator Parks' staff might be involved in any of the plans you just uncovered?"

Before Morton or Clayton could answer, the president added, "Doesn't the congressional staff undergo the same background checks our staff goes through before coming on board?"

President Cumberland did not want to think that Senator Parks might be personally involved in the plot against him and other members of his administration, but his line of questioning gave away his fear.

"We are not ruling anyone or anything out, Mr. President."

Mort confirmed that the investigative team was going over Ms. Black's computer files at work and running tests of their findings in both her home and office files through the Wringer to unveil any potential connections to congressional members and staff and individuals in other public and private institutions. The Senate, in its finite wisdom had forged a truce between the advocates of openness and members intent on keeping the Ethics Committee investigations under wraps. Senators were divided along neat partisan lines on the issue.

✡ ✡ ✡

Senators supporting the President argued that Americans had a right to know the findings of the committee and should have a front seat to watch the proceedings via C-Span. The argument was sound on grounds of the impending presidential campaign. Voters would be electing a president and deserved full disclosure of their government's accountability. Senators supporting Senator Parks managed to peel support away from moderate colleagues across the aisle, contending the findings would jeopardize national security. Ironically, the president's party supported a strong defense, while Senator Parks' s party platform advocated sharp reductions in funding for national security.

The justification for secrecy was far more elitist than the apparent concern for the safety of the nation. Senator Parks supporters argued that the American people would not understand the complexities of the matter. This was not a new claim. For some public officials elitism came easy. Ensconced in the pomp and circumstance of their positions, they underestimated the average citizen.

President Cumberland was not willing to give up the fight for the truth. The power of filibuster had won the day, but the war raged on. He was determined to win it. He got up, walked to his credenza, and picked up a picture of his eight grandkids. Pointing to the happy faces, he smiled.

"I will continue to fight regardless of the outcome of this election for them and for all future generations. Freedom is in peril. The threat from our foreign enemies pales in comparison to the threat from within. When corruption creeps into the system and the highest bidder puts a price on our institutions, we are on a path of self-destruction." He paused. Still holding the family photo, he walked to the window facing the Washington monument.

Mack Cumberland was a simple man. He had faith that God was the captain of his ship and the architect of his house. The president had navigated rough seas and had always sailed into a safe harbor. He had built a house with a strong foundation that withstood inclement weather. He never felt alone. He knew that his Creator guided his decisions ever since he stepped into the White House, the people's house. He was a mere occupant of this venerable home for a brief time. Alone in his office, he often prayed for the wisdom to make the right choices. He was optimistic about the future of the nation and had a deep appreciation for the lessons of the revolutionary war.

"Benjamin Franklin warned us that a republic can only survive, if we can keep it. General Washington did not waver on that cold Christmas night in 1776."

Mack Cumberland turned to the two men who remained in his shrinking circle of trusted advisors. His eyes were moist, his voice firm.

"Fellows, your loved ones fought and died to preserve and protect the legacy of our Founders. Both of you have paid the high price of freedom. In the last decade, another generation full of promise sacrificed for the same reason quiet men took the battle to the enemy across the Delaware, the Rhine, and the Mekong Delta. None of them died in vain." President Cumberland set his grandkids picture back on the credenza. A thin smile crossed his lips.

"Gentlemen, I trust you understand where I am coming from. Our families share a tradition of service that goes back many generations. You are my brothers, and I appreciate your loyalty to country. I am grateful for your personal loyalty to me, but I want to remind you we are a nation of laws and not of men. I know you will do what is right for our country."

Mort and Clayton walked out of the Oval Office in silence. They understood the president's order; within the limits of the law, they now had a green light to dig as deep as necessary to find answers. Only five days away from Election Day, they knew they had to proceed with caution. On normal Friday afternoons, Mort and Clayton got together for a drink at the end of the day to recap the week's events and plan strategy for the upcoming week. On this day, both men left the White House and drove to their respective offices to join their teams in the war theatre.

The notion of a war room was now obsolete. The InterIntel war theatre was a global network of real time interactive virtual labs interconnected twenty-four hours a day, where analysts, intelligence field officers, investigators, and officers in various agencies at the federal, state, and local levels of government exchanged information and analyzed data. Within this network, only a selected group of individuals had access to the Wringer outputs. This elite team was now under direct orders from the President of the United States to use all available tools to connect the dots. It was not the first time in American history when the most creative minds were encouraged to roam free and deploy their imagination to defend the nation.

✲ ✲ ✲

During WWII, Clayton's grandfather and a small platoon of unlikely soldiers became Eisenhower's powerful weapon of deception against the German *Wehrmacht.* They took the fight straight to the Nazi enemy pretending to be three regiments of the 9th infantry division. They landed on Utah Beach the morning after D-Day. Their code name was Troutfly. Their artistry included fake artillery fire, scripted radio transmissions, and sound effects. The original plan did not work out. Instead, they joined the 82d Airborne on a crowded beachhead fighting the enemy to the last man standing. When orders came to head inland, Clayton's grandfather stayed with the brave men leading the charge against the Germans. He recorded the brutality of the battlefield in his journal. The vivid imagery defied the passage of time. The smell of death and the blast of German artillery punctuated with the rattle of anti-aircraft fire filled the stained pages written in a deep foxhole.

Clayton's grandfather had been a prolific writer, a famous novelist who never recounted his bloody journey through Normandy. He never talked about his work during World War II. He had been a quiet professional. His grandson learned about his valor when the records of his unorthodox service were declassified. After his grandfather's death, Clayton discovered the old man's diary buried under faded family photos. Some torn out pages kept secrets away from prying eyes, as if the author decided to keep parts of the story from ever seeing daylight.

✲ ✲ ✲

The 360-degree screens in Clayton's InterIntel headquarters enabled his staff to monitor incoming intelligence analysis, events, and threat scenarios around the globe, around the clock. Data gathered from Cory Black's ongoing interrogation had priority routing, which enabled analysts to link findings to FBI background files for individuals not flagged under normal high-risk potential terrorist lists. Initial analyses uncovered a close link between Cory Black and Senator Parks. Both women sat on the board of directors of a local charity, The Children's Future Fund. This organization raised money in the United

States for children in war-torn countries and provided a credible cover to funnel funds to less noble causes. InterIntel had discovered increasing fund flows to the Kahnpur region, where the Tansari brothers centered their arms smuggling operations for TOVAIR. Many of these fund transfers coincided with The Children's Future Fund fundraising campaigns across the United States, Canada, and Europe.

Since authorities had confiscated the first shipment of several hundred shoulder-fired missiles intended for secret locations near North American airports, the Tansari brothers had managed to execute operation Harun without much trouble. Increased border surveillance had not completely closed off porous entry points along the U.S.-Canada border. The hardware was now in place to launch planned civilian attacks on Election Day. With Autumn's arrest, TOVAIR aborted the mission to kill the President. In spite of a breakdown of communications to carry out orders for attacks against civilian and U.S. official targets, Autumn's agent received orders to proceed with the rest of the plan.

"She is not talking. She probably has a backup plan; someone else is still out there able to execute orders."

Clayton handed Morton the latest interrogation report. Morton glanced at the printout and set his glasses on the conference table. Both men looked exhausted from lack of sleep and the strain of the last few days. Weak evidence pointed to links among

Cory Black, Senator Parks, The Children's Future Fund, and the Tansari brothers. Clayton had a hunch that Cory Black and the Senator had more in common than their official ties to the children's charitable organization.

"Is there a way to get to someone on the Senate Ethics Committee to talk?"

Morton hoped that a staff member would come forward to disclose the committee's findings and shed some light on the proceedings behind closed doors. He knew that during a peak political season someone might be willing to break the silence and reveal the workings of the committee.

"We have tried all possible official contacts. There is one last avenue we might be able to pursue," Clayton paused. He knew that crossing the fine line of using the media to bridge information gaps was a treacherous venture, but he was willing to take the risk.

✲ ✲ ✲

The White House Communications Director kept a thick file of friendly reporters. He dialed the number highlighted in his fat Rolodex and asked Matt, a young investigative reporter from Eagle News to pursue "the story all the way." The request was unusual but Matt was eager to prove his mettle and dismiss claims that he owed his job to his father's prominent position on the Hill.

Matt Thomas' future at Eagle News was going to be on a fast track if he could only break the story of his father's Ethics Committee investigation. He would breach his father's trust, but he would do so to reclaim his own place in his chosen profession. He would finally break the filial cord and strike out on his own. The incentive to pursue the story in exchange of joining the elite pool of White House reporters was enough to get Matt Thomas moving fast to retrieve the information he needed to expose his father's protégée and derail her imminent move into the Oval Office.

Senator Parks arrived at the small reception in her honor and greeted guests and her hosts, Senator and Mrs. Thomas, with the charm and poise she had learned to perfect during her meteoric rise to a leadership role in the U.S. Senate. She looked confident in a bright red suit with black trim. Her double-digit lead in the presidential polls seemed to be narrowing. President Cumberland continued his unrelenting attacks against her record. Negative ads worked and news of renewed terror threats helped his campaign. Her opponent seemed to be gaining ground ever since the press conference announcing the arrest of a suspected TOVAIR mole. Cory Black worked right under the president's nose, and her arrest gave Senator Parks much reason to worry. She had met Cory Black at the home of a mutual Georgetown friend, Sanford Gillman.

The two women soon found out that they had much in common. Both were Berkeley graduates, had participated in anti-war demonstrations during the

Vietnam War, and had moved to Washington early in their careers to carve a niche in the nation's capital. While Priscilla Parks polished her image to enter a career in politics, Cory Black softened her political rhetoric and joined a reputable newspaper to establish her credentials as a mainstream reporter. When their paths crossed during one of Gillman's notorious parties, their host suggested they join an organization he had founded, The Children's Future Fund. The two women complied without realizing that the organization was set up with seed money from TOVAIR.

Cory Black learned of this connection through her friend Lyn Chang, and decided to serve on the Executive Board to gain control over the flow of funds. She convinced Senator Parks to join the Board and requested her unquestionable support for selecting recipient organizations across the globe in exchange for a hefty percentage of the proceeds, which were routed back to Priscilla Parks election coffers through Americans For Fairness and other friendly organizations.

Senator Parks stayed at the Thomas reception long enough to circulate among the select guests and thank each one of her major campaign contributors for their support. She excused herself before guests moved from the library to the dining room; her schedule showed yet another campaign stop at the end of a grueling day. Her chauffeur drove her straight to her Watergate apartment. Her husband was campaigning on her behalf in California. She looked forward to a quiet evening before leaving for a last round of speeches in key mid-Western states in just a few hours.

✲ ✲ ✲

President Cumberland boarded Air Force One after a major swing across Western states and was heading to the Midwest. His strategy for the last days of the campaign was to shadow the trail of his opponent. Wherever Senator Parks went, President Cumberland followed with a strong message.

"My record is open for all to see. My opponent hides behind a congressional ethics investigation. Sealed records hold information that might connect public officials to a deadly network of terrorist intent on destroying our values and institutions. The American people deserve a better deal from their government."

The president urged voters to pressure Congress for the release of their findings before Election Day. He reminded his audiences about the very survival of the republic. His speeches were almost a lesson in American history. He quoted the Founders and recalled the tough decisions many of his predecessors had to make in times of war. He called for a close reading of the Constitution.

"We are a nation of laws, not men. The secrecy of your elected representatives on Capitol Hill now compounds the ongoing threats of terrorist attacks against innocent civilians."

The president had turned his campaign into an indictment of congressional ineptitude and obfuscation. He spoke with passion and determination to preserve the legacy of a great nation. His stump speech was getting traction. The crowds grew larger.

✡ ✡ ✡

Clayton remained in his office throughout the night and caught one or two catnaps while his staff continued to search for missing links. Before daybreak, one of his assistants woke him up with a fresh cup of coffee and the latest news. A courier had just dropped off three computer disks from an unidentified source with a message to watch the 6 am news. As Clayton's team began to analyze the content of the newly arrived information, a newscaster announced that an unidentified source had just delivered a copy of the transcripts of the Senate Ethics Committee investigation to federal investigators.

Later that morning, the media reported that federal authorities were now analyzing the transcripts and would release information to the public as soon as investigators could confirm the authenticity of the material.

Clayton drove up to Senator Thomas's office just a few minutes after he read the first assessment. The evidence linking Senator Parks to Cory Black's nefarious activities remained inconclusive, but the official transcripts did suggest the two women had recent meetings. The phone logs in Senator Parks's office and Cory Black's cell phone records revealed a pattern of frequent communications between them, particularly after the Senator received campaign contributions from Americans For Fairness. So far, Cory Black was not cooperating with investigators. Clayton was intent on getting Senator Thomas to corner Senator Parks into telling the truth.

Senator Thomas had a reputation for being a hard-nose negotiator, who made full use of his seniority and rhetorical skills. He twisted colleagues' arms hard to get his way, and would not let go until he extracted a pound of flesh for each of his demands. His tactics worked with junior Senators and staff, but many of his senior colleagues disliked such unseemly behavior. His peers considered him a lightweight, a man of little intellectual depth. Political cartoonists loved to depict Senator Thomas as a street fighter, a barking dog with no teeth, a sheep in wolf's clothes. For all of his rough behavior on the floor of the Senate, he never once introduced a piece of significant legislation. His most ardent supporters were labor unions, anti-war activists, and radical college students. His family trust kept his campaign coffers full, relieving him of the need to campaign or raise funds to keep his job.

"Come on in Mr. Harcourt, make yourself at home."

Senator Thomas greeted Clayton putting emphasis on the "Mr." The title of "Dr." always made him feel inferior and he was not about to let that feeling creep up on this occasion. The tall man now sitting across his desk looked too secure in his own skin to be intimidated. Senator Thomas knew that dismissing this character would not be a simple matter of talking tough. He measured Clayton's demeanor and figured this man was an opponent, who would not go away any time soon. He looked like a man who knew what he wanted and knew how to get it. This "Dr." looked like a difficult customer.

"Senator, I appreciate your time. Clearly, you must have an idea as to why I am here." Clayton paused and handed Senator Thomas a copy of the transcript from the Senate Ethics Committee investigation. "My office has already determined the documents we received earlier this morning are legitimate. I believe you recognize the evidence on this page."

The transcript excerpt addressed a question to Senator Parks regarding any contacts she might have had with officials who knew Sanford Gillman.

Senator Parks: "Many officials in this town knew Mr. Gillman. I cannot think of any in particular."

Question: "Senator, do you know Ms. Cory Black?"

Senator Parks: "Well, ah. Let me think. She is at the White House. Deals with domestic policy, I believe. I am sure my staff has dealt with her."

Question: "Senator, do you serve on the Executive Board of The Children's Future Fund?"

Senator Parks: "Yes."

Question: "Does Cory Black serve on that Executive Board as well?"

Senator Parks: "Well yes. Now that you bring it up. Of course. That board meets twice a year and I have missed the last two meeting due to my campaign schedule. I do not know the other members very well, including Ms. Black."

Senator Thomas recalled how agitated Senator Parks had become under this line of questioning from a partisan colleague who kept bringing up Ms. Black. At the time, Senator Thomas had dismissed the questions as irrelevant. Now, he wondered if there was a smoking gun and decided to keep his observations private. He leaned back in his leather chair and set his reading glasses down. He handed Clayton the transcript back.

"This is a leaked document. I can assure you that the Senate will investigate and find those responsible for this criminal act. My staff does not leak to the press or anyone else." The Senator's face was turning beet red, his anger rising with each word. He continued, "Our investigation is thorough. I will not allow leaks to jeopardize our work. I trust that your office will keep this information confidential until we complete our findings."

"Senator, our office is not in the business of broadcasting confidential information or obstructing justice. Our business is to find the truth and protect our nation from enemies within and outside our borders."

Clayton paused to let Senator Thomas digest his message. The Senator looked somber as Clayton explained how Cory Black had implicated Senator Parks in a scheme to funnel funds through The Children's

Future Fund to organizations contributing to the presidential campaign.

"That's not all. We also have evidence that The Children's Future Fund is funneling funds to organizations used by TOVAIR's network to supply weapons to sleeper cells in our country. Many of these cells are ready to target civilians and disrupt the presidential election."

Clayton showed Senator Thomas a summary of findings in the latest Wringer report and then popped the question that brought him to Senator's office.

"Senator, will you help us communicate to Senator Parks that it is in the best interest of our nation for her to clear this matter once and for all?"

Clayton appealed to Thomas's own credibility, his chance to make a mark on the history of the United States Senate by preserving the honor and legacy of his revered institution.

"Senator Thomas, your country needs you. We are at war and the enemy knows no boundaries of decency. They target vulnerable officials and use them to execute their evil plans. Perhaps, they have used Senator Parks. Perhaps they are using other members of Congress and the administration to destroy our way of life. In the next couple of days, many Americans will perish because the Senate chooses not to act. You have the power to avert a national tragedy. Convince Senator Parks to tell what she knows before it is too late. Sir, the American people will be grateful for your courage and leadership."

No one had ever spoken to Senator Thomas this way. No one ever mentioned courage and leadership as part of his character. He liked the sound of these words. He could envision his legacy as a referendum on his public service. He would no longer be the butt of jokes around town. His name could rise to national preeminence. Maybe even a run for president might be in the cards.

✲ ✲ ✲

The two InterIntel analysts assigned to the Cory Black interrogation submitted their report to Clayton just as he returned to his office. Interrogators informed Ms. Black that Senator Parks had implicated her in a scheme to funnel funds to finance her presidential campaign through The Children's Future Fund. At the same time, Ms. Black learned that Lyn Chang was now collaborating with investigators and had implicated her in funding TOVAIR's secret activities in the U.S. and abroad. Evidence of arms purchases in India made with diverted funds from The Children's Future Fund corroborated Ms. Chang's claims.

Clayton set the trap of the prisoner's dilemma with the same skill he presented a dry fly to a reluctant trout. He knew that when two suspects are taken into custody separately, each has a choice to confess or not confess. He was certain that both Cory Black and Senator Parks were guilty of supporting and abetting the enemy, but the evidence against them was not adequate to convict them at a trial. He instructed his staff to give the women three alternatives. If both do not confess, they will both face minor campaign finance charges leading to jail time. If they both confess, both will be prosecuted for treason with less than the most severe sentence, the death penalty. If one confesses and the other does not, the confessor will receive the most lenient sentence for turning state's evidence while the other will face the death penalty.

Cory Black was not prepared to make any decisions after three days with little sleep and a barrage of questions from two sets of interrogators. The friendly ones offered food and some rest; the others were rude and did not seem to care that she was after all the president's Senior Advisor for Domestic Policy. The friendly cops had just left after telling her that Senator Parks and her old pal, Lyn Chang had met with investigators and had implicated her. She now had to decide whether to confess or not confess. Her interrogators would be returning for an answer soon. She decided to put off any decision until her head cleared up. She stretched out on the hard cot and stared at the white ceiling. Her cell looked surreal. She had seen such Spartan quarters in movies; the cement floor, the stainless toilet and sink were a stark contrast to her plush décor at home. Home seemed so far away. She did not belong here and wondered when she would wake up from this nightmare.

Senator Parks took the call from Senator Thomas on her way to the airport. He wanted to meet with her right away. That was not possible, she explained, because she was on her way to Chicago. Her speech in Iowa was a success and she planed to attend two functions in the Windy City before heading back to Washington.

"Cancel Chicago. We need to talk right away."

Senator Thomas was a trusted friend. His voice sounded grave. He had never used that tone of voice before and Priscilla Parks did not want to upset such a loyal fundraiser. She glanced at the latest poll numbers from Illinois and scrolled down to see the breakdown for the two districts in which she planned to speak. Her lead was no longer in the double digits, but it was enough to win.

"Okay, dear. I'll change my schedule. I'll see you in a couple of hours."

She wondered if the report of the leaked documents had set off Senator Thomas and she searched for the latest news items. The leaks from the Senate Ethics Committee were generating a frenzy of media activity. She speculated that her colleague wanted to discuss media strategies for the last stretch of the campaign. There was no need for nasty surprises. If her staff and his staff were on the same page, if Thomas was able to do some damage control, all would be fine. She smiled as she thought how much she enjoyed being at the center of attention of her colleagues in the Senate. Senator Thomas always looked after her well-being. No doubt, his call was to alert her of some possible danger ahead. The last days of a campaign were like the first and last days of a war, the risk of casualties was highest.

Chapter 27
Fatal Mistake

The coded message Tom Munroe received from Khalid Hassan kept him awake all night. His instructions were to deliver the message at a specific time to his assigned prison contact. The exchange of information was to take place during the first exercise break during the following morning. Tom memorized the coded message and decided that it was time to risk it all. He had only deciphered part of the message, but that was enough for him to spring into action. After breakfast, on his way to the gym, Tom Munroe slipped into a phone booth and made the call. When he hung up, he knew someone was watching and would report his action. He also knew he had done the right thing. The truth was going to set Tom free.

Clayton had spent the night in his office and was ready to get some fresh air before the daily morning briefing, when his secure phone line transmitted Tom Munroe's message. The decoded message was chilling. TOVAIR was activating sleeper cells in selected NFL cities across the country. The target date was Election Day. Detailed instructions would reach the leader of each cell via e-mail. It was clear that the purpose of the terror campaign was to strike at a nerve center of American politics, the presidential election.

Only minutes after InterIntel analysts had deciphered the entire message, the guard who had just received the same message in a prison gym, walked out to the hallway and placed a call. When he hung up the phone, his boss summoned him to the main office, where FBI agents were waiting to take him into custody.

* * *

Secretary of State Vivian Lacey called Alex Keynes III into her office to inform him that his request to be transferred to Cairo as Consul General had been denied. She wanted to relay the news personally at the risk of compounding the impropriety of her personnel actions. The Foreign Service panel in charge of the review of applications had denied the request, but the Secretary had insisted that the Mr. Keynes record be reconsidered. Her undiplomatic maneuver did not sway evaluators. Mr. Keynes record kept him from receiving his coveted assignment in Egypt. An internal investigation on Mr. Keynes conduct was still in progress after nearly three months. There was no end in sight to the collection of evidence, but at least the State Department kept the dirty little secrets of its own out of the reach of other government agencies. The panel decided that until the end of that investigation, Mr. Keynes was to remain in his present post, a non-descript assignment researching the history of ethnic conflict in the Sudan.

"Alex, I did my very best. You'll just have to sit tight until the Personnel Office completes the internal investigation."

Alex Keynes III did not like to hear the Secretary's excuse. He knew Vivian Lacey had the power to stop that investigation in its tracks. She needed to keep appearances with the Cumberland administration, but his needs came before her interests. Alex Keynes was not about to give up on his plan to leave the country within the next four days.

"I'm afraid your explanation is not good enough, Madam Secretary." He paused and taking full advantage of the weight of his threat, he continued, "Let me remind you that I am able and willing to disclose your relationship to Senator Parks the minute I walk out of your office." He pulled his cell phone out of his pocket to emphasize the point. "My contacts in the media deliver." He did not add, "*unlike you.*"

Keynes did not have a chance to continue with his diatribe. Vivian Lacey shot right back: "Don't you dare blackmail me, Keynes. Do not tempt me to expose you for what you are. You are pushing me a bit far."

Vivian Lacey had agreed to help Alex Keynes III circumvent the Foreign Service Assignments panel before she realized that he had set up a trap to implicate her in a conspiracy to undermine the Cumberland administration. He had gotten hold of documents showing her close collaboration with Senator Parks's office. He had acquired a secret memo that compromised her future. The memo guaranteed Vivian Lacey a prominent place in the Parks's administration in exchange of her support for negotiations with TOVAIR's leadership, a position President Cumberland opposed publicly. Now Alex Keynes threatened her career and she was not about to let that happen.

"Madam Secretary, you have much more to lose than I, if you choose to disclose the preliminary findings of the investigation. I suggest you forget your lame threat. I suggest you figure out an action plan to get me assigned to Cairo before it is too late."

He held the cell phone up to remind her of the possible consequences of a call to Beltway jackals, who were eager to chew up and spit out their prey without remorse.

Vivian Lacey agreed to give Alex Keynes III a temporary duty assignment to the Sudan effective in two days. It would take the State Department that long to process his travel request to study ethnic conflict out in the field. The timetable would work just fine for Alex Keynes. He would be leaving Washington according to schedule. For now, his plan seemed to be working out. The next couple of days were crucial for his survival, and he was determined to execute his instructions with surgical precision.

✲ ✲ ✲

Tom Munroe noticed the absence of the guard who had been his contact for all communication from Khalid, and knew Clayton had received his message. He also knew that he was a marked man. It was difficult to know who was working for TOVAIR's network within the prison system. When he first arrived at this federal penitentiary, Tom thought that the likely candidates for recruitment were prisoners belonging to a tight circle of Islamic radicals. He soon realized that prison guards were also targets of TOVAIR's tentacles. Most of these low-level officers earned meager salaries; many had barely received a high school education. The promise of money enticed these people to collaborate with the enemy. This was a low cost operation for TOVAIR. Prison guards could be bought at a lower price than white-collar officials. The guards were in close contact with criminals who had networks of collaborators outside prison walls, and who were always ready to peddle their skills.

"There are rotten apples in the barrel." Tom had communicated his grim assessment to Clayton leading InterIntel to plan a nationwide sting operation to catch a select number of guards who became government informants in exchange for less severe sentences.

One of those informants was assigned to protect Tom. They seldom talked to one another, but Tom knew about the man's designated job. He was always nearby when Tom was working out in the prison yard or when he joined other inmates in the dining hall or library. Tom was glad to see his protector when he walked out into the yard to collect his tools late in the afternoon. The man smiled and walked towards Tom as two other inmates approached the tool shed from the opposite direction. Tom caught a glimpse of the men from the corner of his eye. He turned to take a closer look. At that very moment, he felt a blade slice the base of his neck and tasted his own blood before passing out.

The morning headlines about a prison beheading did not surprise Clayton. Although the short story did not mention the name of the victim, he knew Tom had met his fate. Morton had dispatched two undercover officers to the prison, but they had arrived too late to save Tom's life. Clayton set the newspaper down and dialed Morton's number.

"It was Tom wasn't it?"

Morton confirmed Clayton's guess and expressed his regret of losing a colleague who had made mistakes, but who had served his country well nevertheless.

"What drives a man like Tom to the right thing most of the time, to have the courage to put his life on the line for his country, and then to make stupid choices that land him in the big house?"

Clayton's question made Morton remember a conversation he had with his Jeff shortly before his son's last deployment. Jeff had asked his father what he needed to do to lead his men and help them avoid mistakes in the battlefield. Morton had answered that a leader should lead by example not just in battle, but also in every aspect of his life. Morton recalled the advice he gave his son just minutes before he hugged him for the last time.

"Son, show them your character, your heart, your intelligence. Tell them that you believe in them, that you expect them to lead and succeed. You will be amazed what men do when you show confidence in them. Share your values with them. Forgive their mistakes but remind them of lessons learned on and off the field. Be fair. Be tough. Always listen. Never let them down."

His son's reply was still fresh in Morton's memory. Jeff's last spoken words brought calm and comfort to Morton Rourke, "Thanks. That is how you taught me to lead by example. Love you, dad."

After he shared with Clayton his last conversation with Jeff, Morton added, "I don't know if this answers your question, but I think Tom did not have anyone who taught him how to lead, who had confidence in him, who listened."

"You're probably right. His work and his private life twisted him into knots that got more difficult to untie with every turn."

Clayton paused. He recalled his grandfather's simple advice about the quiet sport he loved. "Tom's work was his life. Greed and pride got in his way and led him astray. He should have taken up fly-fishing. It keeps a man focused and humble."

Morton chuckled and thought about his own life. He was grateful for his faith and family. They provided the compass for the pursuit of his happiness. His work was very important, but it was not at the very top of his list. His work was what he did to serve his country. It was his duty. It was nothing more and nothing less. There was nothing complicated about Morton's priorities. Right now, he had a job to do. Innocent lives depended on his ability to lead his team to stop an enemy for whom life had little value.

"Clayton, we have to move fast on the Black case. Have you heard from her attorney yet?"

"I just got an e-mail as we speak. She certainly picked an old horse trader, Sam Smelter. He wants to meet this afternoon. Maybe he'll accept a plea bargain. I have the legal team in place."

"Didn't he handle Tom's case?"

"Same one. The old boy is a piece of work, a smooth operator. We are ready for him."

Clayton's legal team was reviewing Sam Smelter's record. He had represented many high-profile cases. He was able to ply the media with the skill of a master sculptor. Clayton instructed his attorneys to offer a plea bargain only if Ms. Black agreed to provide hard evidence of operational details including names and addresses of sleeper cell leaders and other related parties. She had to testify against each defendant in the case against the TOVAIR network operating within the United States.

InterIntel's media relations office was busy analyzing news clips of Sam Smelter's cases. A savvy media strategy emerged after analysts identified a pattern of crafty approaches designed to rally public support for Smelter's clients. This time, Sam Smelter was going to face a tough competitor in the public square.

☆ ☆ ☆

Mack Cumberland read Clayton's briefing, while flying back to the White House for a short break before a virtual coast-to coast campaign "whistle-stop" that would bring live, interactive town halls to every major city and selected small towns across the country. The president's poll numbers were climbing at a steady pace. With only three days left before Election Day, pundits now predicted the horse race to be dead even. The numbers might even reverse and give Cumberland the lead over Senator Parks in the next seventy-two hours. Voters continued to respond to the president's insistence on opening the Senate investigations to public scrutiny.

"You deserve an accountable government. You pay for it. Your children pay for it. Demand answers from your elected representatives on Capitol Hill. They owe you an explanation."

President Cumberland repeated his call for public action in each one of his campaign stops, and voters responded in kind. The virtual town halls packed voters ready to hear the president's confident and calm explanation of how TOVAIR was trying to disrupt the election and corrupt public officials. He promised a clean sweep once his administration had the vote of confidence to serve a second term.

The battle cry "Four More Years" began to drown the negative ad campaign lobbed from Senator Parks's headquarters. The president ended each speech with a warning and a plea.

"My fellow Americans we are at risk. As we speak, our enemies are right next to us, plotting to kill thousands if not more of our citizens to weaken our will on Election Day. We must hang together to stop them. I need your help. Thank you and God bless the United States of America."

President Cumberland knew that Clayton and Morton's teams were working around the clock. He knew that time was running out. In just a few hours, TOVAIR might have a chance to pull off simultaneous attacks that would forever change the American landscape. He was determined to stop the enemy, but knew the long odds of betting that they would not strike under his watch. Civil defense personnel across the country were ready to respond to the impending emergencies. The response system had been tested and worked well, but the president had raised the bar. His goal was prevention not just response. He wanted to eliminate the enemy before it had a chance to act.

The threat of simultaneous attacks in all major cities was rising by the hour. Clayton's latest briefing outlined InterIntel's latest findings in the Cory Black and the prison guard interrogations. Investigators had reached a dead-end street with the cell phone number the guard had contacted to relay Khalid's instructions. The coded message had left little doubt that the person at the other end of the line would be contacting those in charge of executing the plan. It was less clear how that individual would be passing on the message to those in the front lines of terror. A national sweep of registered cell phone numbers had yielded little hope of finding the culprit. More than likely TOVAIR communicated through a network of criminals who operated in the shadows of the law.

✲ ✲ ✲

Alex Keynes III looked at his watch and calculated that he would be on a flight out of Dulles in exactly five hours. He hated to fly the "red-eye" to London, but it was a cheap flight, the only one approved by State's travel office. He walked into his apartment and realized that he had left his personal laptop at the office. He had drafted a short message and was planning to mail merge the missive to the e-mail list in his home computer's address book. He would be delayed by at least a half-hour, the time it would take him to walk the seven blocks back to the State Department. On this late Friday afternoon, Foggy Bottom seemed deserted, as most bureaucrats had left early for the suburbs. He walked briskly congratulating himself for packing his bags the night before.

"One less thing to worry about, before heading to the airport," he muttered to himself as he approached the guard at the north entrance. He showed him his pass. The guard checked his screen and handed the ID back.

"Sorry, Mr. Keynes, the weekend emergency security procedures are now in effect until Monday morning. We can only allow authorized personnel into the building."

Keynes hid his displeasure and tried to persuade the guard to let him into his office. He pleaded and begged. "Please, I am catching a plane in a couple of hours and need to take my laptop. Contact the Secretary's office if you need to confirm my travel."

The guard was not impressed. He had no interest in Alex Keynes's problem. He was trained to follow rules. He was not about to put his job and more importantly, his pension and health benefits in jeopardy. Besides, this Alex Whatever, "the third," seemed to be a typical spoiled diplomat type. The State

Department ID tag with a name highlighting a Roman numeral behind the last name and a gold ring with the family crest showed off his pedigree. Anyone with such superior airs should have a better memory. Forgetting a laptop in the office on a Friday afternoon was plain dumb. Moreover, that business of putting a number behind a name, that just seemed very phony. The guard shook his head as Keynes finally gave up and walked away.

Back in his apartment, Keynes rewrote the message, merged it with his e-mail list and pushed the send button. In his haste, he forgot to activate the program that encoded his messages and secured his e-mail communications from prying eyes. He grabbed his bags locked the door behind him and hailed a taxi; he would barely make it in time to get through the security checkpoints and board his flight. Once on board he would relax with a Scotch on the rocks.

Chapter 28
Serendipity

Clayton's elite team was overworked but never complained. The analysts had a job to do and like their boss, they seldom watched the clock when on duty. Many of them had been taking short breaks to call their families, grab a bite to eat, or just take a short nap. The senior team managing a large volume of incoming intelligence had logged over thirty-five hours of non-stop analysis, and Clayton decided his people needed a break. He walked into the lab and announced that he was treating everyone to dinner. The pizza arrived as he thanked everyone for their hard work.

The staff knew this break would be short, but they admired the quiet professional who never seemed rattled by events. He seemed to work harder than anyone else, getting to the office before daybreak and leaving long after the last staff member had gone home for the day. Clayton kept his nose to the grind, encouraging his team to dig deeper, while the entire country was in a state of hyper-alert. He was a tough act to follow. No one else seemed to be able to function on just a couple of hours of sleep. He managed his team by wandering around and gave his troops praise and encouragement. He reminded them that their 21st century lab was no different from the battlefields of previous generations.

"Folks, we are in the front lines of this war. We will win. The country expects no less from us. Let's not disappoint the American people."

A junior analyst dashed across the room and handed Clayton the first good news of the day.

"Sir, I just noticed this flash link." Flash links showed positive correlations between bits of data. These links identified invisible dots and connected them to reveal causal relationships. The analyst had just spotted a flash link connecting the text of the decoded message Tom had sent to InterIntel and a similar text sent via e-mail somewhere in the United States.

"The message was sent at 18:45 hours, just a couple of hours ago, Sir."

"How fast can we ID the point of origin?" Clayton's question made three analysts spring into action. Before they had a chance to get back to their desks, Clayton gave them an additional challenge.

"At the same time that we figure out the point of origin, let's figure out the destination point." He paused and corrected himself: "Remember, there could be multiple destination points. Ah, and don't forget to get your pizza. Hope you like it cold. It's Friday night guys."

Clayton made young analysts feel good with his energy level. His enthusiasm for discovering nuggets of information and his ability to speak their own language was very cool. Many of his best analysts were recent graduates of the top universities in the nation, who had received graduate degrees years ahead of their peers. The flash link gave Clayton's team a boost; this small piece of good news came at the right time. On other investigative fronts, the news was less sanguine.

The meeting with Sam Smelter had yielded a possible plea bargain, but Cory Black refused to testify against any accused member of the TOVAIR network. Her reason was fear of retribution. Her attorney argued that she would never be safe. Clayton's legal team stuck to its original position, there would be no deal without Cory Black's testimony. After four grueling hours of negotiations, the lawyers on both sides agreed to reach an agreement by 6:00 am the following morning. The deadline was not negotiable.

Cory Black had agreed to turn in evidence that compromised Senator Parks's campaign. Sam Smelter had insisted that this evidence should immunize his client from any claims made by Senator Parks to implicate her in any kind of conspiracy or treason. This was a point of contention, and one that remained on the table for further discussion. Clayton was growing impatient with his own legal team, but knew the wheels of justice turned at their own pace.

Sam Smelter had not yet reached out to the press, as was his usual practice when defending high-profile cases. He was playing it safe. He no longer had to prove his legal prowess; his reputation was sterling and he was determined to keep it well burnished. He had the luxury of picking his fights and he had little desire to wrestle with Clayton. More than likely, Harcourt had the support of the president. Sam Smelter read the polls. Cumberland had a better chance to win the election than at anytime in the last year. Smelter figured it was smart to keep a low media profile, at least until all votes were counted on Election Day.

In the meantime, Senator Thomas had been unable to convince Senator Parks to meet with Clayton's legal team. For the first time in their long friendship, Senator Thomas detected a streak of stubbornness that kept Priscilla Parks from considering alternative options. She focused like a laser on her election. Her obstinacy blinded her from the facts of the investigation and she no longer trusted the advice from a friend, who might see his own political fortunes rise as hers fell.

Senator Thomas began to think that a Parks's victory would prevent him from running for president for another eight years. He would be eighty-three years old by then and over the hill as a presidential contender. A Cumberland second term would give him an opportunity to launch an exploratory committee right away and begin to lay the groundwork and collect the necessary IOUs to win the nomination of his party. In fact, if he could just expose Parks enough to trigger an investigation, she could end up with a bloody nose. She would be out of commission to compete in the next presidential election cycle. In four years, Thomas could be the nominee.

The timing of his public announcement, just before the election, would position him as a leader of his party. He would put country ahead of partisanship, appeal to the opposition, garner their vote, and reach the Oval Office. Senator Thomas was pleased with his action plan. He scheduled a press conference in his office for Monday morning to give his staff time to prepare a press release outlining key findings of the Senate Ethics Committee.

✲ ✲ ✲

After encouraging his team to dig deeper into their latest discovery, Clayton walked out to Inter-Intel's courtyard. This was an inner sanctum built on the roof of three interconnected glass towers. He enjoyed the Zen inspired calmness. Subtle spotlights made the simple lines of the Noguchi stone sculptures glow. One piece named "Brilliance" consisted of a massive rock broken into three pieces and then reassembled. Noguchi united ancient craft and traditions with modern technology. The 20th century master of clean forms had created powerful art; it reminded Clayton of the creative energy of his own team.

InterIntel analysts toiled with the ancient craft and tradition of great nations and they employed the latest technology to break up and put back together bits of information. Their business was to solve complex puzzles and uncover secrets capable of destroying an entire civilization.

Clayton knew that his team was now getting close to discovering the source of the e-mail. Internet access providers did not need a court order to report client records to InterIntel. Once analysts were able to narrow down possible points of origin, it took a matter of seconds to access provider databases and troll for suspects. Clayton climbed the stairs back to the lab and soon learned that there were one hundred and twenty possible matches for the point of destination, but at least the search was now focused on only three possible locations along the East Coast. Clayton paced from one end of the lab to the other watching flashing screens around the room for clues. All of a sudden, one of his analysts called out:

"Checkmate. We got it!"

For Clayton, the rush of adrenalin felt like the magic moment when a trout hits a dry on the water surface. He knew that the next step would be to find the destination points, which in turn would result in a multiplier effect of discovery and action. Once analysts identified destination points, federal and local authorities deployed around the country would receive orders to move in and arrest the culprits before they were able to execute TOVAIR's attacks. That, at least, was the hope. Preemptive strikes against TOVAIR operators were never a matter of simple logistics. This time, the task was monumental. In less than sixty hours, voters would cast the first votes to elect the next president of the United States.

Clayton and his team needed to get actionable intelligence out to the field. He knew that the probability of total success was in the single digits. The complete sweep of sleeper cells ready to execute their orders was improbable. Capturing some cells before they could strike was necessary to discourage others from carrying out their plans. In addition, knowing where TOVAIR would strike could put in motion defensive measures to prevent large civilian casualties. The best outcome was to reduce risks and deflect the impact of the intended attacks.

When Mort walked into the InterIntel lab, Clayton had just sent out the emergency alert to local authorities for the arrest Alex Keynes III. Clayton was downloading the e-mail list retrieved from Keynes computer and his team was already in contact with authorities in target locations.

"It looks worst than we thought."

Clayton was pointing to the screen in front of him. A digital map of the US showed red dots in cities across the country. These were the destination points for the instructions Keynes had sent out only a few hours before. Next to some of the red dots, yellow dots showed the position of swat teams ready to round up suspected TOVAIR terrorists.

"We will need to deploy people to over a hundred smaller cities with populations between 50,000 to 200,000. These were not places we thought they would hit."

Mort did not need additional information to realize that a massive mobilization had to take place to secure these unprotected, smaller urban centers. He had discussed this scenario with a close friend and had made contingency plans to cover this possibility. He conveyed these plans to Clayton with confidence.

"The Defense Department is on board. Mike Perry is in charge of the operation."

"Terrific. He's the right man for the job. It's not going to be easy to move within the short time frame we have. Take a close look at this pattern."

Clayton pointed to a cluster of red dots in key states and near critical facilities. He was concerned that TOVAIR was planning to execute multiple attacks to disrupt the election.

The major concerns were schools and other facilities where large numbers of Americans would be casting their votes. The high concentration of red dots around sensitive infrastructure raised the possibility of serious transportation and communication system disruptions threatening the effectiveness of any homeland defense operation.

"We'll have to move fast and roll out the emergency public announcement campaign and activate the secure online network for voters to cast their ballots from their homes or the online voting booths around the country."

In close cooperation with state and local authorities, InterIntel had developed an electronic voting system. In case of a national emergency, the system assigned a code for each registered voter to access online ballots. The system gave voters a two-day window to cast votes in case they did not have online access or they had trouble getting to a designated and secure voting location. On Election Day, voters received instructions on how to reach secret locations when they logged on to their electronic ballots.

Local elections officials had launched educational campaigns months in advance to inform voters about the emergency procedures they would need to follow in case of electoral disruptions. Now it was time to get the media on board to announce the steps voters needed to follow on Election Day. InterIntel had tested the system only once. There was no additional time to correct any potential malfunctions. Clayton decided it was time to test-drive the emergency voting procedures and sent out the order to initiate program implementation.

✡ ✡ ✡

Alex Keynes III was upset. His flight from Dulles to London had been delayed over an hour. The plane had been sitting on the runway for another hour waiting to take off. Keynes did not want to miss his connection to Khartoum, where one of Assoud's drivers would pick him up for the long journey to Egypt. There he would collect his pension and retire to a life of leisure in some tropical island. Finally, it looked like he was finally going to be airborne. Suddenly, the pilot announced that due to an emergency, they would need to wait a bit longer. Keynes noticed that the crew blocked the aisles and closed the curtain separating business class from coach. It sounded as if the crew had opened the hatch to lower the emergency staircase.

Before passengers in business class could process what was taking place, an air marshal emerged from first class and joined two FBI agents. Their 9mms drawn, the three men moved in unison towards coach class. They approached the passenger in seat 12D and ordered him to stand up.

"Mr. Alex Keynes, you are under arrest. You have the right to remain silent."

Clayton received the news of Keynes capture, and wondered aloud how the State Department's Personnel Office had managed to botch the internal investigation of one of its own. State's unwillingness to share information with Clayton months before the election was proving to be a costly mistake.

"Knowing then what we now know about Alex Keynes would have saved the country time and lives."

"Yeah, in this town bureaucracies rule. Turf matters." Mort sounded as if he was resigned to accept the power of unelected public officials to decide the destiny of a free people.

"There is much blame to go around, Mort. The bureaucrats are not accountable. Congress shuns its oversight responsibility and the president has to use his political capital where it yields the highest returns. Cleaning house is a low priority, when more pressing issues like homeland defense rise to the forefront."

Clayton recalled his conversation with President Cumberland just before they boarded Air Force One months ago. On that late summer day, sitting at a coffee shop in Driggs, Clayton believed the President had a chance to reform the same bureaucracy that had caused him much aggravation during his tenure at the CIA. The president seemed concerned about finishing the job he had started, but his initiative dubbed the Cumberland Purge had had limited success.

Since arriving in Washington, Clayton realized the president's personnel review and reassignment effort was a facelift, a short-lived experiment with little impact on entrenched bureaucratic politics. Alex Keynes was a product of that system, a system that guarded his privacy, revered his seniority, and allowed him to deceive his superiors. He had committed treason without fear of retribution from unaccountable bureaucrats. The price was high.

Clayton believed that the failure of a great nation to live up to its legacy was rooted in ignorance of its own history. He often recalled a short quote from the author of the Declaration of Independence. In 1790, Jefferson wrote: "John Locke's little book on government is perfect as far as it goes." Jefferson was a great admirer of John Locke, the most ardent spokesman of the Glorious Revolution of 1688. Locke's ideas fueled the English quest for representative government, established the foundation of universal rights, and inspired the American Revolution a century later. In *The Second Treatise of Civil Government,* Locke explained why the rights of the people were a fundamental pillar of the best form of government. This was a radical idea in the seventeenth century.

For much of the world's nations, the idea was still radical four centuries later, but Clayton believed that individual rights remained at the core of the American creed. American governmental institutions, values, and traditions rested on the principle that the individual had an innate ability to discern truth from lie and exercise reason in matters of order and justice.

The primacy of the individual justified the political and social equality that gave each citizen the same control over the actions of his government.

"Only the American people can demand that their government live up to its expectations. I'm afraid we confront something bigger than the war we fight against our enemies. We have a crisis of expectations. We ignore the legacy of this great nation at our own peril. We the people, no longer understand what keeps us free. When a civilization fails to teach each generation the lessons of the past, it forfeits its destiny."

"Are you suggesting that it's up to the American people to change the way our government functions, the way bureaucracy gets in the way of results?"

"Yeah, that's exactly what I mean. Government needs to be accountable and that means public officials and bureaucrats need to justify their existence. Our team lived up to these principles, but not all who serve the public do so. Often, the people pay for a lot more government than what they get. In the real world, job security comes from satisfied customers. For some public servants job security has little to do with results. To me that is very disappointing. Any business that operates the way our government does at times would be out of business in less than a year." Clayton paused. "Oh well, I'm going home as soon as this job gets done."

For a moment, Clayton thought about a favorite passage in a classic work of another century. Henry David Thoreau had said it best:

"I went to the woods because I wished to live deliberately, to front only the essential facts of life, and see if I could not learn what it had to teach, and not, when I came to die, discover that I had not lived."

Clayton was ready to return to the place where he could once again get in touch with the very roots of his existence. He longed for the peace that came when a man had time to spend his days in harmony with his purpose, no matter how modest his ambitions. He knew why a mountain stream calmed a man's soul. He understood the thrill of sneaking up to a seemingly unsuspecting trout, only to discover one cannot fool such an evasive creature.

In the last few days, Clayton had made decisions affecting thousands of people and he had improvised as he went along. He knew that it was possible to win the battle and lose the war. There were no blueprints for this protracted fight. This war had no exact beginning or end.

"Clayton, you know the president wants you to stay and finish the job." Mort suggested the possibility of a promotion, and as he spoke, he noticed an open fly box on Clayton's desk. Tiny dry flies snuggled against thin foam ridges and lined up in neat rows as if they were toy soldiers ready to go to battle. The upright wings of a Royal Wulff looked silvery under the florescent lights. For some strange reason, these delicate lures did not seem out of place.

"The president trusts you and needs you. This war is far from over." Although Mort realized the odds of changing the mind of a man ready to wade into a slow stream, he reminded Clayton that nobody ever turns down a presidential offer.

✲ ✲ ✲

President Cumberland was on his way to gain re-election in a country under siege. American voters seemed to favor the incumbent by a narrow margin. The country was numb from isolated but deadly attacks and a barrage of speculation about an upcoming announcement by the Chairman of the Senate ethics Committee. A long and nasty campaign was to end in a matter of hours and even the media seemed battle fatigued. The case against Cory Black was set to go to trial after Sam Smelter agreed to turn in evidence wanted by prosecutors.

Clayton's senior analysts were already jockeying to move up to the corner office. Even an acting position gave career folks a shot at a more permanent appointment. The staff did not know of Clayton's plans to return to his cabin, but some veteran analysts had experienced the ebb and flow of political appointments right after an election. Regardless of election results, there was always an exodus of appointees out of the capital and a wave of fresh faces arrived, eager to step into the temporary seats of power vacated by their weary predecessors. Soon it would be time for a change of the guard.

The emergency voting procedures implemented on Election Day had averted massive casualties in cities and towns across the country. Multiple raids had resulted in the swift capture of sleeper cells in major metropolitan areas, but isolated terrorist attacks had killed several hundred civilians.

A month after the American presidential election, the Tandori brothers were still operating in dark alleys frequented by arms dealers and terrorists. Ahmed Assoud, still had deep pockets and dark secrets. By year's end, his daughter had assumed the presidency of Egypt after the sudden death of her husband. Aisha Al Ramzi wrapped herself in populist causes gaining the support of masses far beyond the borders of her adopted country. She was fast assuming the reigns of TOVAIR and she deeply mistrusted Khalid Hassan's motives.

The competition for Chinese control of TOVAIR heated up but ended with the sudden death of Liao Chang. The Chinese papers reported that the oil magnate had passed away gently in his sleep. U.S. intelligence reports suggested a different demise. Shortly after the patriarch's death, his son Tsu had become a Buddhist monk and had retreated to a monastery in Nepal. His sister, Lyn still lingered in a U.S. jail unable to overturn a life sentence in spite of her high-powered Washington lawyer's best efforts to free her from solitary confinement. The Chang oil fields in the Tarin Basin and at Turpan now belonged to the Chinese government. A wave of nationalization of key industries had followed the rise to power of Prime Minister Chui. He had been the first foreign dignitary to congratulate President Cumberland on his reelection.

Afterword

On the cold January morning when President Cumberland takes the oath of office to serve a second term, Priscilla Parks resigns from her Senate seat. Far from the nation's capital, not much has changed in Driggs. The rhythm of life remains undisturbed since the president's entourage landed at the edge of town on a late summer morning. The tourists are gone now. The locals gather each morning at the Grand Old Grill to catch up on the news of the day. Rumors of the president's late summer visit abound, but few can confirm the stories. Few know the local man who met the president on Main Street. Fewer still know his name.

There is a sense of calm in the air, particularly across the vast Teton Valley. John Colter discovered this region on his way to Yellowstone in the early 1800s. Time seems to stand still while the jagged Teton peaks guard the town from afar like invincible warriors. A thick layer of ice covers the mountain streams. Large brown trout linger in their favorite hiding places waiting for a chance to venture upstream. At the foothills of the Teton Range, Ski Hill Road winds its way up the mountain. Snow covers the ground. Patches of ice crack under the weight of a doe. She sprints across the road leading up to Clayton's cabin, then stops, and looks back before disappearing into the forest. Nature, in its grand splendor is at home here.

About the Author

R.G. Dierks earned a Ph.D. in Political Science after a career in government and the financial services industry, and is the author of two non-fiction books. *Troutfly* is the first novel of a trilogy honoring the patriotism, courage, and sacrifice of American war heroes of the 20th and the 21st centuries.

988747

Made in the USA